Texas Soundtrack

Texas Soundtrack

Texas Stories Inspired by
Texas Music

Terry Dalrymple, Editor

INK
BRUSH
PRESS

ISBN: 978-0-9835968-2-0
Library of Congress Control Number: 2011932125

Cover photographs by Terry Dalrymple
    Front cover photograph taken at Blaine's Pub, San Angelo, Texas

Ink Brush Press
Temple and Dallas, Texas
www.inkbrushpress.com

This book is dedicated to Lorraine, my wife of thirty-five years,
And to Joshua, Phillip, and Sarah, my children,
Music lovers all
And my inspiration.

It is also dedicated to great singer-songwriters,
Texan or otherwise,
Who inspire us all.

Other Fiction from Ink Brush Press

Laurie Champion, editor, *Texas Told'em: Gambling Stories,* with an introduction by Doyle Brunson

Terry Dalrymple, *Fishing for Trouble*

Andrew Geyer, *Dixie Fish*

Andrew Geyer, *Siren Songs from the Heart of Austin*

H. Palmar Hall, *Into the Thicket*

Dave Kuhne, *The Road to Roma and Other Stories*

Myra McLarey, *The Last Will and Testament of Rosetta Sugars Tramble*

Jim Sanderson, *Dolph's Team*

Jim Sanderson, *Faded Love*

Jan Seale, *Dearness Happens*

Melvin Sterne, *Zara*

CONTENTS

From the Editor

Songwriters, Texan or otherwise, are storytellers. Most of the time, anyway. Their stories are brief, maybe three or four verses that take three or four minutes to sing. So the writers must be by nature or training masters of minimalism. Their work is not dense with detail; it is dense with implications that grow from just the right details. Consider, for example, Guy Clark's "Step Inside this House." A few details about the persona's belongings reveal to alert listeners his entire life. Texas songwriters tell hundreds of such suggestive stories.

So how, I wondered, might Texas fiction writers use some of those musical tales for inspiration? Would they retell the same stories in more detail? Would they create entire lives for songs' characters? Would they find some of those just-right details somehow significant to entirely different stories? Would they be reminded of particular times or places with stories of their own?

The challenge was simple: write stories somehow inspired by songs of any genre written or performed by Texas musicians. The best results are the thirteen stories selected for inclusion here, and they amply demonstrate that the answer is yes to all of the questions above as well as to some I never thought to ask myself. What these stories do and how they do it reveals the same great diversity as the songs that inspired them.

As editor, my final question was what to say in an introduction. That question was heavy on my mind one day when Daniel Makins waved from his yard as I drove past. Who better to write an introduction than a singer-songwriter from Texas, one who has written plenty of fine songs that tell plenty of fine tales? And, I might add, who has now written a fine introduction.

And now, enjoy.

Terry Dalrymple
San Angelo, Texas
June 2011

Introduction:
Made In Texas?

Daniel Makins

Daniel Makins is a songwriter from San Angelo. His songwriting accolades include winning the Gig Harbor Folk Festival competition and reaching the finalist stages at the Kerrville Folk Festival and the Wild-flower Festival. *The Daily Texan* called Daniel "One of the best new artists most likely to be seen on *Austin City Limits*" and said his "poignant lyrics [are] indicative of true talent." In 2004, he established the San Angelo Concert Series, which continues to bring internationally known songwriters to West Texas in an acoustically superb, listener oriented format. He serves as Executive Director of the San Angelo Cultural Affairs Council and produces and hosts the KNCH 90.1 FM Public Radio San Angelo-Songwriter Showcase radio hour. Daniel says his goal is trying to live a good life. Visit his web site at www.danielmakins.com.

In the year 2000 I made the big move to Nashville. All aspiring songwriters must, at some point, make this pilgrimage. Like big dumb bugs to the yellowed porch light we amble in wanderlust northward into our perceived potential. I suppose, for most, a better analogy for the exposing experience of "the industry" might be more akin to dimwitted gnats flung headlong into the windshields of as many semi-trucks.

Upon arrival from Texas one is assumed to be a Texas Songwriter. The immediate necessity to have the nonchalant, professional ability to explain that you are in fact not a "Texas Songwriter" but a songwriter from Texas is an intriguing realization. As in all other forms of commercially viable art which, by nature, tend toward the median of society, our music and literature is often hijacked by what is marketable.

The paradox of existing as a songwriter in Texas is that you can connect with many and often make a decent living without ever escaping her borders; concurrently, those beyond our welcome signs often don't know what to make of our self-conscious pride or our artistic expression and this leads to a sort of self imposed isolation. Perhaps due to our state's previous existence as "a whole other country" we relish feeling self-contained.

We are comfortable. We love our home because we are products of its environment. We love it because it is in us. Our Mexican food is actually Texan food. We are drunk with nostalgia because you will not find an Ohio Edition Ford F-150 and the marketing masterminds will most likely pass on the Delaware package Dodge Ram.

Sudden for this young Texan fan of southern literature transplanted to Tennessee was the splash of cold water epiphany that Texas is not the South. However, the expression of the Lone Star State is certainly, at its unmolested, un-marketed core, similar to that of the South in its concurrent romantic reminiscence for the good old days and its stark acceptance of the present. Our best songs contain slow, focused observation of the people and places unique to our sphere of existence. Our exceptional songs reason through this familiarity to stumble upon some deeper metaphorical truth, even if it is a lie. So do our exceptional fictions, as illustrated in these pages.

Pulitzer and Pen/Faulkner Prize winning author Richard Ford recently stated that "the writing of the South brings deeper insight or intelligence to something we thought we knew about." I suppose the old adage of writing what one knows stands incontrovertibly affirmed.

So why is Texas different? Our experience of the Civil War is different. Our settlement and frontier narrative is different. Unfortunately the loudest and proudest of mass marketed sounds originating in both the Nashville and Texas Music scenes seem to be saying to the most talented and introspective of southern writers, "Get over it, tonight's the night, look at her, this is my truck and that's my beer . . . Yee-haw . . ."

Despite these "character" flaws, our worthwhile songs and stories contain scenes depicted with a similar southern, gritty accuracy that paints pictures.

It is the spontaneous ability of lyrical imagery to connect and take an audience to a place familiar, or at least recognizable, that generates space in which real movement, empathy and self-actualization can occur for both writer and audience. Author and humorist Tom Bodet cleverly describes these as "moments meant to take the loneliness out of being human."

The rhythm of good music written by Texans contains a wonderful mix of southern calm that lends itself well to melody and phrasing. We have all day to fit those words in with just the right emphasis and accent. Even when you think him impossibly behind the beat, Willie Nelson finds a way to say it all without being left behind.

These observations might prove useful for writer and listener alike, but what of process? Process comes from within. A collection of stories inspired by songs or their attachment to a given memory is a study in process. Laurence Musgrove's story in this collection, "Shambala," speaks of an artistic life and its anxieties. It features the line, "I go in for color, and in color, I go in." This sentiment is one that translates well for the songwriter. It seems to smack of devotion or an intentionality which is, to me, the most important trait a keen observer can possess. Most all songs contain happy accident, struck-by-lightening lines, but completing a complimentary work around their foundation takes intentionality. It takes purpose.

Contained in this collection are stories inspired by songs which were mostly inspired by stories. As a songwriter I'm fascinated that complete narratives can be derived from once familiar songs popping into one's head. Or that innocent mention of individual words or places such as "Econoline" and "Guanajuato" can manifest in further creative roaming as in Amanda Gann Churchill's included story. Vocal inflection and timing must surely play their parts well.

Don't worry if the songs used for inspiration in this collection are unfamiliar. Read Laurie Champion's tale "How to Listen to Country Music," wherein she posits comforting advice in her closing lines: "The songs will always, always make perfect sense."

The stories contained here will also, I believe, always make perfect sense. As varied as Texas music—from "The Song of Four Snakes," Chris Ellery's tale of the magical powers of snakes and songs, to "Ridin' My Thumb to Mexico," Dave Kuhne's nostalgic look back at the freedom of youth in the 1970s, to "The Deacon's Horse," Clay Reynolds's western tale of horse thievery—these stories and others presented here represent truths as only fictions can.

One thing is for certain, whether you are a native or a proud, time-tested transplant to our state, you will find within these pages both familiarity and truth.

The Song of the Four Snakes

Chris Ellery

There was old man Perkins sittin' on his stool
Watchin' Butch and Jimmy John talkin' loud and playin' pool
Robert Earl Keen, "Feelin' Good Again"

Chris Ellery teaches literature, folklore, film criticism, and creative writing at Angelo State University. His short fiction has appeared in numerous journals, including *Concho River Review*, *descant*, and *CCTE Studies*. He is co-translator (with Asmahan Sallah) of *Whatever Happened to Antara* (2004), a collection of short stories by the award-winning Syrian writer Walid Ikhlassi. His three published collections of poetry are *Quarry* (2005), *All This Light We Live In* (2006), and *The Big Mosque of Mercy* (2010).

Chris explains, "'The Song of the Four Snakes' owes its existence to Robert Earl Keen's 'Feelin' Good Again.' My older daughter included the song on a Father's Day mix she sent me from Nashville, so I would feel her company as I listened to the lyrics in the backyard over Lone Star and barbecue. Something in it—the sublime pathos of homecoming and reunion, I guess—grabbed hold of me from the beginning. Then one Sunday I was out walking with my headphones on and was struck by the lines about old man Perkins. Who was this old man? Why was he there? What was he thinking and feeling as he watched the boys line up their shots? I hit the replay button on my iPod a dozen times, listening to those lines over and over and thinking about old guys I'd seen over the years sitting alone in various taverns and bars in Texas and Oklahoma. I had to give the old man a life. At the time, I was preparing to teach a folklore class focusing on folk and fairy tales and was immersed in Karl Jung, Joseph Campbell, Marie-Louise von Franz. To a large extent, that accounts for the mythological and folkloric elements— the magic—of Joey's tale. The good feeling of this plunge into the

5

unconscious I owe to my daughter—and to Robert Earl: 'It feels so good, feelin' good again.'"

A breath of the beast is the morning fog. In this land it rises twice a year: late, when the beast goes to its winter sleep, and again in the spring, when it comes once more, fresh and eager.

We all know from the old tales that the dragon which guards the maiden is the lowest level of being. His name is Joey Perkins and he married, just before turning 30, a barely-legal former cheerleader, Mary Fae Zest. Trust me, she is not the maiden of the myth.

Joey was the only child of a gas station owner who lived and ran his garage on the easternmost edge of San Devacas. A barbed wire fence separated his place from a field of mesquite, scrub oak, and tall, wild grass. Far beyond that field was Blue Butte, a lonely and magical place. Winter and spring, Joey would stare across the deserted field at the butte, wrapped in the breath of the beast, and feel its mysterious and elusive power. It rose above him and blessed him, and as he grew, a wild, hilarious boy, he came to know its every ridge and draw. By the time he reached puberty he could overhaul an engine and shoot a .22 through a grackle's eye. He was bronze and blond, built like a hero, and eager to indulge every sense.

When he was 18, Joey went away to fight in the War of His Time. He was taken a long way from his home to a country where a dragon seemed always to grip the land. In some seasons, it spit monsoons from the sky, apparently determined to wash away the mountains and jungles and sunken, overripe fields. In others, its hot breath scorched the land for weeks on end. It made men crazy, eager to kill.

In the War of His Time, Joey saw many terrible things and did some terrible things. Because he was a crack shot, he was often sent away alone to hunt down some dangerous prey. He disguised himself with bits of the landscape until he felt he had become the place itself. He would come back to his buddies and for days not say a word. They respected his silence. They had a name for him: The Assassin.

Once, he was lying on his belly, hiding in a flooded field, waiting for his moment. Out of the water a snake appeared and slithered directly up to his face flicking its forked tongue like a black flame. It stared at him with a look so self-assured it seemed a demon. It was yellow and red with black markings like thorns along the spine, and its skin seemed to ooze some

6

kind of transparent jelly. Of course the boy's instinct was to kill it, but Joey kept his head. A ripple in that flooded paddy would almost certainly draw mortar fire, so he stared past the snake through the scope of his gun, all the while telepathically transmitting a message to the snake: *I am not here to harm you.* Later, he thought perhaps he had said these words aloud. The memory played with his mind, for the snake had stayed there until he finished his work. After an hour he fancied that it wanted to protect him, after two that it loved him.

After that, there seemed to be snakes wherever he went.

One time, his platoon was cresting a hill, following a dry road on the way to set up an ambush. A thick, green snake lay heaped upon itself in the way. The point man raised his machete. Joey caught his arm. "It ain't poison," he said.

"This is the perfect spot," the point man said, "and I don't want to lay in them bushes and worry about no snake."

"We can't set up here," Joey said. "That's what it's telling us."

By then the whole platoon had gathered to listen to the conversation. The lieutenant stared at Joey. "This ain't no chicken parade," he barked. "You jawing with snakes now, civilian?"

"No, sir."

The lieutenant stood there and stared at Joey, then stared at the snake, then at Joey. "Goddamn egghead," he said. He stared down the road for a minute, then ordered the platoon to move out.

The snake slid away as the men passed, and they could see its belly was swollen. That got the boys talking. "The Assassin is soft for snakes." "Brother to a python." "King cobra to a queen cobra." "He got the daddy down his pants."

Another night he woke in the jungle to a monsoon and a shiver of sudden and deathly fear. All the threats of the country came against him. The tree he was under gave little shelter, and rain pelted his face. His eyelids flickered. As suddenly as it began the rain stopped, the clouds parted, and when the moon showed pale and full, he could see the head of the serpent like a black diamond against it. The snake dripped from the tree but seemed to hang out of space. Between Joey and the snake there was an instant of recognition, and Joey felt protected. Suddenly he heard music. Music so faint and fragile he could not tell where it was coming from. A sweet and winsome melody played on some instrument he'd never heard before, a kind of whistling, but from many lips and of many tones. Where was it coming from? The snake? The moon? His own head? Maybe it was all of them. Maybe it was the whole land whistling, every living thing, tree and bush and brier, and every inanimate thing, stone and dust, and all the dead, animal and human, enemy and friend. He considered that, and listened. He listened until the music was inside him, inside his head and inside his soul, for good.

When the War of His Time morphed into the Next War, Joey was discharged and returned to San Devacas. He took his pleasure for many years with no thoughts of either leaving or settling down. He followed the way his wild will led, which just also happened to be exactly the Path of Least Resistance.

The years came and went. He pumped gas and tuned a fleet of engines. On long hunts he chased deer and turkey, sometimes rabbits, quail, dove, even feral hogs and the occasional bobcat. Most of all he chased tail. Certainly a powerful need drew him to women, of a certain sort. And lots of women, of a certain sort, were drawn to him. Every encounter left him broke, breathless, somehow empty, yet craving more. By and by his father went with the breath of the beast and Joey found himself owner of his own business and alone in the world.

His tavern of choice was the Welcome Come On In where he hung out sipping longnecks and dropping quarters in the jukebox. He was there most every Friday and Saturday night. Most everybody who came in knew Joey. He filled their tanks and kept their old trucks together. "How y'doing, Joey?" they always asked. "I'm feeling good," Joey would say.

The place was owned and run by the daddy of an old high school buddy, Jesus. There were jars of pickled eggs and hotlinks behind the bar along with a big can of crackers, and about once a month the Silver City boys would show up and make an evening of it, eating supper out of the jars of pickled food. Joey liked the boys, but could hardly stand this ritual of eating rubbery eggs and links. He always made fun of the Silver City boys for eating those eggs. "Them eggs'll hatch a dragon in your belly," he liked to say as the briny smell saturated the tavern. The lobster-red skin of the sausages made them seem like little sections cut out of the Devil's tail. "Demon dicks," Joey called them.

One night a girl came in. Every head in the place turned, for she was a beauty, just coming into womanhood. The place was not exactly off limits to females. Couples were pretty common on weekends, and once in a while a biker or cowboy would bring a woman in, but it was rare to see a woman, much less a mere girl, enter alone. This one wasn't shy about being among all the men there. Her sentience seemed to crave attention.

"Can I use your phone? I've got me a flat tire down the road a piece and I need to call my daddy."

8

Jesus was tending bar that night. He set the phone in front of the girl. "Course you can use the phone, honey. Or maybe old Joey here could help you out. He owns a garage. Bet you fix a hundred flats a day, Joey, am I wrong? What's one more?"

The girl's Mustang was pulled over to the curb a couple of blocks down Main Street. She didn't have a spare, so Joey pulled the tire and they went back to the garage, just on the edge of town. This girl was not afraid. Beyond Joey's wood pile, beyond the barbed wire, Blue Butte was wrapped in a cool breath.

While Joey was patching the tire, the girl asked, "What's that you're whistling?"

"Huh?"

"That tune. It's so pretty."

Joey had not realized that he was whistling, and he felt embarrassed. "I don't really know. I wasn't paying attention. I guess I whistle sometimes."

"Do it again. Please."

The Song came out of him as if it had been waiting to be born from the world below. He whistled it softly, with perfect pitch and feeling. Pretty soon the girl started humming along. Joey's song filled her with all the sweetness and sadness of life, all that is lovely and true and painful, all that starts out young and grows old. It made her love him.

"My name," she said, "is Mary Fae. I'm a cheerleader for the San Devacas Warriors. I'm not like most cheerleaders. There's more to me. For one thing I'm real interested in music. I play guitar pretty good and piano some and I sing. Someday I'm going to be a star. What do you think about that, Joey? You believe that? Would you like to help me become a star, Joey?"

Joey said he would.

"Another thing. Some'll tell you different, but I'm a virgin."

"Okay."

"What about you?"

"No."

"That's good. I don't plan on staying one forever. There's a game this Friday night. You ever go to the games? Why don't you come to the game Friday night and watch me cheer?"

Pretty soon Mary Fae gave the class ring and letter jacket back to the boy she was dating and started seeing Joey. When they were together, Mary Fae liked to say, "You sure bewitched me, Joey. You cast a spell over my heart and now I just can't help loving you." Joey was glad and hoped the spell would never break. Mary Fae's father, only 12 years older than Joey, disapproved of the relationship. He hissed and threatened, said Joey was too old and Mary Fae just a kid, but he could not put out the fire in either of them. He watched over his daughter with brutal diligence, hoping to catch them together. They outwitted him, however, and as soon as Mary Fae turned 18, they were married.

Mary Fae took Joey's song and put some words to it. But the words didn't matter. The melody was enough. Anyone who heard her sing The Song fell in love with Mary Fae. She got a little band together, got up a repertoire, and took to playing at the Panorama. She packed the place. Everybody wanted to hear The Song, and she always saved it for last. Joey was there every time. He loved her so much.

A baby came and they named her—well, Mary Fae did—Crystal Belle. Joey thought that next to Mary Fae he'd never seen anything so wonderful. She had pink, dimpled cheeks and she would stick her tongue out at him and then smile. Every time she did it, Joey thought of that snake in that flooded field and was happy. He got to thinking that his happiness was a promise that snake had made him.

There were three years of this.

When the breath of the beast brought the fourth, Mary Fae handed Joey a newspaper clipping. It announced a talent search in the Big City for the hit TV show *Path to Stardom*. "Will you take me, Joey?" Of course he did. Mary Fae sang The Song, and all the scouts for the show and the agents who were there fell in love with her. They wanted her so much. And when she sang The Song on the hit TV show *Path to Stardom*, the whole country, everybody who heard her, wanted her, too.

She signed a contract. She sold a million records. She was gone more and more. She stopped telling Joey that he cast a spell on her heart. The spell was broken and she had a new lover, named Myfans. Joey was jealous and yelled at her, as he believed a man was supposed to, but when finally she announced she was leaving for good, he really didn't try to stop her. Maybe some intuition prevented him. Maybe he really just wanted her to be happy. Maybe deep down he simply believed it was just the Way Things Are. Anyway, he let her go. When she was gone, he grieved. So overwhelming was his loneliness and need that he thought he could not live. Possibly he would not have except for Crystal Belle.

One morning he left the girl swinging her feet at the breakfast table and went out to the woodpile to fetch in wood for the fireplace. As he lifted a stump, a rattlesnake slid from beneath it. Startled, Joey grabbed an axe to kill the snake. He was about chop the serpent's head off when it tucked its rattle into its coils and stared at Joey. Its tongue was not darting nor had it fixed its pupils in a threatening glare. After a moment it gently lowered its head and lay it on Joey's boot. All at once Joey sees. He drops his axe and whispers, "Whatever you're doing here, I ain't going to harm you."

The snake lifts its head from Joey's boot, and there is a visible smile on its reptilian lips. Joey is aware of a raw, potent smell, most unusual and fecund. The snake speaks: "Four times you have held your hands. For this mercy you will receive a gift. A day will come when you stand at a precipice and stare into a dark and dreadful abyss. Then a beautiful maiden will come to you and offer a choice of three golden wishes. You must choose, and if you live worthy of me, you will choose wisely."

With this the snake released its coils and whipped itself in its side-winding way over the woodpile and under the barbed wire, disappearing into the desolate pasture of brown grass and scrub, headed in the direction of Blue Butte.

When Joey returned to the breakfast table, the girl stuck her tongue out and smiled, and the loveliness of it jolted every cell of his body. It suddenly dawned that he was not alone in his loneliness, not abandoned in his abandonment. He knew his grief was not his alone but was part of everyone, living and dead, streamed from the very soul of sadness itself, which washes over all, so that within its brutal current he felt a violent, ravishing joy.

Joey raised the girl, Crystal Belle. She was beautiful, like her mother. When she was little, he whistled the melody of the snake. It held its magic, and the girl loved him. He whistled still as she grew bigger and biggest. She took the magic into herself, and it came out of her, not in song, but in strange stories, a brave nature, and gentle ways.

He worked for her without complaining. When an engine fell on his hand, he remembered Crystal Belle and thought, "This is for you." He bought her pretty clothes, ballet lessons, art lessons. He listened eagerly while she read aloud the stories she loved and the stories she wrote, and while she told of her days and her dreams. He taught her things: how to know all kinds of fish and fowl, how to maintain the fluids in her car, how to dance the two-step. And he saw to it that she had good women in her life, a wise old housekeeper and the wives of trusted friends, to teach her what only women can. The cord of his love was strong, but there was an instinct or a wisdom in him that knew not to hold too tightly.

When she reached the proper age, Joey said, "It's time I let you go. You have to find your path. Go on now, and don't look back."

"Good grief, I'm only going to college," she said. But she had chosen a school Back East, and Joey knew she would no longer be his. When they said good-bye, she put her tongue out and smiled, thrilled by all the possibilities of life, by all that she might come to know. To Joey her smile was the dark, delirious nucleus of gratitude. When she was gone, he was lonely for a time, but he felt that he had done right.

Here, you must know, the tale turns almost unbearably sad. This should not surprise you, for we share this world with demons, with not angels enough to stay all their lust and schemes. Evils wait on every road, and no house is safe from the wickedness of men. Violence and disaster, detested suitors, are ever courting innocence and beauty.

Three years after Crystal Belle left, Joey got a call from someone at her college with the news that she was dead. When he went to bring her home, a teacher at the school told him that she thought Crystal Belle had a daughter. How could that be? She had said nothing, and there was no sign.

Only after the funeral did he fully feel the devastating reality of his loss. His Crystal Belle, his little girl. The light of his life was in the ground, a fact outrageous, obscene, unbearably cruel. He went to the woodpile and waited for the snake. In rage and despair he waited. This must be the moment for the promise. He would wish her back from the grave.

No serpent appeared. He waited all night, and again the next day. Then another night and another day, and then another. All the while not a breath stirred. The sun beat down on the brown, desolate field. Under the skull of the moon, Blue Butte squatted gray, barren, bestial, mute.

Had the maiden come with her golden wishes, I doubt Joey could have chosen wisely. Rare is the gift to live in accord with this, with all life is, the Way Things Are. This gift is rarely wished for, more rarely granted. It is hatched below, fathoms down, charmed beyond fear and beyond desire, those demon guardians of Paradise.

Joey closed his business and set out to find the girl. He looked and looked, searched and searched, asking and begging, with prayers and curses. He found no trace in all the wide world. She had simply vanished, as if some fog had swallowed her. After many years, Joey returned to San Devacas and resumed his life there. But sorrow, you must know, is not some bone to be buried in the earth and forgotten, nor a thought to be thrown at the moon like a dream. Neither is love. At night sometimes Joey gazed out toward Blue Butte and imagined his daughter there. He imagined a granddaughter, too. As the years passed, he imagined her—how she looked, how she had grown, who she had become. Though he had never seen her, could never know she ever really existed, he could not be stopped from loving her. She lived her life in his mind, in the magic of Blue Butte. He spoke to her and whistled The Song for her in the night, hoping somehow it might reach and touch her with its power.

In the course of things, Joey's friend Jesus inherited the Welcome Come On In from his father. Joey became a fixture there, an old man full of loud and happy barroom talk, like other men. He had his own bar stool, which the boys called Joey's Throne. There he would sit and sway to the strains of whatever song happened to be on the jukebox. Once in a while it was a voice he knew well, one that stayed young over the years. She was a favorite of all the boys, who knew her only by her stage name. To Joey she was still just Mary Fae.

Jesus enlarged the place, put in a dance floor. Couples came to two-step, to laugh and fight, break up and make up. Sometimes Joey would take a spin. He was a good dancer, a reliable partner for all the wives and girlfriends when the men were tuckered out or more interested in drinking, telling lies, shooting pool than keeping their ladies cheerful. In this way Joey heard happy stories and sad stories, listening on his quick feet to tales of engagements and divorces, to secrets of maternity and hard love, listening, listening, and giving such comfort as he could.

At last his endurance began to fail until a single dance would leave him breathless, a shock of pain hammering through his chest. One day the doctor said his heart might go any moment. That night as usual everybody shook the dice for jukebox quarters. Four dice, high roll, and the winner gets to pick the songs. Joey turned the cup, and the dice showed four sixes. When he got back to his stool from shoving quarters in the jukebox, there was a young woman sitting on the stool next to his. He recognized at once those sparkling eyes.

"Do you want to dance?" she asked. She led him to the dance floor.

"You're the spitting image of your momma. The shine of the full moon is in your face," he said. They danced, moving so easily together that it was impossible to say which of them was leading. This was wish enough, gift enough. Around the floor—how many times?—he held her light body, so light it seemed a vapor, yet so vital that it was he who felt insubstantial.

"People used to call me The Assassin," he said. She stuck out her tongue and smiled. They stopped, and he held her, in the middle of the dance floor he held her. Then he said, "You must know I looked high and low?"

"I know," she said, "it's all right." Couples glided by like ghosts in a dream, seeming to pass right through them. "I am sent to you," she said. "The time has come." She lifted herself on tiptoes and whispered in his ear with barely a breath, and when she had said what she had to say they began to dance again. Then she said, "You choose when you pass through the door of this place. That seals the wish. I will wait on Blue Butte until the moon hides in the breath of the beast. These are the wishes that were promised."

She took his hands and pressed them, and in doing so seemed flesh and blood again. "You did right by us all," she said and smiled. "I know you will choose well."

He nodded, kissed her forehead, and let her go, then returned to his stool at the bar, Joey's Throne. He found his beer still foaming in the clear bottle.

Jimmy John racked the balls as Butch chalked his stick for the break. Joey took a sip of his beer and said to Jesus, who was tending bar, "I believe I'll try one of your eggs."

"Did you hear that, boys!" Jesus exclaimed. Butch looked up from the table toward the bar.

"What's got into him?"

"He's hoping to hatch one them demons he's always talking about," Jimmy John teased. "Let us know how it goes down, Joey. Them sour old things always stick in my throat." Butch rubbed his crotch and leaned over his break. Jesus fished a pickled egg out of the jar and set it on a napkin in front of Joey, a pale, glistening, ovular globe. Overeager for the break, Butch missed cue, and the ball fluttered toward the side pocket. Jimmy John and all the boys howled with laughter at poor Butch's expense. "I never seen nothing like that," Jimmy John razzed. Butch chalked his cue then stuck his left thumb in the cone chalk and chalked his hand, too. Robert Earle dug deep in his jeans and bought a round for the house. "My break," Jimmy John said. He whacked away and the cue ball struck dead center on the one. Balls went spinning and crashing like galaxies. The nine ball dropped and then the ten. "Big un's," Jimmy John declared.

"Good break," Joey said. His chest was pounding, and he pressed his heart to tamp down the pain.

"It was a tight rack," Jimmy John said. "Very tight. How we like 'em, ain't it, Joey?"

"You know it, Jimmy John," Joey replied. "Just how we like 'em." He was sweating.

The egg in his mouth tasted faintly of ginger.

"Que pasa, Joey, how y'doing?" Jesus asked. Joey looked at his scarred, broken hands. Many a tire and sparkplug, many a pulled engine, old desolate dead engines lifted from trucks.

14

"I'm feeling good," Joey said.

As if convinced by this wish, the pain in his chest eased, and Joey started whistling very softly. Pretty soon, Jesus picked up the tune, and then other voices joined, many of them, singing above the noise of the jukebox what they all thought of as a classic country song, Mary Fae's song. The song of the snakes.

Even Jimmy John couldn't resist the notes. He hummed while he lined up his next shot. Butch only watched him and rubbed his crotch, leaving chalk on his pants.

Econoline

Amanda Gann Churchill

Amanda Gann Churchill writes fiction and creative non-fiction. She received her MA in Creative Writing from the University of North Texas and resides in Fort Worth.

Churchill explains, "Two of my favorite songs are Robert Earl Keen's 'Mariano' and Nanci Griffith's 'Econoline.' Because I heard both for the first time in 1993, when I was 15, they will be forever linked in this way. They are also, more importantly, linked by resonant words that sent me straight to my family's crimson-colored set of World Book Encyclopedias back in 10th grade: *where in Mexico is Guanajuato and what kind of car is an Econoline?* While I was slightly disappointed that Griffith's automobile was nothing more than a really big van, I was mesmerized by images of beautiful Guanajuato. So, when I started to write about a girl who is inspired by a stranger's beautiful hometown, these two words, old friends by then, found their way to the story and took over."

I'd always heard stuff about the sky bein' different in different places. I never believed it, though. The sky in Rawlins was your normal blue. There was a lot of it because there wasn't a lot to Rawlins—a few squatty buildings and flat farm and grazing land, far as you can see. But, after watching the sky pass over me for a few days, looking at nearly nothing but a squarish patch of daytime blue and nighttime black, I can tell you: the sky don't care what you think—it changes on you.

By the time I crossed into Mexico, the sky was darker than the blue at home, almost the color of that super-strong mouthwash. A blue that made me stare harder and harder, like it was trying to suck me up out of that van. Hours later, it was even more intense. It reminded me of when my kindergarten teacher had us crayon on waxed paper and then, with another piece of waxed paper on top of the drawing, squished it with a hot iron. It sizzled like a steak on the grill and the colors melted, ending up much brighter and stronger than before. That's what the sky through the van window looked like.

I used to look out the very same window when I was a little kid, watched the clouds move around, watched storms force their way in and water droplets splat against the glass and roll down. But back then the van wasn't moving, it had long since been parked and forgotten. I'd open up the cargo door of the Econoline, crawl in with my bag of supplies and hide out for hours. No one ever bothered me because of the sad state the van was in—faded brown exterior, all the tires flat, weeds growing up around it, window shield pocked with bb pellet shots, stuffing discolored with sun damage and exploding out of the seats. If I had a playhouse like other little girls, I would've been easy to track down. Instead, I'd lie there for hours, alone, and look out at the sky. Sometimes I'd read or draw. I stashed things in the van that I didn't think Mama would miss—an old radio and a couple of blankets to lie on. Sometimes I'd fall asleep out there.

Another good thing about the van: I could lock the doors from the inside. And I had the only key.

The van was my Uncle Beau's. He'd won it as a kid in a contest he found on the back of a cheese cracker box. Told my Mama—his stepsister— that he thought winning it would fix whatever was broken between his real daddy and his mother and that they might travel in it, be happy. It didn't. I'm fourteen and I already know that once a family's broken, there's little anyone can do to ever make it right again. It's disappointing stuff and maybe that's what made Uncle Beau the way he is. Don't know. Don't care, really.

The class was called Life Skills and every 8th grader in Rawlins Consolidated Independent School District had to take it in the spring semester. I tried to get out of it, but Mr. Hobbs, a grumpy old man who used to be a coach but had been stripped of his whistle and stuck in the counseling department summed it up this way for me: I was alive, so I needed life skills.

"But this ain't geography, Miss, why are we doing this?" A tall boy named Josh asked our Life Skills teacher from the back of the class. Miss Gilbert passed out the last of the "Where in the World?" project sheets. She loved projects.

"Because, you need to learn about other places and it's a good exercise in thinking outside the box. The box being this town," she said.

"Where are you going to choose, Sammy?" Jamie H. asked me in a whisper. "I'm choosing Dallas. That's where my cousin moved after college."

I shrugged. Jamie H. probably would make it to Dallas, with or without this project. She just had that look about her—swinging blond ponytail, long limbs, big smile and eyelashes that didn't need any mascara. To top it off, she was smart and nice—the kind of nice that wasn't asking for anything or needing anything. We weren't tight friends, but unlike the rest of her crowd, she was always friendly, saying "hi" in the halls. We were "tablemates"—our two desks pushed up facing each other. It meant we worked on in-class projects together. All of her free goodness kinda bothered me.

"I don't know. Guess I'd better think on it," I said.

"Now, if you can't think of a place, I have a list right up here on the board. Come over and sign up for a location," Miss Gilbert motioned to a list and immediately a line formed at the board.

"Better get up there before they're all taken, Sammy," Jamie said with a grin, twisting her ponytail on top of itself to make a bun, then letting it fall with an elegant swish. "Go for someplace good. Someplace far away."

I tried to smile back, but the day hadn't been going my way so far. I had decided to skip Texas history—my second time to take that stupid class —because there was a test about the Texas Revolution, and I got caught, which was going to be another detention for me. And I wasn't too excited about the weekend. Mama was off from work. That meant everything was going to be topsy-turvy.

I was last to sign up. Minneapolis/St. Paul, Columbus, and Albuquerque. I looked at Miss Gilbert and I must have sighed because she stood behind me, rested one of her cool, freckled hands on my shoulder and sighed herself.

"Well, why don't you think about this overnight and see if you can come up with a better option, Samantha. You can choose anywhere in the world."

"Anywhere?" I asked. A cousin lived in Abilene. It was a reasonable choice, but I couldn't bear standing in front of the class, talking about the benefits of Abilene.

"Go ahead and get crazy with it," Miss Gilbert responded and patted my shoulder. I couldn't tell if she wanted me to "get crazy with it" because she wanted me to dream big or if I was such a lost cause, it didn't really matter what I chose.

I settled back into my seat and pulled out my spiral notebook. Miss Gilbert turned off the lights, flipped on the overhead projector and the whirr of the motor started its magic, lulling me to sleep. I usually didn't sleep well at night, so note-taking times in classes were always hard on me.

"Today, we're going to be talking about self-esteem. . ." Miss Gilbert began. It's hard to sneer when you're falling asleep, but I managed.

Didn't take me two shakes of a dog's tail to figure out who was slid up underneath Mama's car when I got home from school. Mama was still home, which was weird because she always was gone to work by the time I got off the school bus. I didn't even have to ask—I walked up the drive, saw those tan, hairy legs, reminding me of a spider, put my backpack down on the kitchen table and saw Mama there, drinking a glass of pink wine in the middle of the afternoon.

"Uncle Beau's back," I said.

"Beau's back in town for awhile. Just got released. He's looking for a job." Mama didn't look up at me and instead she stared through the window at Uncle Beau, shimmying out from underneath her beat up old sedan.

"Stayin' here?" I asked, not sure why I even posed it as a question. My legs started to itch, so I scratched one leg against the other, my jeans doing the work usually assigned to my fingernails.

"Sammy, I hate that rubbin' noise," Mama said, glaring at me before returning her gaze out the kitchen window. I stopped.

I got a plastic cup full of the store brand Cool-Drink, careful not to spill a neon red drop on the floors I mopped the day before. My heart wasn't beating wildly like I thought it would. I wasn't terrified like I thought I'd be. Guess I knew that the day would come again. I was a little angry at Mama, but even that was a low flicker of a feeling. I decided to try, just to say I did.

"Mama, does he have to stay here? I don't wanna share my bathroom and he's so messy." I tried to sound convincing. It helped that I was indeed a clean freak. Someone had to be around here.

"Samantha Lynn, you and I both know that he's family and he needs some help. Besides, he can share my bathroom. I'll tell him that." Mama took another sip of wine. I noticed that she had lipstick on and that it had smudged the edge of the cloudy old wine glass. I think we had more, somewhere, but since that was the only one that ever got used, it got the brunt of the dishwashing.

Uncle Beau was barely family. He was part of a package deal when my grandfather remarried a woman named Calico from Colorado that he had met at a casino in Oklahoma. Try and say that five times fast. Mama was starting up her associate's degree in nursing and Beau had just left his sophomore year of high school for personal reasons. That's how Uncle Beau had phrased it when I asked once as a kid. *Personal reasons.* He and Mama became thick as thieves for the year he lived with Grandpap and his new bride. Then, things fell apart between Grandpap and Calico—can't expect much out of a woman named after a type of cat—and Beau was gone again.

But, Uncle Beau was like one of those trick frisbees. He came to live with us after my daddy left when I was a little girl, then back again when I was in second grade and again in fifth grade. Every three years or so— seemed to be the average time the state gives to someone like Beau.

I watched Mama pour more pink into her glass with an unsteady hand and my mind was instantly made up. I slapped together a bologna sandwich, slid it into a baggie, grabbed a snack bag of corn chips and a handful of iced animal cookies.

"You goin' someplace? I called in sick from work and don't feel like cookin'," Mama said, her words bumping up next to each other like one stopped too fast coming out of her mouth.

"Yeah, I'm headin' out to the library to work on a project with Jamie. You want that leftover casserole? I can put that in the oven and y'all can eat that for dinner." I put my food into my school backpack and then, after digging through the deep freeze, slid an entire casserole dish, foil and all, into the oven and turned it on low, set the timer for an hour. There was a fifty-fifty chance she'd forget about the casserole and it'd burn up before I snuck back in.

"Mama, just turn it up to 350 when the timer goes off. Should be ready to eat around 5:30 or so. I'll be late because after the library Jamie's mom said we could come over and work on gluing our diorama together."

Because of Mama's work schedule, I didn't have to lie often, but when I did, I was always doing something with Jamie. Luckily, there were four Jamies in my class, including Jamie H. I never specified which one and if Mama ever wanted to find out, that's four mothers to phone, not counting the two Jamies that had step-mothers. She'd be passed out by number three, if she ever got it in her mind to try.

"Bye, Mama." I said.

"Wait, you aren't goin' to say hello to Uncle Beau?" she asked, mid-sip. Then, she got a funny look on her face, looked at me up and down, like she hadn't seen me in ages and was taking me in. I ran my hand over my mouth and chin, just to make sure Cool Drink wasn't dripping off me or something. I thought about what I had on: purple tank top, dark denim jeans, green fake leather flats. I had pulled my thin, light brown hair back on both sides with green hairclips to match the shoes. Thought I looked pretty cute, but had gotten in trouble for the tank top. Have to wear sleeves in middle school. Not that my skinny arms were doing anyone harm. I hated middle school and reckoned that high school wasn't going to be much fun either.

"No, you go on, Sammy. Bet Jamie's waiting," Mama said, waving me off. I ran out the door before she changed her mind, grabbed my bike and took off across the field, beyond the scrubby tree stand, and, confident that no one but Jesus was looking, hid my bike under those trees, and took off in the opposite direction.

Twelve acres—formerly my Grandpap's land, now ours—separated our house from the state highway. Although it was nothing but two falling over fences and a nearly dried-up stock pond, I claimed it as my own when I was a kid and that's where I played, straying out farther and farther as Mama got drunker and drunker. Soon after Beau's return in second grade, I found the van, all locked up, in a tiny dip of land. I was curious. I asked Mama about it and she had told me the story of how Calico had it towed to the land and Grandpap demanded the ugly thing be put off somewhere it couldn't be seen. I asked where the keys were and she said she figured they were in one of the junk drawers. Took me the better part of a Saturday, but I found them.

The van became my clubhouse. The day I took off, dodging Beau with my bologna sandwich snug in my backpack, I hadn't been there in ages. But, I had kept the keys with me for years, just in case. I held my breath as I stuck the key into the cargo door in the back, surprised when I didn't hear the familiar pop. It was already unlocked. My left foot crunched down on a plastic water bottle, the paper wrapper still new and clinging tight. My heartbeat sped as I opened the door, catching a whiff of hot air and body odor. I didn't run, though, when I saw two dark eyes staring back at me.

I don't remember much about when Beau came to live with us in second grade—just bits and pieces, like when you are trying to recall a movie you've seen years ago. The stuff I can picture in my head is everyday occurrences. Eating a sandwich in the kitchen and realizing that if I took my fingernail and scrapped the table, the tired old wood allowed a shallow mark. Watching the trees bend nearly in half, like they were doing aerobics, during a tornado warning. Standing outside Mama's bedroom door, waiting for her to hear me, and then walking away, placing my feet directly on the tile squares, not touching the grout in between. Sitting in the chair next to my teacher's desk, her asking me why I hadn't been bathing and staring at my feet, wishing the carpet would split open and devour me whole. But to each memory, Uncle Beau is there, somewhere on the sides, his shadow stretching across the scene. And, there's a feeling of trouble in the pit of my stomach when I think back, a low rumbling like right before you're sick and you know that you have to get to the bathroom fast.

His stay in fifth grade wasn't that long—only four months. But I remember those months pretty well, starting with seeing him for the first time in so many years. It was a Thursday and I got off the school bus at the end of the road and started walking toward home. It was fall, but still hot like summer and I was wearing matching shorts and t-shirt—orange with pink polkadots on the top and pink with orange stripes on the bottom—my favorite summer outfit. I heard someone come up behind me on the road, the gravel crackling slow under the tires because they were creeping along.

"Sammy! Hey, Sammy!" The voice was familiar. I knew if I turned, I would see him, his hair the color of old hay cut short because the state gives you a haircut when you're let out.

I heard another voice and then Uncle Beau said, "Yeah, I'm sure that's her." Then, he started yelling again, closer this time. I cut across the ditch, through the stagnant water, getting green scum wrapped around my shins and my canvas shoes. I dodged quickly behind tall grass, knowing that chiggers were probably attacking my socked ankles and where my underwear hit the top of my thighs. I was still just walking fast, pretending I didn't hear him, but as soon as I cleared a low-slung part of the barbed wire fence, I took off running, my soggy, untied shoelaces slapping my ankles. At an old chimney that was half knocked down, a place I had hid notes to my future self just a few summers before, I made a left and ran through the trees toward the cemetery, entering through a little arched passageway at the back. I passed by the age-worn headstones over a hundred years old and then the newer ones of people I had heard about but couldn't ever recall meeting. I stepped in the center of the graves, running with every bit of energy I had until I just stopped. My lungs locked up.

"Why you doing this?" I wheezed to myself aloud. He would be there when I got home. Mama would be smiling and hugging him. He'd sleep in the room next to mine, share my little bathroom at the end of the hall. Something fragile, like the blue shell of a robin's egg kicked out of the nest, was crushed inside me.

And, just like that, next to Charles Brayburn who was an Oddfellow and had a fancy monument—a tall pillar with three interlocked chains and two hands shaking in friendship—I fell to my knees, wrapped my arms around the pillar and launched a short, choppy scream into the stone.

"Who are you?" I asked, not certain if the man in the van understood me. As my eyes adjusted to the shadows in the Econoline, my nose adjusted to the smell—a hot musty smell from the baking old van, and something sharp like the smell of saltwater I gargled every time I got sore throat.

Soon I could see him, shirtless, but wearing boot-cut blue jeans cuffed at the ankle. He struggled to get his shirt on—a Western cut shirt, light blue, with snap buttons. He tried and tried, but his left arm wasn't working properly. He looked like a bird stuck in a chimney, flapping and flapping but getting nowhere.

"Who are you?" I asked again. "This is my van," I said.

"So sorry, so sorry—" the man said, breathing hard. "I hurt. You see?"

His face was still hidden in shadows and as if he knew that I couldn't see him well, he pushed his head into the light just enough. Half of his head was swollen, a festering, angry reddish purple. His left eye was nothing but a slit, reminding me of the steam vents my quiet grandmother had once made in the tops of her pies, the fleshy crust folding in where she stuck the knife. I couldn't tell if the man had been beat up or run over by a truck—or both, perhaps.

"You need to be in a hospital," I said. "Do you understand? Hospital."

"No, no—I get better soon. No hurt soon." The man's one good eye frantically looked from side to side. He was scared and I was the one doing the scaring. An odd feeling of power shot through me as I realized this, followed quickly by remorse. I wanted him out of my van, but something about the way he was trying to button his shirt with the hand he didn't usually use, his brown face creased with lines and the few gray hairs budding at his temples, made me wonder about him.

"Can I sit down?" I asked as I lowered myself onto the bumper of the van. "Here," I said, reaching into my backpack and pulling out my bologna sandwich. "You want this?"

The man seemed to think about it for a second and then reached out for the baggie. "Gracias, gracias," he said as he opened the zip bag with one hand. He ate one half in three bites, the other half in four.

"De nada," I said. I only knew a little Spanish. In fifth grade, Mrs. Hernandez, my homeroom teacher, taught us some sayings and common words. I enjoyed learning something that my Mama couldn't understand and took to speaking simple Spanish phrases to myself around the house.

"My name is Ignacio," the man said. I could tell that he had said this phrase before and was confident in his words. I could say "Mi nombre Samantha," with the same ease, but I didn't want him to think I spoke more than I did. I reached my hand back into my backpack and handed him my corn chips.

"My name's Sammy. I live right over there—" I pointed toward our house. "This is my van," I said again, feeling bad about the lie.

Ignacio nodded and crunched away on the chips, salt sticking to his unshaven chin. He wiped it away and I noticed he wore a beautiful ring on his pointer finger. Gold and intricately carved, it took up half his knuckle and in the center was a smooth moon-colored stone that looked like marble. A vein of red ran right through the center of it.

"So, what happened to you? Why are you hurt?" I slowed my words down to give him time to chew on each one. I pointed to his arm and to his swollen head.

Ignacio nodded. "Coyote. Ask for more money, so—" Ignacio kicked his leg a little bit to show how he had been injured. I had heard about coyotes, people that smuggled Mexicans across the border some ninety miles from Rawlins for a fee. The summer before, five men had been found dead in the back of a U-Haul, locked in and left because they didn't have enough money to continue their journey deeper into Texas. The truck was found in a nearby town, a town we shared the local newspaper with. The article had been cut out, photocopied onto a transparency, and we talked about it in social studies one day.

I nodded. "I'm sorry," I said. I looked over my shoulder, back at the house, worried that for some reason, I'd see Beau loping down the slope. "Hey, I'm going to scoot in here a bit, okay?" I pulled myself into the van and crossed my legs. It felt good to be out of the sun, which for April was pretty darn warm. My relief, though, was quickly exchanged for the stifling heat of the back of the van. I waved my hand at my face, but it was as helpful as a gnat's wing.

"Your English is good, Ignacio," I said, trying to figure out his age. His face looked older than Mama's. Ignacio didn't seem much taller than her, either, maybe five eight or so, and he was thin like most of the boys in my class.

"Where you from?" I asked.

"Eh, I am from Guanajuato."

I must have looked confused because he drew an imaginary Mexico—a long shape that was a mix of the letter J and a hammock—on the floor of the van and pointed toward the center. "Guanajuato. I learn English in school and from my daughter. She work at hotel. Big hotel in Guanajuato." His right hand fluttered through the still van air, creating a large squarish shape, which I figured was the big hotel. I realized that if his other arm could help, the shape would have been that much clearer.

"Oh. Is it pretty there? Bonita?" I asked.

"Pretty, yes, very pretty. Big town. Very grand, old." Ignacio tried to smile, but the scabby looking scrape on his lip moved when he tried. It must of hurt because he grimaced. I imagined it was from where his face was rubbed against concrete as he was kicked. I slid my hand back into my backpack and pulled out the cookies. I took one out—what appeared to be a pink iced camel—and handed the bag over.

"Gracias," Ignacio said.

"How long have you been here?" I asked.

"How long in van?" He asked, wiping a crumb from his chin. "Four, five days. I need to go to Oklahoma. Have work there."

"Work? What kind of work?"

"Eh, work is rock. I put up rocks," he said. Ignacio took his good hand and mimed laying a rock down, spreading it with something, and putting another up next to it. "Hard work."

"Yeah, I bet," I said.

"You want me to go," he said, and I wondered if it was a question or a statement. I actually hadn't thought much about that. The van really wasn't my property and as far as wanting people to stay or go, I'd never had much say in those matters. My dad left and I never got to say goodbye and Beau just came as he pleased and left when he got crossways with the law. It was nice for someone to ask, for once.

"Well, this van isn't really mine. But, I'm the only person to use it ever, you see." I looked down at my feet. I didn't know how to tell this stranger the truth. But, seein' as how he might not understand me totally, anyhow, I tried. "Things aren't too great at home. This is where I hide out sometimes. You know, get away from things." I looked in his eyes for comprehension and I saw a flicker of something warm and kind. I wondered if he was someone's father.

"You can stay for a little bit, but I'll need you to move on soon."

"Thank you, I only stay until no hurt more," Ignacio said. "You come visit. And I pay you somehow."

I thought about that for a second. "Well, there's something you can do. You said this Whatta-what-o is pretty?" I knew I slaughtered the name of his hometown.

"Guan-a-jua-to." He said slowly and, then, turning with a painful jerk, he opened up the outside pocket of a backpack that clearly had once belonged to someone else—a daughter perhaps. It was dirty neon yellow and had several flowery patches sewn on the front. He pulled out a photo that looked to be several years old of four children in front of a church.

"You see—very pretty," he said. "My children at Templo de San Diego."

Ignacio's kids stood on walkway made of stones, flanked by hot pink flowers. The church itself was mostly stucco and painted a bright peach. The entry was stone made to look like a fancy carved candle. It was the prettiest building I had ever seen. The kids in the picture smiled back at me.

"There's this project at school. It's due at the end of the week. I'm going to need your help. We have to choose a town to talk about—one we'd like to live in when we grow up. I'm going to choose your town. That okay?"

Ignacio nodded and smiled. "Cool," I said and then shrugged. "I guess I'll leave you be. Unless you want the company." Ignacio shrugged as well. I didn't want to face Beau. I didn't want to sit in the quiet library until I was shooed out by the old bat who ran it, wanting to get home to her programs and her parakeet.

"So, tell me about your family," I said, trying to sound grown up, and leaned back on the van wall, listening to the evening set in outside and the baby grasshoppers making their first noises of the spring.

The next morning, I sat cross-legged in the back of the Econoline even though it was first period and I was missing Texas history again. I was still tired from the night before. After leaving my new friend in the van, I watched from behind the gas tank shed as Mama and Beau drove away for a night out. I slept alright until I heard them clatter back in the early morning hours. After that, I got dressed and waited for charcoal gray of first light, my shoes on my feet and everything.

"I brought the stuff, show me the photos," I said while chewing on my pointer-finger nail, watermelon lipgloss smudging across the chipped paint.

Ignacio nodded and carefully tore open the box of Cheese Nips because his ribs were still aching. I had brought a plastic bag of stuff I grabbed from the cabinet before leaving the house for the day. He had already eaten most of the pizza-flavored potato chips.

"Now, I need to learn how to say this right." I said.

"Guanajuato?" Ignacio said with a full mouth.

"Wahn-ah-wah-toe," I repeated. "That's where you went to school, right?"

"Only for a little time. Then I started the working."

"And you were only eleven, right? You gave tours," I said, smiling at the thought of this man walking backwards through a whole city.

"Yes, like you said. People come from all over to see this city. It looks like a—" Ignacio shoved another handful of crackers in his mouth, "Give me bag. One moment."

I pushed the backpack toward Ignacio.

He fished his hand inside and pulled out a paper clipped stack of papers and photos. From the inside of the stash, he pulled out a couple of color postcards, the edges soft and curved with travel. "Here. You see? All the colors?" He held the cards out to me and pointed with the fancy ring finger.

I held them up to the light filtering in through the van window. The first photo was of a shady square—a large, marble fountain was in the center, surrounded by stuccoed buildings in red, gold and pink. The windows and doors were trimmed in carvings that looked like decorations on the top of a wedding cake. Under one tree, a woman sat reading a book. I tried to make out her face but couldn't because of her large sunglasses and floppy straw hat. One curl the color of molasses lay on the woman's shoulder. A cat was perched on the edge of the fountain, getting a drink. I flipped to the next postcard of a large stone theatre surrounded by manicured palm trees. What looked like a hundred skinny steps led up to the doors.

"Es Teatro Juarez. Very old," Ignacio said. "The next one es Cristo Rey."

"Cristo Rey?" I flipped to the last postcard and smiled. "Jesus, right? And what does *rey* mean?" A large figure of Christ stood in front of a brilliant blue sky with his arms out, one palm facing down and the other reaching in a sideways handshake. On either side of him, small curly-topped angels held up crowns.

"Yes, yes—Jesus. Rey es king. You pray at that place, miracles happen. I know. This ring I wear, it has same stone as mountain under Cristo Rey. Old ring—from father. You see?" He took off the ring and held it out to me. It was much heavier than it looked, as if it were made of iron, not gold and stone.

"My father went to pray one day. My mother had baby—my sister—and she not . . ." Ignacio took his hand, pressed it against his heart and breathed in deep. "You know what I say? Not good. But father go up mountain to pray. And then, go home. Sister living and ring . . . " He pointed to the line of bright red that ran like a river through the center. "Ring get that."

"Really?" I said loudly. I loved stories where something magical happened—something good that no one was expecting. "That's so cool!"

Ignacio put his finger to his lip to quiet me down. Worried, I pulled myself to a squat and peered out the front windshield. The field was empty, just waving weeds and bugs slamming into the glass. Just the same, I held still there, making sure no one was coming. Uncle Beau was probably still asleep. Reassured, I settled back into place and thumped the cards with my left hand.

"Hey, 'Nacio. Listen, I'll go by the DQ and get you a burger if I can have these. I'll get you fries, too. You like fries?"

"And a blanket? It getting cold at night." Ignacio said.

"Sure, sure. A blanket and a pillow. I'd better get going. If I'm not there by second period, they'll call home for sure. Don't need that." I grabbed my backpack and scooted to the cargo door.

"I'll stop by after supper, 'Nacio. You keep these for me until then." I handed the postcards back to him, then thought about it a second. "I'll keep this one," I said, pulling out the first postcard of the sunlit plaza. "I think this is my favorite."

I had just stepped onto the black-topped basketball court as the tardy bell rang. I hated that sound—half fire-engine clanging, half game-show buzzer—and so loud that it stayed in your head for a second or two after the darn thing was turned off.

Rawlins Middle School sat in the middle of a flat, dusty field. On one side was the state highway that cut right through our town like a knife through a cake, on the other side, Rawlins Elementary and Rawlins High. Next year, I'd be back there, if I passed Texas history, of course. I swung off my backpack, searched for the note I'd written and forged my mother's name on, and headed to the main office.

"Late again, Samantha? Let me see that note," Miss Marla, the attendance lady, said. "Goodness, girl, you've been sick again?"

"Yes ma'am. It's the spring winds. Pollen." I unpeeled the taped edge of the card stating that "all visitors sign in here" that was stuck to the Formica-topped counter the color of nacho cheese. I wasn't the first peeler—

the tape was gray around the edge and curled—and I wondered how many kids had stood there, peeling and lying.

"Allergies?" Miss Marla asked, barely looking up as she wrote out my pink hall pass in old lady script.

"Uh-huh." I said, rubbing my nose with my sleeve for good measure.

"Bless your heart," Miss Marla noted the time on the pass. "Get on to class, you don't want to miss any more of Life Skills."

The halls were empty except for the custodian and his trashcans and a few crumpled sheets of paper, moving as the ancient air conditioner puffed to life. I took my time going to my locker and taking out my binder. I checked my lipgloss in the mirror inside the locker door and applied a little more eyeliner. Mama said I looked like a raccoon, but I thought it looked pretty glamorous and mysterious, like the fashion magazine had told me it would.

I slipped into my seat as Miss Gilbert was explaining the "bellringer" writing exercise. *Gilbert and her damned bellringers*, I thought. I pushed the pass to the corner of the desk and started writing about what I thought the difference between morals and ethics was.

As Miss Gilbert stood at the overhead projector, the copies of her notes fuzzy against the white back wall of the class, I slipped out the postcard I'd traded a DQ hamburger for. The woman was still reading her book, the cat was still getting a drink from the fountain. Behind the colorful pink shutters, closed to the light of day, I imagined a perfect bedroom to live in, soft white sheets and a cold tile floor. I wondered how far of a drive it was to Guanajuato, how many tanks of gas it would take. I wondered if it was hard to learn how to drive on the highway. I'd only circled the driveway a couple of times.

"What's that?" Jamie whispered, reaching out and touching the card with her perfectly manicured pointer finger.

"Postcard. Guanajuato. It's in Mexico," I said, flipping the picture side to Jamie and then quickly slipping it under my binder. "Might go live there one day." I could feel the words accumulating in my mouth, fighting each other to be first out of the hatch. "Got family there, actually. They might want me to move in with them, help them run their business."

Jamie's eyes opened wide and I knew I had her hooked. "Is that what you're doing your project on? You going soon?" Jamie whispered, trying to keep up with Miss Gilbert's notes. "I mean, before the summer? What kind of business?"

I hadn't thought that far. "Mmmm. . . tours for visitors. They need a tour guide to walk through the town and point out things."

"Don't they speak Spanish in Mexico?"

"Yes, but all the visitors speak English. That's why they need me."

"Wow. That's kinda cool, Sammy," Jamie smiled and I felt myself sitting taller.

"Don't tell anyone, okay? I don't want everyone asking questions—"

"Samantha Rodgers. Please stop whispering in my class. This is your warning." Miss Gilbert walked to the board, wrote down my name and put a check by it. Two more checks and I'd be in detention, which wasn't all bad—it would keep me from the house for awhile in the afternoon. Maybe Uncle Beau would get tired of waiting on me to get home, go grab a beer or something. But then I thought about Ignacio, waiting on his burger and fries, and decided to shove all the sass back into my throat.

"Yes ma'am. I'm sorry ma'am," I said and began to write furiously to catch up, stopping ever so often to stare at the corner of the postcard that hung out from under my binder.

I enjoyed working on the Where in the World project more than I cared to admit. I went to the library twice, photocopied pages from travel magazines and from encyclopedias and even requested a book from another library that was called *A Photographic Journey Through Mexico*. It came in twenty-four hours and I was back again, using up all the dimes in the house on the Xerox machine that sat hot and cranky in the corner of the librarian's office. I overdid it, I guess, because I had far too much information and pictures for my poster and report.

The night before the project was due, I closed my bedroom door and struggled to push the over-stuffed recliner against it. I picked up my backpack from the floor and slowly unzipped it, letting each tooth release from its counterpart, until the opening was like a large, yawning mouth. Mama was at work and Beau was out with a friend that he had made years ago who happened to turn up, just like Beau, every couple of years. I pulled out my geometry book, let the pages flip open, and pulled out the extra photos, already cut out and ready to be used. I spread them on the floor, moving them around into some order and they took up the entire oval rug. I peered over them, lightly touching them, flicking away pieces of fuzz from the floor, finally choosing a photo of a mauve, stuccoed church. I don't know what I was thinking, except I didn't want to throw them all away.

Placing the photo on the edge of the dresser, I opened up my closet and removed the winter coat that was hanging on the hook in the door. It was a three-sizes-too-big pass-down coat and because it never got that cold in Rawlins, it had dust on the tops of the shoulders and collar. I then balled up some tape and stuck it on the back four corners and middle of the photo. With light hands and squinted eyes, I placed it in the dead center of the door.

Next, I picked up a photo of a young child, dressed in bright blues and greens, on the back of a donkey. A black and white mutt of a dog with long legs stood next to the donkey, panting. In the background was a yellow house and a tree with large, waxy leaves. I hung this photo under the church. Next, a café, empty except for tables decorated with tissue paper flowers and pink pottery plates and teacups. I looked closer, to see if I could see into the background, but my own shadow darkened the photo. I did notice that a fountain peered through the arched window of the restaurant. I placed this picture above the church and slightly to the left.

For two hours, I created a collage in the shape of my winter coat, occasionally hanging the ugly thing in its spot, checking to see if any of the photo corners were visible. Mama rarely made it to my room, but I still didn't want anyone to know about my city. Over the course of the week, that's how it had begun to feel inside me: like my city. I hadn't even been there, didn't know anything about it other than what the books and Ignacio had said, and still I felt like I knew it.

I stood in front of my photos, hands on my hips, and listened to the wind outside, bringing in a spring storm, my ears straining for the sounds of Uncle Beau's car and just stared at the blue buildings, the sunset, the gardens, the woman in the floppy hat. I hoped my presentation would go well the next day and was about to sort through my stack of notecards and practice when I heard the screen door squeak open and then slam closed.

Shit. Shit. Shit.

I had worked hard to dodge Uncle Beau since his arrival. Mama had also been a distraction for him, fawning over Uncle Beau in a way I hadn't noticed before, laughing extra loud, taking time off of work. Now, I was alone in the house with him and nothing but an old recliner was pushed up against the door.

Don't freak. He might not be the same way as he was before.

I heard Beau talking to someone, his friend I guessed, and listened as the fridge opened and closed. They swore and laughed about something that had happened in the grocery store parking lot. I heard the pop of cans and then the hum of the television set—wrestling had been turned on. I switched off the overhead light and stood in the closet, the single bulb bright against my forehead, my brain jumping from one idea to the next. *Fake sleep? Hide? Sneak out?* Maybe, I thought, I could just walk out there casually, feel out the situation, and everything would be just fine. No big deal.

"Sammy, you up? You in there?" Beau slurred at the door. I could tell his lips were next to the door jam, as his voice had a close, wet sound. The doorknob jiggled open, the lock long since broken, and the door made a hollow thud against the recliner.

"Sammy? What the—" Beau said. "What you doin' in there?"

I quickly tiptoed to the bed, slipped under the covers and called out in my best fake-sleepy voice, "Huh? Who's there?"

"Come on out here, girl. Want you to meet a friend of mine," Beau said.

"I have a presentation in the morning for school, Uncle Beau. I'm tired."

"You haven't even talked to me five minutes since I got here, Sammy. You gotten rude in the last few years? Why, you better'n me now? Big middle school girl?" Beau started laughing at his own ribbing and then pushed harder against the door. "What is this here, anyway?"

"Needed the room for my project. Had to move the chair," I said and then paused. My armpits and the place behind my knees began to sting and itch with sweat. I could feel my chest getting tight. I looked at the digital clock that sat high on the chest of drawers, glowing yellow green like cat eyes in the dark—10:30.

"Oh, crap! I totally forgot. I need to print out something for school tomorrow. I'm goin' to race over to the neighbors and print. Won't be gone long at all . . ." I hopped out of bed, grabbed my backpack and squinted at the door. It was a flimsy lie. Our closest neighbors were elderly and definitely didn't own a printer. I rolled up my poster and zipped the pack around it. Might get a little dinged up, but it'd survive.

"Can't you do it tomorrow? Come on out," Beau said.

"No, need to do it now. I'll hang out with y'all when I get back in." I unlocked my window and thanked God in heaven that my father decided not to build a two-story house. I wiggled out the window, closed it lightly and raced around the side of the house toward my bike. I was down the drive when Beau realized what had happened—the porch light flipped on, but I was already to the road. I would head like I was going over to Granpap's old place, then cut through the back way.

My bike wheels crunched over gravel and then, off-road, sliced through grass and weeds. The wind picked up a bit and I shivered because I had sweated right through my t-shirt and my hair, all the way back to my ponytail, was wet like I had just finished gym class. I was among the trees, dodging the skinny, scrubby ones with my front tire. It would have been easier to walk my bike through the tree stand, but I kept pushing, standing at some places to get me going just a bit faster. Then, the trees opened up to the field, the familiar decline started and I was whooshing toward the Econoline, not caring that I was getting slapped around by the tall switchgrass that hid my van so perfectly through the seasons.

Ignacio had been asleep, curled up in the stinking van on his side. His eyes were wide and confused as I hopped inside, closing the door with a bang behind me. I heard his hands look for the lantern and then turn it on. I'm sure he was searching his English for "what the hell are you doing here," but settled on a quiet hello.

I couldn't talk and so I wrapped my arms around my knees and buried my nose into the valley created by my kneecaps. I stayed there, still and thinking, trying to slow my brain down. I used to like to ride my bike up to the railroad crossing and as the train was going by, I'd fix my eyes on one point in front of me and let them relax. They'd almost cross and the colors of the boxcars would fly by, looking like the rag rug that ran the length of the hallway that connected my room to Mama's. That's how my head felt—everything was a blur of colors and sounds.

"Trouble in family." It wasn't a question. Ignacio was a smart man.

"Yeah. Something like that," I said. My nose was running uncontrollably and that's when I realized that I'd been crying. I wiped my nose on my knee and a string of snot hung in the air. Ignacio held out a Dairy Queen napkin and I rubbed my nose right over the embossed logo.

"It's my uncle—the one that's not really my uncle. Beau. Well, he drinks . . . " I started, not exactly knowing how to jump onto the next idea that was forming in my head. I didn't know how to say it out loud. I felt like I was crossing a fast moving creek in the spring, standing on a rock, trying to figure out where I could land that would lead to the next rock that would lead me to shore. "He drinks and then he acts all crazy. At first, he acts like he's playing and then he's not anymore and . . ." I looked for some sort of understanding in Ignacio's eyes. *Maybe it's my fault. Maybe it's no big deal.* But Ignacio's eyes were downcast. He was looking at a hole in his sock where his big toe and longish toenail stuck out. He saw me looking and he ducked his toe in, as if ashamed.

"I have daughters. Trés. Ana *diecinueve*, Lucinda *catorce*, Lupita *once*." Ignacio spoke slowly. My brain chugged at the numbers—19, 14 and 11—and I nodded. *"El mundo esta un lugar peligroso para niñas."*

I didn't catch it all. I shrugged.

"World," Ignacio said, making a circle with his finger. "Bad for girls."

"I wish I could leave. Just get out of this place. But that'd mean leaving Mama. She needs me—I keep the house up and make most of the food. I go to the store, I get her scrubs ready for work."

I tried to add *and I love her*, but lately those words always made me want to cry. A sob would come up out of nowhere and get lodged in my throat and choke me. Before Beau came back to town, I'd tried to tell Mama I loved her in the morning before heading off to school. She'd be asleep on the couch, her hair plastered to her face with who-knows-what, and I'd cover her up with the blanket that I kept folded up on the arm of the old wing-back that sat in the corner. I kept it there just for this purpose. I'd tuck the blanket in around her feet, so she'd have a hard time kicking it off and then I'd lean in close. *Mama*, I'd say, but then I'd stop, not being able to continue. The blanket was wool and heavy. A thought would run through my head of its own will, run like mad as if on fire and I'd imagine me grinding that rough material into her mouth, the fringe hanging out like baby fingers waving goodbye. There was a time I'd imagine just the opposite, a happy Mama, one who would open her eyes and say, "have a good day at school, sweetie."

I wondered sometimes if I was going crazy.

"Sí, your mama fear if you go far?" Ignacio stared at me and I shook my head. "I say wrong, maybe?"

"No, you said it right. Most mamas might be afraid if their kids went off. Don't know if mine would. She's not like most mothers."

Ignacio nodded. "I see," was all he said.

"How are you feelin'?" I asked, wanting to fill up the quiet.

"Good. Strong. Leave soon, no more van. No more problem for you," he said, and I felt suddenly uncomfortable, my legs itching like fire ants were crawling up my shins, under my jeans.

"You haven't been trouble, Ignacio. Wish you could stay longer. It's been fun talking to you. When you leaving?"

"Tomorrow. In morning I go early." Ignacio watched my face and I looked at his. I barely knew him, but I was suddenly so sad to be facing an empty van the next afternoon. "I have a friend who has truck. Come meet me at highway. We go together."

"Yeah, I have to go to school early. My project is due. Poster looks really good. I think I'm going to get an 'A' on this one. I need it, too."

"I need to give you money. I have money. You buyed me food, medicine. You take care—"

"Nah, Ignacio. You did enough. The postcards are enough." I said.

"Okay, no money." Then, after a second, he smiled and handed something to me. I didn't know what it was a first, until its heaviness snapped something in my brain.

"No, Ignacio. This has been in your family. This is special and you need it." I handed the ring back to him and scooted toward the door. "You need sleep if you're leaving. I'm going to go now . . . "

"You go back to house?"

I hadn't thought about where I was going. I knew I couldn't go there. I shook my head no.

"I sleep in seat of front. Take pillow." Ignacio crawled into the passenger's seat and stretched his legs across to the driver's side. He folded a t-shirt and laid his cheek against it, as the vinyl was split open and rough.

"Maybe just awhile." I curled up, thinking I wouldn't be sleepy at all. But, the stress of the night, combined with the shrill of the cicadas and Ignacio's snores, lulled me to sleep.

I awoke with a start and looked around. It was no longer dark, but the light thistle gray of morning. Ignacio was still asleep. I didn't want to wake him. I didn't know how to say goodbye and thought maybe it was best if I just left. I put on my shoes and slung my backpack over my shoulders. I'd have to clean myself up at school. The locker room would be empty and I just hoped that no one would say anything about my crumpled day-old clothes. I opened the cargo door, thinking that Ignacio might wake up a bit, but all he did was smack his lips a couple of times and continue sleeping. His arm was lodged next to the van wall and wrapped around the seat back like he was hugging a person.

"Thanks, 'Nacio," I said in a whisper. Then, I reached out and did something weird, my hand drawn away from my body as if it were connected to an invisible string. I slid my finger along the stone of Ignacio's ring, right along the red river. *God protect us*, I whispered, *please.*

My presentation was perfect. I didn't stumble once over my speech and everyone was impressed with the poster. Miss Gilbert seemed pleased and as I was leaving class, she called out to me, *adios!* with a beaming smile. It was a nice gesture, but I felt numb. My eyes burned with exhaustion and something inside me had given way to a silent sadness.

I didn't go by the field where the van was parked on my way home from school. I didn't want to see it all empty. Instead, I walked right home, hoping for a trouble-free shower and a nap. Somewhere, between the bus drop-off and our long driveway, I decided that I wouldn't dodge him anymore. I couldn't keep it up.

Mama and Uncle Beau sat together at the kitchen table, smoking, laughing loudly. Beau looked up and grinned at me when I walked in.

"What y'all doin'?" I asked.

"Just talkin'. Beau here made one hell of a deal today. Lucky bastard!" Mama cackled and took a deep drag. "Get me some more wine out of the fridge. Stuck a new bottle in there this morning."

I obeyed. There had been a time I would have said something. Now I just twisted off the cap for her.

"Yep, free money. I'm taking it to a jeweler tomorrow and I'm sure I'll get a lot for it. Some kind of special quartz the guy said."

"What are you talking about?" I asked, knowing full well that they'd both been drinking for quite some time.

"Some Mexican dude came up to the house this morning, gave me this ring for the van. He spent all afternoon putting some used tires on it and someone's coming tonight to tow it off. Goddamn thing doesn't even run, but he don't care. Said he always wanted an Econoline." Beau was drumming the table with excitement. "Ring's real gold with this huge stone. Come here an' look at it, Sammy!"

I shook my head, my hands shaking.

"What's wrong with you?" Mama glared at me and then reached across the table and slid her hand onto Beau's knee. "You gonna buy me something with your ring money?"

Beau squeezed her hand. "'Course, Missy." He took a long swallow of his beer and turned to me and, with a sly smile, said, "Think I'll be staying on here for awhile, Sammy. I think we need to have a talk about the way you've been treating me . . ."

"Coming to tow the van tonight?" I asked.

"Yeah—don't know where the keys are. That's his problem, though. Shit, talk about the luck!" Beau grinned and reached his hand towards me. He was drunk enough to think I'd reach back. Mama leaned across his body and slapped his arm down.

"C'mon, Beau," she said. But, I knew she didn't do it for me.

I left the kitchen. I went outside and climbed through the bedroom window, remembering the recliner slammed against the door. I didn't think. I grabbed a few things from my top drawer, pushed the wad of clothes into my backpack and tossed it out the bedroom window. I ripped down the collage behind the winter coat, folded it up, and stuffed it in a duffle bag I rarely used. On top, I put a few books, my favorite perfume, my jewelry box, and whatever else my hand touched as I tore through the room.

Before long, I was pumping my bike across the field. Tires, all different shades of nearly worn-out, propped the van up higher than usual. No one else was there. I threw my stuff in the back and lifted my bike inside. I squeezed into the small space next to it and covered myself with a blanket. Before I threw it over my eyes, I saw something sticking from the rubber around the back cargo window. I reached out for a postcard. It was of Guanajuato. An illustrated map of Ciudad Viejo was on the front. On the back were the words, *"Dios es nuestro protector"* written in a sprawling script. I didn't read much Spanish, but I understood what it said.

Shambala

Laurence Musgrove

Laurence Musgrove is professor and head of the Department of English at Angelo State University in San Angelo, Texas, where he teaches courses in composition, literature, creative writing, and English education.

His work has been published in *Inside Higher Ed*, *The Chronicle of Higher Education*, *JAEPL*, *Southern Indiana Review*, *Christianity and Literature*, and *Concho River Review*. He also blogs at *www.theillustratedprofessor.com* and *www.handmadethinking.com*.

Musgrove says that his story "was inspired by the opportunity to retrace events I experienced in my early college years. I happened to see B. W. Stevenson perform live in Austin in the early seventies while attending Southwestern University. Classmates and I regularly hitch-hiked down I-35 to Austin for good cheap Mexican food and to catch a set or two of music by the likes of Stephen Fromholz, Uncle Walt's Band, and B. W. Like the mythical kingdom Shambala, Austin in those days seemed to me to be the center of everything beautiful and good. I dedicate this story to Guss Farmer, now deceased, one of my favorite professors at Southwestern."

It was probably about time I told Paul I was gay. But I couldn't do it at school. He was a student of mine at Southwestern in Georgetown. Not an art major, but still someone who paid attention and listened. A good listener I'd say—and that's saying something for a college student. Most are just drifting in and out, self-absorbed or stoned, just getting the credit and drawing a bunch of nonsense. And not listening. Even the majors, especially the girls, aren't interested in listening. They just want to play with their colors. Make it pretty. "Don't bother me," they say with their eyes and shoulders and pouts.

So after class one day near the end of the term, Paul said he was meeting some friends on Saturday night at Saxon Pub to catch B. W. Stevenson, and wanted to know if I wanted to join them. I figured it would be a good time to tell him. Besides, it was only a couple of minutes from the house Roger and I shared.

Like I said, he was a pretty good student. He really tried to do what I asked, even though he was very raw. I mean, he really didn't have any drawing talent to speak of. He tried hard and usually had to go through a couple of efforts before he felt like he could make a go of it. I liked talking to him about what he was working on and leaned over to him quietly, reminding him how best to hold the charcoal and "draw big." But he seemed more interested in focusing in on me, really wanting to chat more than draw.

That was okay with me. I guess I was more interested in talking than teaching anyway. I've always been what Mother called her "Little Extrovert." To my father, I was a "Chatty Cathy." He couldn't wait for me to shut up. He had a sermon to write or meetings to make or eggs on the plate to finish. There in our little eat-in kitchen before school, Father wasn't interested in a dream about a boy standing on an elephant's tusk.

The sun setting beyond a golden wheat field, two animals stand in the open landscape—a horse on the left facing right, and then in the left foreground, an elephant with a small boy shirtless and in shorts, center of the frame, balancing on one foot on the left tusk.

Dreams pretty much explain me and why I am an artist. I have very vivid dreams, and I share them with anyone who will hear me out. In fact, I begin most of my classes talking about my dreams from the night before. My students think they are there to learn a new technique or continue working on a project from the week before, but they are really there first and foremost to think about images. And I think the best way to think about images is to think about what we see in our sleep. I am a big believer in sleep and what I see there. Dreams fascinate me. They are a place of escape and comfort for me. And they are the source material and inspiration for my drawings and my teaching. My paintings come from a different place altogether.

Roger is a good listener, too. He lets me sleep late because he knows that's when my dreams are most active and memorable. He fixes breakfast and lets me lounge around into the morning, waking slowly and sketching images from my dreams. We both schedule our classes in the afternoon so we can have our mornings together. Most couples spend their evening dinners together after a long day at work. But Roger and I spend the mornings together, leaving for school around 11 am. He teaches south of Austin, and I'm north. After the evening rush on I-35 passes, we arrive home and have a light meal and some wine. And I paint late into the night.

My paintings are not like my drawings. First of all, they are abstract. I go in for color, and in color, I go in. That is, when I paint I am interested in seeing how much depth I can create. Roger converted the large attic of our Austin Victorian into my painting studio. It's a large, open and simple space. Up against the west wall always stand at least three canvases— works-in-progress—each 5 X 5 feet square. Opposite, just in front of the east wall, Roger and I sit in lawn chairs, open a bottle, and I try to see just how dark and far and deep I can take our eyes into the brushwork.

Night after night, it's like this. We sit and drink, and I paint. And we talk very little. Roger may nod or shrug when I send a look his way, wondering if I'm heading in the right direction. But by nightfall, I'm all talked out. At that point, I'm just trying to send all colors blackward.

Paul visited Roger and me at our house a while back, and so he's been up to the studio, too. He called to say he was out eating some Mexican at El Patio, and wondered if it would be alright to stop by. He said he was by himself. I must have given him my number after class. He often lingered while the rest of the students scattered. I don't really remember why I gave it to him. Maybe I liked him. Maybe I knew he was in Austin often enough with his friends from school, listening to music, eating Mexican. So before I really knew it, I must have given him my number and said to call anytime. So he called. I said to come on over, and I gave him our address. It's not that far off of Guadalupe with plenty of tall oaks and fraternity houses in the neighborhood.

His eyes really popped when he stepped upstairs into my studio. He had so many questions about my paintings. Why I chose that particular size of canvas. (It wasn't too large to get down the stairs.) Why I chose those colors. (Spontaneous decisions mostly.) How long the paintings took. (Not sure really.) When I would know I was finished. (When I grew tired of it or had an idea for something new.) Where Roger painted. (He was printmaker and had a studio at school.)

On that night, I had never seen him so animated, so full of questions. In truth, I was startled and bristled a little. He seemed so aggressively curious about my work I felt like it had been a mistake to invite him. He was my student after all. He was shining a light on me I'd rather he didn't shine. I suddenly felt my studio had been invaded. No telling what he might tell others.

After Roger announced it was time he got to bed, I told Paul I had better turn in, too. He looked a little disappointed, but quickly acknowledged it was late and had a long drive back. I showed him out, and he told me how much he appreciated seeing my studio and work, and how much he enjoyed my class. He thanked me for treating him more than a student, like a friend. As he waved from his car, I smiled and felt my anxiety about Paul vanish. I don't know why I felt uncomfortable. He was an honest, innocent sort. He didn't want anything from me other than what I wanted to give him. And what did I want to give him?

Well, I wanted to give him a better idea of who I was. He was, after all, one of the bright spots in my teaching that year. To be honest, of any year. In class, I could count on his eyes, the nod of his head, his concentration and attention. That was deserving of something. And that something had to be what I couldn't really share with very many people at all. I might lose some students. I might lose my job. And losing my job was not what I wanted for myself or for Roger. Roger, of course, already had tenure, so it wasn't the same for him. In fact, his dean knew, his department head knew, the head's wife knew, his art department colleagues knew, his graduate students knew. His was a state school. Mine? A tiny church-affiliated college in a dry county, thank you very much. And it was 1974 after all. A very, very long time ago.

So after some hesitation and a cool glass of Riesling with Roger, I drove the short winding way over to Saxon Pub along the dark, up and down streets above Barton Creek. Paul said the first set was scheduled for 8, and it was already almost 9 by the time I arrived and paid the $8 cover. The club was pitch black except for the bar, and the lit stage where the band was banging away. I wasn't familiar with B. W. Stevenson and "progressive country," as Paul told me this brand of music was called. I was easily older by ten years, and my favorites in college included Simon and Garfunkel, some Dylan, Joan Baez, and in high school, I was a Beach Boys fan. I even had a few Jan and Dean records and one or two by Herb Albert and the Tijuana Brass. I also listened to my mother's records, Billie Holiday and Miles Davis and Sinatra, lots and lots of Sinatra.

But here was this chubby cowboy with a high baritone singing his heart out. He wore a faded pair of overalls, white t-shirt, and one of the biggest cowboy hats I had ever seen. It sat atop his long shaggy brown hair framing his bushy beard, rosy cheeks and dark brown eyes. And the room was his. No doubt about that.

I wondered how I would find Paul among the packed house, but as the song ended, I could see his shining blonde hair at the front of the room. He and his friends had a center table right next to the stage, and as I began to make my way toward him, he seemed to sense my presence, turned around, smiled, stood up, and motioned for me to join them. Then, he leaned over to the folks at the next table and asked if he could have their empty chair. They nodded happily, and again, he waved me forward smiling broadly.

At his table were three of his friends, all glowing and sunburned from one of those glorious Austin Saturdays in early May. And like the rest of the college kids in the club, they were all about two or three years from their last haircut. Even the two halter-topped girls across the table had hair half way down their bare backs, shoulders glowing freshly pink and tan. They were all so fresh and young and happy in this music, in this club, and in their lives.

Paul introduced me around to his friend Mike and to Janice and Susan. They attended UT he said, but they all went to high school together back in Houston. I shook hands with Mike and waved across the table and its collection of plastic beer cups to the girls. Mike had a scruffy beard and curly red hair haloed around his freckled face. The girls smiled and turned back to one another, talking intensely. They were what I would call "hippy beautiful," eyes like flowers.

On stage, B. W. was a jolly sort. Perhaps a young Santa in the making. But he was also high as a kite and staggered a bit as he tried to explain how he came to write the next song. The rest of the band wasn't listening, and most of the crowd wasn't either. The bass player was downing a longneck, a couple of waitresses were taking orders while the band was between songs, and a few folks were heading for the restrooms.

Paul stood up a bit to call over a waitress, and as I looked up at him, it struck me just how tall and thin he was. He then turned and looked straight up at B.W. Paul wasn't more than ten feet away from him, and Paul just stood there, locked in and listening. B.W. stopped, looked down at Paul, and said, "Hey there, friend, looks like you're the only one paying attention to me."

The crowd suddenly went quiet. Paul shrugged slightly, and said, "Yeah. I guess so."

B.W. laughed and swung around quickly to the drummer and yelled, "Let's do it!" And the next song crashed over the room.

Chuckling, Paul sat down, smiled at me, and shrugged again. He leaned over to me, half-shouting: "That was kind of weird."

I shook my head. "No big deal," I shouted back.

Suddenly, a waitress was at my shoulder, stooping down next to me. "Pabst," I told her.

The music was an obstacle. I didn't like clubs like this. No chance to talk. I felt trapped and silenced. I didn't even like the music. The sooner I told Paul what I had come to say, the better—and the sooner I could get out of there. But it was too early. I just couldn't come and tell and leave. I had to sit there, and listen, and drink a beer I didn't really want to drink.

Every once in awhile, Paul would look over at me and nod, raise his beer cup and smile. He clearly enjoyed the music and his friends, this place, and he was happily sharing it all with me. I couldn't help but smile and nod, and raise my bottle back at him. I guess I could see why he was enjoying himself even though I couldn't. And I couldn't wait any longer to tell him.

I leaned over to him. "Paul," I said loudly.

He leaned over toward me, still looking at the band. "Yeah?"

"I'm gay you know."

He nodded and turned to look at me with a smile. "Yeah. I guess I knew that." And then he moved back and continued a rocky kind of bounce in his chair, absorbed and awash in the music.

I didn't know whether his answer was an end or a beginning. I just felt a deep dark blur all around me, like when I wake suddenly in the night and look around our blackened bedroom.

I remember enduring a few more songs before telling Paul that Roger was waiting up for me and I needed to be getting home. I didn't even finish my beer. I just parked it on the table, waved goodbye quickly to Mike and the two girls, put my hand on Paul's shoulder, and then weaved my way out between the crowd and the maze of chairs and tables into the clean air of the night.

As I walked to my car, I could feel the heat still coming up off the sidewalk. As I drove home, shifting up and down and around the quick sharp turns, the neighborhood streets lined and crowded with shining parked cars, the streetlights passed over head. And once or twice I could see bats dive and nab the circling moths.

I was very tired. I was ready for bed. I was ready to sleep in.

Ridin' My Thumb to Mexico

Dave Kuhne

Dave Kuhne is Associate Director of the William L. Adams Center for Writing at Texas Christian University, where, since, 2000, he has been the editor of *descant*, TCU's literary journal. Kuhne is the author of *African Settings in Contemporary American Novels* (Greenwood Press, 1999) and principal editor of *descant: Fifty Years* (TCU Press, 2008). His fiction has appeared in *New Texas* and *Concho River Review,* and his story "Magic Coins" was anthologized in *Literary Fort Worth* (TCU Press, 2002).

Kuhne says of the story's inspiration, "I love the Rodriguez tune for its sparse lines, haunting spirit of wanderlust, and its notion that the character would simply keep traveling until, some way, some day, he 'sees her again.' The Johnny Rodriguez song, like my story, is about a quest for freedom and failed (or soon to fail) romance. Ultimately, my story became as much about escaping the time and place as about the actual journey. Like the characters in the story, a girlfriend and I hitchhiked 600 miles from north Texas to the border, so the Rodriguez lyrics inspired me to write about the times, lost youth, and first love."

Dad was big-time pissed with me that year because the university at Austin had transformed me from a "never broke a rule" highschooler to a "never follow a rule" hippie. He hated my long hair, my dope smoking, my anti-war rants, and my screwing his friends' daughters. He had recently caught me puffing on a joint out behind the parts room, and that, of course, had not helped things one bit. He had clearly had enough and was probably glad I was going to spend a month in Mexico.

"Maybe after a month in Mexico, after you see how tough it is down there, you'll realize how good you have it and stop bad mouthing America," he told me.

Dad was suspiciously quiet as he drove me to the edge of the suburban metromess so I could catch my first ride. He pulled the car onto the shoulder of I-35 just south of the Fort Worth-Burleson line. The radio blared more of its same sad song about Watergate and Nixon as I pulled my pack from the back seat and tossed it onto the grass. It was already ninety degrees, and heat waved off the fields beyond the interstate.

"Don't worry. I'll be back to inventory the parts before school starts."

"We won't wait up."

Dad was a real Texan, one cut from the "old rock." His great grandparents had come to Texas from Germany, his father had lost everything in the Depression, and Dad had lied about his age to enlist in the service after Pearl Harbor. He believed pot was something like heroin, that only "bad" girls had sex before marriage, and that fooling around was a dangerous step: "You keep messing with those girls," he'd say, "and you're going to get yourself shot. Or worse, you'll get one of 'em pregnant."

He had never met Christi, but he could quit worrying about facing down his buddies at church now that the object of my affection was from Waco. Yes, it had been a difficult year, but I still tried to help my folks out at the family business. It was tough going, what with Mom doing the books and Dad selling stoves, range tops, vent hoods, and garbage disposals from the "showroom." But it was what we did, and the store had provided us all a living and given me a chance at college. I had spent all of June organizing the parts room, sweeping floors, polishing dishwashers, saving every dime for my escape to Mexico with Christi. July was for Christi and me; I didn't want to think about August.

Even though Dad seemed cool to me on that hot morning, his eyes looked a little foggy as he wiped his glasses, glanced in the rearview, then at me and my pack, and pulled away, driving south to the next exit so he could make a turn back toward town and the store that was eating away at him and Mom. My mother wasn't very pleased with my summer plans, but Dad had said that if, as a twenty year old, he could survive a hike across Germany with people shooting at him, then I, as a twenty year old, could probably survive a month in Mexico. Since Mom was a worrier, I told her that I'd be Greyhounding, not thumbing, my way south.

Within minutes I was speeding along in the cab of a junker pickup driven by a cowboy with a hangover.

"I don't usually pick up hippies, but you looked harmless enough."

He was right. I looked like what I was: a skinny, long-haired kid from the suburbs—like John Lennon without a guitar, an English accent, or wire-rimmed glasses.

He offered me a brew, which I turned down since it was nine in the morning. He was obviously one of those fellows who measured the miles across Texas in beers. The morning beer was apparently needed to steady his nerves. He looked a bit bleary eyed under his sweat-stained Rudolf's Plumbing gimme cap, and I hoped he could keep the old pickup in the right lane.

"In fact, we used to kick the shit out of hippies, you know—if we were drunk or pissed enough. Those were the days, huh?"

The cowboy shot me a sinister grin and pushed his Rudolf cap a bit to the left side of his head to block the morning sun. He turned the dial on the radio till he tuned in a station playing the number one country song of the summer of '73: "Ridin' My Thumb to Mexico" by Johnny Rodriguez. The tune reminded me of my mission.

"I guess we hated you hippie guys because most of you are just rich college kids and you get all that college pussy plus draft deferments, too."

"Even college boys have draft numbers now."

"Yeah, well, maybe so. But I know you guys get laid more than eggs. All I got was a wife who turned to ice when the money ran low. Then she started messing around with some dude from work, and now she's PG'ed and I'll get to support a kid that's probably not even mine. God bless America! Just let me warn you boy. You knock up one of them college chicks and that'll be the end. Then you'll be just like me, paying, paying, and paying while your ex is partying every night."

"You sound like my dad."

"Listen to your father, son."

We didn't talk much the next hundred miles to Waco. The exits for the little towns clicked by, and I just let the rolling, burnt-brown fields flow along to the country music on the radio. But just as we pulled into Waco, a patrol car snapped up behind us, red lights flashing.

"Shit, where'd he come from?"

Rudolf tried to push the empty beer cans beneath the seat. We pulled over, and the officer appeared at the driver's window.

"I need to see a license."

The cop had a cold, professional expression. Then his nose wrinkled.

"I smell beer. Step out of the truck."

Rudolf got out of the truck and two empty beer cans bounced out behind him.

"You been drinking?"

The one thing I hated more than Nixon was the cops, and before I could stop myself, I blurted out "They're not his. They're mine."

"Is that so? Then you get out of the truck, and bring that pack with you."

The cop checked the driver's papers, then turned to me.

"You two are an odd couple."

"He was hitching. I picked him up. Next thing I knew he was pulling beers out of the pack."

"You don't look old enough to drink."

"I'm legal." He didn't need to know about the half ounce of pot in my boot.

The officer checked my license and patted me down. He made me walk the white line, but I clearly wasn't drunk. He dumped my pack and went through everything: the micro-tent, the sleeping bag, the clothes, the rain gear, the tiny backpacker's stove, the cook kit, the first aid kit, my Spanish dictionary and spare canteen of water. He knew what he was looking for, but he couldn't find it. After twenty minutes of searching, the cop gave up and let us go our way. Rudolf dropped me off in front of the McDonald's across the interstate from Baylor University, and I unloaded my pack.

"Thanks, kid. For a hippie, you're okay."

Christi and I had planned our escape for months, but I figured the odds were only fifty-fifty that she would actually show up. But she was there, standing in front of the McDonald's, dressed in a white, long sleeve shirt, faded blue jeans, and good hiking boots, pack leaning against the golden arches and hair pulled back under a straw cowgirl hat. Even in those clothes she was beautiful—five foot six, plenty of curves, chestnut hair and green eyes—and I knew I'd have no trouble getting a ride so long as Christi stood beside me. A friend had dropped her off at the McDonald's because her parents would never have allowed her to ride a thumb to Mexico with me or any other boy-man. They were still spooked about what had happened in high school—the baby and all. So Christi had lied to them, told them she was going to spend a month with a girlfriend on the beach at South Padre.

I had met the parents once. Her dad was a tax lawyer, tall with a thin face the color of pink granite. The house was a four bedroom ranch style on five manicured acres—a far cry from the apartment my folks had moved into to save money. "Father" led me through each room, explaining all the photos on the walls: lots of shots of him, his rifle, and dead animals with large horns.

"Got that one last year in South Africa." He pointed to a picture of himself standing beside a downed Cape buffalo. "I would have mounted that one, but Christi's mother doesn't want a bunch of dead animals on the walls. You do any shooting?"

"Only a little pool."

It was clear that Christi had gotten her green eyes and her curves from her mother, who was kindly, but concerned. Later, I learned that when Christi told her folks, they sent her away, to Fort Worth, of all places, where she spent her senior year at the Gladney Center, waiting to deliver the baby to its adopted parents. Then her parents dispatched Christi to Guatemala—charity work. Her Spanish was nearly perfect.

I examined Christi's pack.

"We'll need to wrap that sleeping bag in your ground cloth. First rule of the road. Keep the sleeping gear dry."

"You'll have to teach me."

We crossed the bridge over the freeway to the motel that advertised, ever so discreetly, on its billboard: "Couples—$12." We spent the day playing with our gear.

Early the next morning, the soldier gave us our first ride. He was in uniform, sergeant's stripes and all, driving an older Chevy four door. Christi sat in the back seat while I got in up front.

"Name's James. I can take you to Belton. I'm going to the base in Killeen."

Killeen was the home of Fort Hood, a large base where the draftees were trained for duty.

"Thanks for stopping," Christi said.

"I've done my share of hitchin', but I never had such a pretty partner as you when I was on the road."

He looked at Christi in the rear view and gave her a wink.

"You know, a lot of military types won't talk to people like us," I said, "much less help them out or give them a ride."

"Yeah, and a lot of people like you spit on people like me—call us baby killers."

I hated Nixon and the war, but I had never gone that far, and I remembered the soldiers who had come from Fort Hood to Austin for one of the demonstrations—GI's against the war. Feeling guilty about being safe in college while they risked everything, I had let four of them stay in my dorm room. They didn't seem much like baby killers; they were victims of the draft, forced to join or be jailed. With a little less luck, I might have been one of them.

As he promised, James dropped us outside of Belton, and we were picked up in just a few minutes by a red-faced, red-haired hippie named Bob who nursed his old VW van down the interstate at fifty miles an hour. A student like me and Christi, he was going to Austin to start the second session of summer school at the university. Bob fired up a joint, the sacrament of our tribe, and we passed it around.

"Why don't you two stay over at my place a couple of days? My girlfriend and me have plenty of weed, and Kinky Friedman is playing at the Armadillo."

The Armadillo World Headquarters was the cultural center of our hippie nation. A gutted National Guard armory, the Armadillo was a large tin building with a high roof and a stage at one end. It was justly famous as the home of some of the hottest music in the Southwest. In addition to hosting rock and country bands, the 'Dillo was the birthplace of the odd, underground effort to establish the armadillo as the official state animal of Texas. In fact, a local artist had recently painted a mural on one side of the building: a giant armadillo attempting to mate with the dome of the capitol. The governor had denounced the painting, claiming that the picture was an obscene slander on the honor of Texas.

"Sounds like fun, but Mexico calls."

We puttered down the freeway past the university; the campus was anchored by the Tower, the million-volume library that was one of Austin's tallest buildings. Ever since Whitman went on his shooting spree, the Tower had made a lot of people nervous. In fact, the university had recently closed the Tower to visitors due to a string of suicides—student jumpers who cracked under the pressure of school, or, in at least one case, a fellow who had been drafted decided to go down before being sent to Nam.

Bob drove out of his way to drop us on the south side of town where we could snag a ride easily. Back then, we all helped each other since we were all we had. Too often it was just us, our stoned tribe against the redneck army that occupied all of the state except for Austin. It seemed strange to pass through town without stopping, but we were making good time and wanted to reach the border by dark so we could score a cheap room in Reynosa.

"You see," the foreigner said, "it's so different in my country."

He was a petroleum engineering student at Texas A&I in Kingsville. He pushed the new Mustang to a hundred miles per hour.

"It looks a lot like here, in some places." He nodded to the blur of brown brush and rocky rises that clouded the windows of the car. "But we don't live like you do."

"Where's that again?" I asked.

"Saudi Arabia."

The Saudi floored the car to a hundred and twenty; the lines on the highway didn't seem to have any spaces between them.

"Better slow her up."

He slowed to ninety.

"How's it so different?" Christi asked. "Back home, I mean."

"You see, we don't drink the beer like the Texans do, and never there would be a pretty woman like you standing on the side of the highway seeking a ride from men. Never would the mullahs allow that."

He took one hand off the wheel and patted Christi's thigh.

"And we don't have the hippies." He shook his head. "You hippies, you are something. You take the drugs and you sleep with anyone."

He shot me a glance in the rear view.

"I mean, maybe the three of us could . . . ."

He moved his hand higher on Christi's leg.

"I don't know what they told you about hippies, but if you can't keep your hands on the wheel, just pull over and let us out."

The Saudi laughed.

"Here? You want out here?"

We were south of Alice, in the true middle of nowhere: nothing but open highway and scrub desert between us and the Valley.

"Yes, just let us out. Now."

"A-okay, mister hippie."

He slammed on the breaks; Christi braced herself against the dash.

"Out! Get out of my car!"

Christi cleared the front seat and stood safely on the shoulder of 281, and then I pushed our packs onto highway and climbed out. The Saudi sped away with screeching tires and a cloud of burning rubber. Christi and I stood on the shoulder of the road, bathing in the heat. There wasn't a car or truck in sight.

As the sun slid across the western sky and the temperature settled down to about 100, we waited, and waited, and waited: nothing but wind and heat.

Christi tucked her hair into her hat.

"If we ever get to Mexico, we're going to take the bus. I've had enough of this fun for a while."

I could only agree.

I didn't like hitching at night, so as darkness shadowed the brush, we jumped a barbed wire fence, walked into a ravine, and settled down. We didn't need the tent since it hadn't rained in about a month and there would be no rain until the next tropical storm curled its moisture off the Gulf of Mexico. Instead of starting a fire, we ate peanut butter and crackers washed down by water and an after dinner joint. We spread out our bags and lay down, counting the stars as they appeared until darkness grew and the stars outnumbered our math.

We were quiet for a long time, lying there, watching the sky. Once in a while we heard a car or truck on the highway.

Finally, Christi turned to face me.

"Don't fall in love. I'll be gone in the fall."

"It may be too late."

The stars continued to multiply above us.

"You'll never know how much it meant to me, that first time. You asked if I had taken any *precautions*. That was the word you used. But I can't stay, can't change my plan. Lack of planning led to my first disaster."

Christi's plan was a good one: transfer to Stanford to improve the odds of getting into med school. We would return from Mexico in late July; in August, her father would drive her to California. I planned to stay in college and avoid fighting with my father. In other words, I had no plan.

"Plans change all the time. I could go to California. Cut my hair. Get a job."

Christi was silent; tears shone like stars in her eyes.

The night I met Christi I was running down Guadalupe Street about fifty yards ahead of a cloud of tear gas and maybe a hundred yards in front of the first line of riot-geared police who were swinging night clubs and bashing the heads of anyone who was too slow or too stoned to move. The regular Saturday afternoon antiwar demonstration had evolved into a Yippie street party complete with red flags and a bonfire in the middle of Guadalupe. The cops had been content to wait out the party, wait until the hippies had smoked enough dope and the Yippies had burned enough junk furniture to lose interest and wander home. But before that could happen, some crazy ran down the sidewalk, hammer in hand, smashing storefront windows like he was playing a cymbal. That was too much for the cops.

They lowered the visors on their helmets, fired off a volley of gas, and proceeded to march, nightsticks swinging, into the crowd. I had just passed the university bookstore when Christi opened a door to the stairs leading up to the offices of the *Rag*, Austin's underground paper, and Middle Earth, the drug crisis intervention center.

"Here. In here."

I ducked through the open door and onto the stairs just yards ahead of the police. Christi locked the door behind me, and we hurried upstairs and stood at the window of the crisis center, frozen as we watched the cops club protester after protester. The pavement turned red and the tear gas wafted over the street and onto the campus.

In the corner of the room, a Middle Earther watched a "patient" moan and toss. The Middle Earth staff was famous for talking down the victims of bad LSD or those with weak psychological constitutions—those who should have never experimented with hallucinogens. There were many drug victims among our tribe, a lot of crashes and causalities: kids who got lost when they moved from pot to acid to speed.

"He's okay. Needs a few more hours to come down, is all."

"I'm Kent." I looked out the window as more cops rushed past the building, chasing the protesters north on Guadalupe. "Thanks for saving me."

The next morning, we stood in the early sun waiting for a ride south.

"You know what I liked best about Guatemala?"

"What?"

"I liked that it's not here. It'll be that way in Mexico, too. When we cross that river we're in another country, a country that doesn't own us."

"What exactly were you doing in Guatemala?"

"Well, after the event, I mean, after I delivered the baby girl, I couldn't just return to school for the senior prom. Waco is still like a small town. My folks have a 'position.' When I think back, the whole thing was just a stereotype. But I was only sixteen."

The way she said "I was only sixteen" made it sound as if turning nineteen had brought a century's worth of wisdom.

"Anyway, my father had one of his doctor buddies arrange for me to work in a clinic in the highlands. That's where I developed my plan. Up in those mountains, it's easy to forget. That's what I'm looking forward to in Mexico."

Finally, an eighteen-wheeler hauling an empty trailer pulled over. The driver rolled down his window as I walked up.

"Where you going?" He mopped the sweat from his bald head with a rag.

"Mexico."

"Think the girl can ride up back?"

"She'll be okay."

"Then come aboard. I'll going to cross at Reynosa. You'll have to climb down there to go through customs."

I helped Christi scramble over the truck's tires and onto the trailer, and then I handed up our packs and jumped onto the truck bed. The driver gave us a minute to situate ourselves behind the cab window, and we were gone, cutting through the miles of brush country toward the Valley.

The land began to change, to flatten; finally, the scrub and brush surrendered to the Rio Grande delta. Before too long we were passing fields that stretched straight-rowed to the horizon. And in those fields of cabbages and onions the people, the Mexicans, worked, looking like dots on the gridded rows. I had never been to the Valley before, and I couldn't help but wonder what it was like in Mexico, what could make people move north to pick crops in the blazing humidity for a few dollars a day. I remembered what my father had said: "When you see how tough it is down there . . . ." Maybe Dad was right: I was just a spoiled kid wasting my time chasing dope and skirts.

Then there was development, some motels, a shopping center, Edinburg, McAllen, and, after a few more miles, Hidalgo, the bridge, and the border crossing.

"Mexico."

The way Christi said the word made it sound magical.

The big truck took us across the bridge, past the U.S. flag. Below, the Rio rolled fast and green with water released from Falcon Lake. The driver pulled into a lane for Mexican customs, and we climbed down from the bed of the eighteen wheeler. I remembered my father's silence as he drove me to the outskirts of Fort Worth. I remembered "Rudolf," the beer-drinking cowboy who gave me my first ride. I remembered his battered pickup truck and the radio blaring out that Johnny Rodriguez song. We had ridden our thumbs to Mexico, ridden away from the USA, away from our parents, our troubles, and our separate futures, at least for a while.

Bring Lyndon Home

Mark Busby

Mark Busby, a native of Ennis, Texas, is Director of the Center for the Study of the Southwest and the Southwest Regional Humanities Center and Professor of English at Texas State University-San Marcos. He received a B.A. and M.A. from Texas A&M-Commerce and a Ph.D. from the University of Colorado-Boulder. He is author of the novel *Fort Benning Blues* (2001); *Larry McMurtry and the West: An Ambivalent Relationship* (1995); *Ralph Ellison* (1991); and is editor or coeditor of *John Graves, Writer* (2007); *The Greenwood Encyclopedia of Regional American Culture: The Southwest* (2004); *From Texas to the World and Back: Essays on the Journeys of Katherine Anne Porter* (2001); *New Growth/2: Short Stories of Contemporary Texas* (1993); and *The Frontier Experience and the American Dream* (1989).

Professor Busby taught at Texas A&M University, College Station from 1977-1991, and he has also taught at Texas A&M University-Commerce, Indiana University-Purdue University at Indianapolis, the U.S. Army Adjutant General School, and the University of Colorado-Boulder. At Texas A&M-College Station he received an Association of Former Students Distinguished Teaching Award for 1988-89. In 1996 he was inducted into the Texas Institute of Letters, served as the TIL secretary from 1999-2001, vice-president from 2001-2002, and president from 2002-2004. He served as President of the South Central Modern Language Association for 2002 and the American Studies Association of Texas for 2009. He received the Texas State University College of Liberal Arts Award for Scholarly and Creative Activity for 2010.

Of the story-song connection, Busby says, "The song that inspired this short story is 'Song of Peace' by Shiva's Headband. This story is based loosely on my own experience: I *did* travel to Austin in late March 1968 a few months before I got drafted. There *were* signs up and down I-35 that said 'Bring Lyndon Home' for a man named Fagan Dixon who was running against Jake Pickle for Congress. And I *did* hear Shiva's Headband at the Vulcan Gas Company on that trip. The narrator in this story is the same one as my novel, *Fort Benning Blues,* which takes place a couple of years after this story."

Billboards along I-35 leading to Austin proclaiming "Bring Lyndon Home" made me laugh almost uncontrollably. A few weeks before, I had depleted the appeals to my draft board to extend my deferment for another semester, and I knew what that meant: the letter beginning "Greeting" would be in the mail shortly. After a spring break road trip from my East Texas college to Marfa and Big Bend, I was stopping in Austin to tell a friend goodbye before my draft notice arrived.

I wasn't sure what to think about the war in Vietnam. I had been raised to believe in my country and its leaders. I had read about military heroes and had seen Audie Murphy, an orphan boy from Texas, in *To Hell and Back* at least five times as a kid in the 1950s. I had grown up tempted by the belief that each generation had a war in which the boys became men. I had been brought up believing Americans had a God-given right to lead the world and that American leaders sought truth and justice against the forces of darkness, in this case the Communists working through the Vietnamese. And growing up, I had also learned to believe that the little peoples of the world needed our help in learning to walk the straight and narrow way.

So I would soon have to decide what I would do when I got that dreaded letter. Could I forsake my country and go to Canada or accept the draft notice knowing that I would have to support a war many had decided wasn't worth the costs? I felt split by fears of participating in the war and of war itself and by my desire to experience life. I also feared being exiled from my family, my country, everything that made my history.

It wasn't just the fear of losing my country, but I also thought of my grandfather, the first Jefferson Bowie Adams, the man for whom I had been named. Granddad was a veteran of World War I and then worked for the railroad before settling on his ranch in Mariposa, Texas, to raise a few Herefords and a lot of hell with his neighbors. He was a curious combination of Southwestern independence and patriotism, and he spoke with pride about his military service. He had joined the cavalry before the war broke out, and he would bring out his pictures of himself in uniform riding his favorite mount, Chief Bowles, named for the leader of the Cherokees in East Texas. Then he would tell war stories about the Argonne Forest and Bayou Woods. They were still called cavalry units, even though horses weren't effective in war by then and were mainly ceremonial. So it was for Granddad that I, Jefferson Bowie Adams II, found myself in this quandary, knowing that if Granddad's namesake hightailed it to Canada, his disgrace would be too great a burden for him to carry and maybe for me to live with. This trip was intended to help clear my mind and decide on the path I would take.

When I got to the apartment overlooking Lake Austin where my friend James lived, I asked him about the billboards along the interstate.

"There's a local politician named Fagan Dixon who's running against LBJ's man for Congress, Jake Pickle, but he's really running against Johnson and the war. Some of his hippie supporters came up with this slogan that has caught on here."

Decidedly antiwar, James had joined Students for a Democratic Society (SDS) and participated regularly in protests against the war. I knew his point of view but thought it would help me decide if I could hear his arguments about resisting the war, since I had heard the other side regularly from my family. James knew the purpose of my trip and began his discussion before I got my suitcase in the door.

"Look," he said, "our friends are dying over there for unclear reasons. The country shows no unity of purpose, and the war is cloaked in ambiguity. The Gulf of Tonkin resolution was a sham. This domino theory is a crock. The only certainty is confusion and death. Look, no country should make war without knowing why or shed the blood of its sons without a united sense of purpose. No war should be waged without the support of the people, and this war is losing support. The reality is that the guys who die over there will stay dead, even if the reasons are obscure."

It was a good argument, one I needed to hear, but it didn't make my position any clearer.

We stayed up late, and James continued trying to convince me. The next day we were going out on Lake Austin, a lake created from a series of dams on the Colorado River. The day started out warm and sunny. The apartment owned canoes that residents could check out, so we loaded our fishing gear and a cooler of beer and paddled toward a nearby cove.

We soon reached the cove, dropped a weight overboard, opened our tackle boxes, and attached cork and hooks to the cane pole lines. James was a serious fisherman, but he knew I wasn't much use with a rod and reel, so we rocked quietly in the canoe, watched the bobbers, and talked some more about the war.

"Jeff, it's too bad that draft lottery hasn't been instituted yet. It might have given you some chance if you had any luck. Have you tried the Reserves or Guard?"

"I've been to the Army, Marines, Navy, Air Force, Coast Guard, the Boy Scouts, Girl Scouts, Cub Scouts. The only way to get one of those prized spots is to know somebody, to have a congressman or senator call for you. I'm just a poor boy from Mariposa with no connections. I even signed a contract to teach English to tenth graders down on the border, but my draft board didn't buy that as a critical reason for a deferment."

"Well, you ought to apply as a conscientious objector."

"I've looked into that, too. It's Catch-22. To be declared a conscientious objector you need a history with a religious tradition that opposes war. I fled my mama's Church of Christ as soon as I could. And I don't oppose all war; I just question this one."

"You know," James said, "people have ways to fail draft physicals. You can get fucked up with drugs or herbs that spike your chemicals, mimic diabetes, anything to get you 4F. I wish you'd gotten in touch with me before your physical."

"Me, too," I said, although I wasn't sure I would have taken anything. If my family thought I had some dread condition that would keep me out of the Army, it would have scared them more than my getting drafted.

"Then, you have to go to Canada. I have contacts. When you're ready, you call me, and I'll get you in that Canada pipeline."

"I'm a warm weather boy. What about Mexico? It's closer to home."

"Better than going in and becoming a war criminal by participating in that illegal, immoral war. But you'd have more support in Canada or Sweden. Mexico officially deports U.S. citizens, so you have to lay low there."

Before long, the sky grew cloudy, the temperature dropped, and a Texas norther was rolling in. With the temperature change, a light fog rose over the lake, and we knew the storm would soon arrive.

"We better get off the water," James said. "Let's paddle to the shore and look for shelter. I don't think we can make it back to the apartment before this hits."

As we pulled the canoe up on the bank, a driving rain pelted us. We followed a trail, saw a cabin, ran to it, where an old man motioned us in. On the porch he told us to take off our wet shirts, went inside, and came out with some towels.

"Well, you boys kindly got drenched," the man said. "Good thing you come here and not that other trail. You wouldn't a' found nothing there but a dead end. Name's Ledbetter," he said, holding out a rough hand.

We introduced ourselves. He was wearing a straw cowboy hat and walked with a limp—a short, broad man, a fireplug with a hat and a smile. I noticed that he was wearing black, hightop Keds like I wore in junior high.

"You boys from around here?"

James told him that he lived at a nearby apartment and I was visiting, waiting for my draft notice.

Ledbetter sat for a minute.

"This Vetnam war is a tough one," he said quietly. "I lost my son Tommy over there last year."

We gave him our condolences, and James said something about how this was an awful war.

Ledbetter cut him off. "Ain't no war any good. But you know we got to do them. For me it was Korea. Stepped on a mine and screwed up my foot. That's why I wear these here shoes. My old nub of a foot just won't do with boots any more, hard as I've tried.

"Anyway, I was proud of my Tommy for joining up with the Marines. You know, a man's just got to step up some time. These here protests ain't right. I grew up knowing our job as Americans was to take care of people like Hitler and old Ho She Min."

And it was just then, as I sat looking down toward that rainy, foggy lake, that I could see home, my brother in a cowboy hat, the Boy Scouts, Kiwanis and Lions clubs, the Avenue Church of Christ, picnics by Lake Bard-well, Fourth of July parades, John Wayne movies, Little League baseball, Friday night lights on the stadium, the Southern Pacific railroad line, the Czech polka halls outside town, my small college square. The weight of my short past pressed on me in images. For a moment, I thought Ledbetter looked just like my grandfather.

Although uneasy, James said, "I'm sorry for your loss, Mr. Ledbetter, but this is a bad war. The TET offensive was bad, and it showed that the government has been lying about how much progress we're making. I'm ready to bring LBJ and the troops home."

Like many of his generation, Ledbetter picked up on James' anti-government comments.

"Well, it's true, I don't much trust the guv'ment. They gonna have to step up. We cain't let them Communists take over Vetnam, 'cause all them other countries will follow. But you cain't trust anything the guv'ment says. When my Tommy died, they sent some major who tells me some shit about how Tommy had been shot in the back by a sniper and died instantly. Talked about how them Cong was cowardly shootin' a man in the back. But when they shipped his body home, I went to the funeral home. They'd closed the casket, and I called that wimply little man in that shiny suit to open it up. He told me the guv'ment had told him to close the casket. Well, I raised holy hell until he agreed to open it up. By damn, when he opened that thang up, I could see Tommy's whole face had been blowed off. Shot in the back, my ass. I seen men killed in Korea, and it ain't easy. But I didn't expect to see my own son like that. I thought maybe it wasn't him, so I rolled up his sleeve and seen it was his tattoos all right. I sat down there and cried like a baby. I was cryin' for my dead boy and then for a guv'ment that'd rather tell a lie than the truth."

His voice broke, and I could feel the depth of his sadness.

"But I'm still proud Tommy died serving his country. He made the sacrifice. These Vetnam vets coming home and gittin' spit on and yelled at. That ain't right. It ain't them boys' fault. They're supporting their county.

He stopped and glanced at the sky. "Lookee here," he said. "Looks like that storm's passin'. You boys may want to git on back durin' this lull."

We got our things, thanked Ledbetter, and headed for the canoe, as the rain and fog disappeared when the sun broke through the clouds.

That night was my last in Austin. James said we should go down to the Vulcan to hear the regular band that played there called Shiva's Headband. I'd never heard of the place or the band. Right then I wasn't thinking about anything except that my time was running out.

The Vulcan Gas Company was in an old building on Congress Avenue, the front covered with psychedelic posters advertising the night's performers and the special on Pearl beer, fifty cents a cup. The building had a couple of stages and homemade benches and old church pews. In front of the stage was a space for dancing. The whole room was strobed with a psychedelic light show.

James and I got there just after the music started. With all the seats taken we stood near the dance floor. Before long, someone handed James a hand-rolled cigarette. He took a drag and offered it to me. The small college I attended wasn't isolated, so I had been around marijuana before, with plenty of opportunities to join in. But I'd decided that I'd stick to beer as my conventional narcotic, so I shook my head and passed the joint.

Shiva's Headband wasn't terribly psychedelic, more like the Grateful Dead than the Doors, with fiddle and harmonica and a back-to-the-earth sound. But the psychedelic lights and loud speakers created the sense of a hallucinogenic experience. Soon they began to play a song that the leader, a guy named Spencer Perskin, said was called "Kaleidoscoptic." The next song was introduced as "Take Me to the Mountains," and I was soon reliving my drive through the Davis and Chisos Mountains with a hike to the Window in Big Bend. The lines reflected the back-to-the-land, country-rock music that was beginning to take over the music scene.

The next song became the one I remember with both clarity and confusion. It was one of those songs that started with a long instrumental intro before any singing. The drummer began with a gentle rhythmic beat, then the violin broke in, and the instruments went on and on with this dreamy sound. The people all around, mainly long-haired young men in bell-bottom jeans and striped or tie-dyed t-shirts and braless women in peasant or granny dresses or bell-bottoms embroidered with flowers or peace symbols, began to sway with the music. Soon they raised their arms and swayed in unison as the music looped for what seemed like ten minutes. James and I raised our arms and began to lean with those stand-ing packed in near us, and I noticed the haze of smoke as the strobe lights lit the stage. Swaying back and forth, I realized my head felt light, my eyes blurred, my mouth was dry, and I then imagined myself and my family. I disappeared from the setting but saw my mother and grandfather, and both looked far away with longing and sadness in their eyes, as if I had left and not returned. When the band began to sing, I came back to the present and realized with a start that this must be a contact high, as I inhaled the thick smoke in the enclosed space. James was feeling good and continued to sway. The song, I learned later, was "Song of Peace," and the lyrics, the best I could hear, were about reaching personal peace, not peace in Vietnam, and urged the listeners to raise their arms and let their burdens go. I raised my arms, opened my hands, but the moment had passed. I felt some release but nothing like a bolt of lighting with the clarity of purpose I longed for.

Then I noticed that just to my side was a young, bearded, long-haired man wearing an Army fatigue shirt with the sleeves cut off. The shirt looked real, not a knock-off, and I could see the U.S. Army insignia above one pocket and the name "Wentworth" above the other. As he swayed to the music, I realized that the man was about my age and that he, too, like most of them here, had faced the same choices that I had before me. The song began to end as it had begun, and it seemed to me that these swaying men and women looked almost like a single entity, morphed from individuals into a whole.

I pulled out of Austin on Sunday night, the last day of March 1968, driving north with a mixture of dreaminess and ambivalence. I snaked slowly through traffic to the interstate. I could see in the headlights that bluebonnets and Indian paintbrush had exploded along the roadside. Someone on the radio broke in to say the station was switching to live coverage of an address to the nation by President Johnson. I half listened because I had heard Johnson speak so many times with no effect as the war droned on. His speech seemed boilerplate about a peace offer Johnson had made to the North Vietnamese, more about how great President Thieu and the South Vietnamese were doing. He talked about his history in public service, all standard stuff, I thought. And then he said with America's sons in the fields far away and the future under challenge at home, he couldn't spend any time on "personal partisan causes," and then he dropped this line: "Accordingly, I shall not seek, and I will not accept, the nomination of my party for another term as your President."

At first I couldn't believe what I had just heard but then began to realize the significance of what Johnson had said. LBJ had just withdrawn from the presidential campaign of 1968 and was coming home; I would soon set out on my next big journey—wherever it would lead me. I thought about my Vulcan reverie, my contemplation of the future, and, with a start, noticed as I passed it, another billboard imploring, "Bring Lyndon Home."

A Proposition

Chuck Taylor

Chuck Taylor has published two previous novels, *Drifter's Story* and *Fogg in High School,* as well as three short story collections, *Lights of the City, Somebody to Love,* and *It All Flows Away.* He has recently published two poetry collections, *Heterosexual: A Love Story*, and *Like Li-Po Laughing at the Lonely Moon*, and his most recent book is a memoir, *Saving Sebastian.* He's worked as a children's magician, bookstore clerk, balloon clown, survey taker, janitor, soft water salesman, maintenance man, and animal lab assistant. For the last twenty-one years he has taught creative writing at Texas A&M University. He is married to Takako Saito Taylor, has three children, and still writes either in bed or at the kitchen table.

Of the story, Taylor says, "In the early 1970's the Austin music and poetry scenes were small enough to interact and learn from each other. The song that seemed to catch the spirit of the 70's Austin I loved dearly and lived in was Michael Murphey's 'Alleys of Austin.' The slow pacing of the song, and the unity of spirit from the rain and rivers in it, captured how I felt at the time and how I thought all of Austin lived. Michael Murphey and I even exchanged a few letters, forwarded to him through the literary magazine of Austin at the time, *Lucile*, where we both had poems. Austin in the 1990's, when the story is set, was a much harder city. The struggle to make ends meet brought out many forms of desperate weirdness. In this story I attempt to use the wisdom of the past, contained in a song written twenty years earlier, to assist a man in the 1990's."

Seems like I've spent half my life in the alleys of Austin. It's so easy to slip out a back door with a couple of buds, and then cut through a back yard, usually with a garden planted, into an alley, when the

63

party you're at gets too crowded and noisy-crazy. The alley's another world and you can hear the insects buzzing and you can catch glimpses of the stars through the pecans.

You can even dream that you're far far out of town, maybe deep in the Big Bend country, where the bears and big cats live and the stars cling close and are your closest friends.

I'm not from Texas, and had never lived in a city where the residential neighborhoods had alleys running through the middle of blocks. In the old days the dump trucks would come up and down and pick up the trash, but the behemoths they use now in the 1990's, to pick up your plastic trash receptacle with a scary robot mechanical arm, weigh way too much to make it down the narrow allies.

In the allies of Austin you drop back into another time when life was easy and cheap, and people didn't rush around so hard working, trying to pay their mortgages and raise their kids. You slip back to a world of long quiet talks with friends, to a world where maybe you shared a few "J's" and didn't have to worry about cops coming up behind you in their squad cars. They'd need to drive so slow in an alley that by the time they reached where you were standing, you'd have thrown your joint in the bushes and melted back into the party.

I never smoked myself because I'd had asthma as a child in the Midwest, spending most of July and August, when the ragweed was taller than a man, in bed and barely breathing. If I puff on the herb my lungs fill up with fluid, but most of my poet and artist buddies indulged, though a few, in their fifties now, have faced honestly their mortality and quit.

I'd found myself at an art party, thanks to my old friend Grey who'd talked me into it and dragged me along. Austin's the only city I know that throws art parties. The organizers haul in a few kegs of beer into their back yards, and they have, amazingly, small stages permanently built also in the back, especially in the older parts of the city close to the university where students live. To be admitted to such a party you are supposed to get up on stage and perform, but of course there are no tickets and nobody enforces the rules.

That's Austin. *Laissez faire.* "Don't tread on me." Southern in its own way.

That night I'd seen a lanky contortionist in a blue bikini bend her body into shapes I didn't know existed, I've seen a troupe of three belly dancers move abdominal muscles I didn't think people had, I'd heard your usual dreadful singer/songwriters—three of them—strumming out of tune guitars, and I watched a juggler, a stand up jokester, and a couple of decent

64

slam poets.

If you grew tired of the performances you could mosey back in the house and mill around, but I'd been enjoying most of what I saw, and had spent the evening standing close to the stage. That night, that July night, while a woman was on stage holding up her paintings and talking about them, a lady I did not know walked up and asked if I was Robin Watson.

No perfect stranger had done that before, and I must admit it was a rush to the head. She was about five feet four inches tall, maybe thirty years old at most, with luminous white skin and wonderful auburn hair. Yes, even in the dark of the back yard, with the lights coming off the stage, I could see her shiny red brown hair.

"I was told to look for you when I got to town," Arkansas said. "I was told what you looked like by Katrina, who I'm travelling with."

That brought a certain deflation to my ego. I'd thought she'd recognized me as a writer, and knew my books, and was in love with my words. In a music city like Austin, we male writers yearn for a taste of the attention lavished on male musicians by the opposite sex. Can't a poem or story be as good as a song?

But now we were walking the alleys of Hyde Park, Austin, Texas— Arkansas and I. She'd come to the party in bare feet and found the gravel of the alley too hard to walk on, so I loaned her my slip-on rubber sandals. During the walk I learned she and Katrina had just arrived in Austin from San Francisco, where they'd been living in a squatters' commune.

As we walked together in the quiet, under the leafy trees, by small funky apartments built in backyards for extra income while husbands had been gone long ago fighting in World War II, I fantasized Arkansas and I lying in bed together naked, with me combing her breathtaking red-brown hair. It might have been just combing her auburn hair, but I desperately wanted to know if that gorgeous hair reached to the upward curve of naked bottom.

"I didn't know any communes were left in the 1990's," I finally managed to say.

"This one only lasted a month," Arkansas replied, "before the police came and ran us off."

"Why did you come to Austin?" I inquired.

"Well, as you know, Katrina used to live here when she was hitched to Charles. The bastard got custody of all four of her kids. She wants to see them."

"I knew they'd split up and Charles had gotten remarried, but didn't know Katrina'd left town."

"Now she's back. She's back with me. We're conscious channels now, you know. I channel the Virgin Mary and she channels Shakespeare."

"Oh," was all I said. A few years ago I'd gotten interested in channels after reading the Seth Books, and had attended a number of sessions and been able to see through the act. Conscious channels say their soul sits on one of their shoulders while the spirit takes over their body and speaks through it. They are awake and aware when the spirit is speaking. Unconscious channels fall into a trance. I'd seen once before another channel that claimed to have been Shakespeare in a previous life, yet she couldn't tell me Shakespeare's birth or death dates.

"I've moved beyond that. So many lives since then," the channel had replied to my question.

The fascinating thing about many of the channels I saw perform was that, out of economic desperation and a desire for status and a better life, many believed they were indeed channeling. The acting job, the voice shifts and the change in gestures, were almost as good as professional actors. In those two years, I'd never seen a male channel perform, though I knew they must exist.

I learned that the Austin channels knew each other and read the same New Age books, and what they said when they channeled was about the same.

"We've got no money left. The drive took it all," Arkansas continued. "Our car broke down out in Llano. We had to hitchhike in. We're hoping we can sleep on your bookstore floor."

Now normally I'd have hung tough and said no to such a request. I'd have made phone calls to see if I could find a woman friend to put them up. In the past I had allowed people to stay in my bookstore. They never bought groceries for the refrigerator I had in the basement, and they ran up huge long distance phone bills on the business phone, being too poor for cell phones. They of course always left before I got the phone bill. So normally I'd have said no, but my girlfriend had left me three months earlier. I was lonely.

A long-term relationship didn't seem possible with these women, but maybe we could enjoy a pleasant fling. Arkansas and Katrina weren't sure whether they were going to set up their channeling business. They believed that they needed to be in a progressive city, but Santé Fe and Albuquerque were overrun with channels, so they were thinking either Austin or Miami.

But they had to make money first. Although Katrina was a doper and cocaine user, she carried a few papers in her purse that allowed her to pass as a fundamentalist Christian. If you claim to be a fundamentalist Christian there's an automatic job network of fundamentalist Christian companies all over the United States that will hire you. Of course the two women said nothing about being channels. They landed jobs the very next day in a Christian printing shop.

To make their act convincing, as they worked in the back of the shop stuffing envelopes, they sang along to the Christian music piped over the business's sound system. Katrina and Arkansas might be called unorthodox Christian channels. They liked Christian rock and knew many of the lyrics. They'd listened to the music driving east from San Francisco, and they'd been working for a month in various Christian companies all the way across the West from San Francisco to Austin.

I was so lonely for company the judgment side of my brain wasn't functioning well. The next thing I learned was that Arkansas had a three-year-old child. This child ended up sleeping with us on rubber mattresses I laid out in the Romance room of the bookstore. Little Eddie had no regular eating times or sleeping times, and kept Arkansas and I awake half the night. This didn't seem to bother the mother, but then she was around fifteen years younger than I. She was a free spirited hippie of the 1990's who didn't believe in discipline.

The sex began that first night with Arkansas on the floor of the romance room—me on top of Arkansas, and little Eddie straddling on top of me playing cowboy. I was, of course, the horse. Katrina must have thought she was the one who was going to get something going with me, but I wasn't about to get together with her. I knew Katrina too well and had not completely abandoned my senses. When she heard Arkansas and I making noises, she got out of bed with a huff, got dressed, left the store, and came back with her own guy a half hour later that she'd picked up at a nearby downtown bar.

The sex I had with Arkansas that night was close to the worst sex I'd had in my life, and not because little Eddie was cramping my style, riding my back. I could tell he was used to his mother doing it with men while he was in the bed. Little Eddie thought it was playtime. The sex was bad because Arkansas hardly moved and acted so passive. She seemed to imply that she was permitting me to have my way purely because she needed a place to stay.

Ten minutes after we were done I got dressed, climbed over Katrina and her bar pickup—they seemed to be having a good time—and went out the front door of the store (left unlocked by Katrina). I went around the store to another alley of Austin, a downtown alley that runs between my business and the law office next door, to try to make sense of what was going on. We were supposed to be in the new "arts district" of Austin, but the kind of art we were doing out of the store—one act plays, songwriter's circles, and poetry readings—wasn't the kind of art the city powers liked that could bring in big spenders and tourist dollars.

The parking in the alley belonged to the lawyers in the building next door. Just a year ago the building had been the Orion Theatre, but the manager of the theatre, a former big marijuana dealer everyone called Joe Willy, had died of a heart attack. We knew each other a bit—had spent hours talking in this very alley. I missed Willy and his death shook me. He was in his late thirties, younger than I.

A month before one of the lawyers, who owned a bright new Mercedes that he parked every day in the alley against the bookstore wall, came in the bookstore for the first time and accused me of throwing a concrete block through his car's front window.

Had I ever had hostile feelings toward that black Mercedes?

Yes. Any poor person, as I was then poor, struggling with a new business and living in the business, would have hostile feelings, but I did not know the Mercedes belonged to a lawyer.

Had I thrown the block through his window?

No. I was a businessman. I respected property. The thought had never occurred to me.

"We have plenty of street people wandering around downtown Austin," I said, "and there's that club on the corner where people go dance all night and take ecstasy."

Getting rid of the accusatory, snot-assed, fancy suited lawyer had been easy. I was not about to confess to something I did not do, and he knew there'd be no fingerprints to dust off a concrete block. The question now was, how to get rid of the two women and the child? The alley was cool, a lot cooler than inside the bookstore. A slight breeze funneled up and down its length between the buildings. Here I could make out a few stars. Here I could think.

Scraps of words from the Michael Murphey song floated in and out of my mind. I'd never been a cosmic cowboy with a cool 1940's pickup back in the 1970's. He was the cosmic side of redneck rock, this blending of country music, rock and roll, and the hippie counterculture that had been centered at the torn down Armadillo World Headquarters, once located in the 1970's about a mile from where I now stood on the north side of the Colorado River. Redneck Rock included diverse artists such as Jerry Jeff Walker, Jimmy Dale Gilmore, and of course Willy Nelson.

Murphey was my favorite because, while becoming a well-known musician, he also published poems in the same magazine my early poems appeared, a local rag that sold surprisingly well called *Lucille*. We had exchanged a few letters, and later he moved to Colorado. His alley song had a lovely line in it about the hill country Pedernales River flowing to the sea. "Pedernales" is a lovely word, and Murphey knew how to draw the sounds and rhythms out right, to catch the river's slow beauty. The song refers to the water washing out to sea, and the same water raining down on Austin, on the singer, and on all the people listening, joining them in a mystic moonlit ring in the alleys of Austin and, finally, in the magic alleys of other Texas cities and the whole world.

Replaying in my head scraps of that old song that you hardly heard anymore lifted my spirits in the downtown alley. It gave me the where-withal to figure out what I was going to do with my two conscious channels and little boy. A side of me I had to watch was the side of me that wanted to stay with Arkansas so I could love and help with her lovely boy, but Jesus drives a Ford in the Michael Murphey song. There's no mention of channels, either the conscious or the unconscious kind.

Should I call Child Protective Services? I knew when they saw how the mother lived they would take the child. I didn't approve of the way the child was being raised, but Little Eddie seemed happy. Would things be better if he were ripped away from his mother? No, not at all, and she would probably get him back in six months. All I would do is create two angry women who would despise me forever.

It was a Sunday, and I didn't open the bookstore till noon, so I let the women and child sleep till ten. I stayed outside the rest of the night enjoy-ing the breeze and the few stars visible above, and then moved down the alley to forth street to watch the sun rise in the east. The man Katrina had brought into the business without my permission fortunately had not taken the cash box. He was gone when I went back in and woke the women up at ten.

They were rubbing their eyes and groggy when I said: "Ladies, I have a proposition. I will buy you both breakfast and buy you both tickets on the bus to Florida, in trade for the title of the '78 Oldsmobile you say is broken down in Llano west of here. I will also give you one hundred dollars travelling change. But, if you don't like what I am offering, I will instead call the police and tell them you broke into the store and spent the night—and I will call Child and Protective Services about Eddie."

The two women looked at each other, their eyes full of surprise, shock, and hurt. Apparently the Virgin Mary and Shakespeare had not channeled any hint of what I had planned.

"The phone's over there by the counter. Make up your mind—or I'll make the calls. Which will it be?"

My bluff worked. Katrina got the title out from her purse and signed the car over. We went to eat in silence at Pete's Bagel, and then I drove them up to the Greyhound Station on Airport Drive.

My business was on the edge but by scrimping on food and gas I made it through the month and got the rent paid. I never heard from Arkansas again, but Katrina, well, two years later I was at a poetry reading at the Salamander Coffee House just off Sixth Street, Austin's entertainment area downtown. A blond woman with sooty bare feet came running in and up to me. A couple of men living on the street came in and stood by the door.

She must have seen me come in the place. Her eyes blazed an exuberant fire.

"I'm so glad I divorced that man!" she exclaimed loudly, and then quietly asked for twenty dollars.

I checked my wallet, found I had the cash, and I gave it to her.

She smiled, muttered thanks, and then dashed back out the door and into the night with the two men. She seemed more bent over, Katrina did, and her spine stuck out her back more than I'd remembered.

Katrina had always been thin, but she seemed thinner now.

Two Men—Three Shoes

A.C. Jerroll

A.C. Jerroll is a pen name sometimes used by a Texas writer who has published two dozen books as well as numerous short stories, essays, and poems in various magazines. He serves as editor for a literary journal and for several literary presses, and he is a member of the Texas Institute of Letters.

"Sometime in the last century," Jerroll says, "Texas song writer A. William Hinson wrote the words and music for a three-act musical drama I had written. Hinson's music was the best part of the play, the part audiences talked about most. Since then I have kept up with his song writing. When I read the lyrics to Bill's recent comical song, 'I'm Her Dog Now,' I combined the humor in the song with some grimly serious characters I had created for a short story set on a river, and the story somehow fell into place."

I lounged barefooted in the front of the canoe with a beer in my hand and singing a Hinson song when the river tried to kill us. "If you've got a girl," I sang,

"that wants to leave you
Every time some other dog sniffs around
Then jump that backyard fence and find a new one
Before that woman takes you to the pound."

Luke chuckled, probably because he is a fine guitar picker and singer and so has a good enough ear to recognize how I can't carry a tune in a bucket.

"So that," Luke said, "is a song that cheered you up when your old lady dumped your sad ass so she could make it with that stupid truck driver?"

"There's more to the song." I started to explain when the river took a notion to divide around an island, and we scooted into the deeper channel. I put the beer down and grabbed my paddle just as the turn in the river showed us a death trap.

The current ran us straight toward a huge tree, one that would have made a fine bridge if we had been afoot on the bank and looking for a place to cross. But we were in Luke's canoe loaded for four days on the river, and that tree had no business acting like a bridge. We ran smack dab into the bank with a muddy thud, into the very spot where the root ball of the tree had given way to the week's heavy rain. The canoe swung hard against the prone tree and tilted over, drinking the river and puking us and all our gear into the water.

I watched my shoes bob and vanish in the rush of current while I found footing in chest-deep water. "Luke?" I looked around in a panic in time to see his head vanish, and I knew the river had him. A glance at the bank told me I could scramble ashore, and in a split second I saw what the river would make me do. I would run down the bank, find Luke's body in a tangle of trees. People who know Texas rivers call a bunch of junk like that in the river a *sieve*. I'd see his red hair flashing in the water like stop light and his blue eyes looking muddy in death. It would take hours to rig a way to pull him out of the sieve, and then what? I would be in the wilds of Texas, a jillion miles into trees and poison ivy, fire ants and ticks, too far to hike to civilization. Not that I could leave Luke because coyotes would see him as a meal rather than the good friend he was. I would whip out my lock-back knife and cut a stick to whack any coyote that took a notion to nibble on him. My eyes stung at the fast vision of the end of Luke.

Then he came sputtering out of the water, a wild and worried look in his eyes. "I can't lift the effing canoe," he said. "I got under it and pushed up, but the current, the current."

With a fast dipping of my face into the water to cover any tears that Luke might see, I started grabbing for camping gear. It floated all around me, and I worked fast, snatching, shoving it into the eddy between me and the bank, waterproof bags of clothing, our cooler full of beer, ice, food; a bag containing the tent. The paddles floated, threatening to dive with the current under the log of a tree to disappear like my shoes did, and I grabbed both paddles.

Luke clung to the canoe, now on its side and jammed hard against the fake bridge by a current that wanted to push us under the log and among other trees jumbled like Pickup Sticks across the channel. The dang river wanted to shove us into the sieve where Luke would be, dead as a hammer, if he hadn't come popping up, swearing and looking wild.

"Good thinking, corralling the gear like that." Luke looked upriver. "I could wade against the current there beside the bank, holding on to roots and vines, and drag our stuff to that grassy spot." He pointed to a place some thirty feet upriver. "You stay here, keeping our gear around you. I could get on the bank right here, and we can haul the canoe ashore, empty it, then reload the gear and go far enough back to catch the smaller part of the river that runs around all these fallen trees. It could take hours, but we can do it."

"Good plan," I said. "Beats the hell out of guarding a corpse with a stick to keep the coyotes from eating it."

As he made it to the shore, Luke eyed me with a puzzled look. "Shove the cooler to me," he said.

His plan worked, and before long we paddled around the river island, beyond the sieve of tumbled trees. As we put ashore on a rocky shoal, a place to dry our gear, I spotted one of my shoes farther down the bank. We pulled the canoe to higher ground with me hopping about, cursing the way the pebbles and rocks hurt my bare feet. Then I went after the shoe.

Luke hooted with laughter when I came hobbling back, a shoe on my left foot, my right one finding every rock on the shoal sharper than the others. I took a few steps, hopped around in a fit of cursing, took a few more steps.

"Want to set up camp now?" Luke asked. "It's early, but we could dry out, rest, have a few beers."

"Wrong order," I said. "We can have a few beers and rest while we dry our stuff. Did we lose much when we flipped?"

"A tarp. The camper shovel must have sank like a rock. One skein of water washed away. But we got lots of beer, and we can drink ice melt in our cooler. We're in good shape for the rest of the trip. Except, of course, for your one bare foot. Having only one shoe ain't worth much."

"It beats a poke in the eye with a stick. I'll rig something for the other foot so I can get around."

It seemed likely that I could make a sandal from using fishing line to tie a flat piece of bark or a bunch of large leaves to my foot. Something. But there was nothing to be had. All the bark I could find was crumbly, and the leaves on every tree and bush around were tiny and brittle.

When I finally figured out that I could empty my fishing bag, step into it and walk around holding the bag's handle to keep the thing on my foot, Luke again laughed like a fool.

"I should have let the coyotes have at you," I said.

"Coyotes?"

The fishing bag was okay, but barely so. Rocks still stabbed through the thin cloth on the bottom. Then it occurred to me that I could wad up one of my tee shirts, put it under my foot in the fishing bag, and get along well enough.

Luke took pity on me, offered one of his shoes. "Too little," I said. "I wear a size twelve."

"My size exactly," Luke said. "I'll take a rest, shoot down a couple of beers, and you can wear my right shoe while you do whatever the hell you need to do around camp."

His shoe fit well enough, though it was almost as wide as it was long. Still, it beat hobbling around on the tee shirt inside my fishing bag.

Luke watched me cast for bass. As he followed me down the bank, he wore his left shoe and the fishing bag. When I saw how comical he looked holding that strap and limping about, I wanted to laugh, maybe loud and in his face. Instead, I turned my back and made do with a few quiet chuckles.

I cast a couple of times, pulled in a bass too small to keep.

Luke watched. "You said there's more to it."

"More to fishing?"

"The song. You know, cheered you up when your old lady up and run off."

I released the tiny bass. "It was a lesson, that song."

"So sing it. I could use a lesson about now."

"You'll laugh. I can't sing worth a crap."

"I might laugh, but so what? Let's hear it." He waited around, watching me cast.

"You laugh and I'll put a bass hook in your ear so it'll take you the rest of the day and all your doctor skills to dig it out."

"An emergency room technician ain't exactly a doctor," Luke said.

"Whatever." I waved my hand. After I heard plenty of silence out of Luke, I shrugged and launched the song way too high, so I growled the first line down to a range I could handle, almost. "I'm her dog now," I sang,

"No longer left to spend the night alone
I'm her dog now
Because she gave this poor old dog a bone."

I cut my eyes toward Luke.

He didn't laugh. "Yeah?" was all he said, then shambled off in that comical gait forced on him by wearing the fishing bag shoe.

It rained some that night, but the tent held. Just when I thought the rain had lulled Luke to sleep, he said, "So it wasn't the song that helped you because that song is supposed to be funny, you know—country and western redneck humor. Right up your alley. But you didn't even crack a smile over it. It was the new girl you found. I got to tell you that I'm relieved you found someone so fast. Still, I wondered when you chose this river if you might be suicidal, given all the rain and the nasty things flood water can do to a canoe."

"Suicidal? Me?" I tried telling myself that the idea astounded me.

"Your new girl—she anyone I know?"

"For a while she was an anodyne," I said and waited for him to express surprise that I knew the word, which I did not until I looked it up just before leaving on our canoe trip. Luke knows all those kinds of medical words, and I wanted to impress him. The rain increased, slapping the tent like water on a shower curtain.

"I was right to worry about rain," he said.

A few days before, when I told him about the stretch of river I wanted us to run, he had objected, but not much. "Lotsa rain lately," he said. "Could mean trouble, unless of course it's trouble that you're looking for."

In the tent he said, "Much more rain tonight and the river can get to our tent. We're not very high off the river." He turned on a flashlight, and I watched him struggle into a slicker suit. "I'm going to pull the canoe to higher ground. If we lose it to high water, we're screwed."

"Need help?"

"From a guy gimped up by having only one shoe? Nope. Besides, it's a one-man job."

He tugged the canoe up close to the tent, but it turned out not to be necessary. The rain stopped while he was fussing around out there, and the next morning I thought the river looked lower, not higher.

Around noon, though, we had to put ashore to get out of a bad rainstorm.

It was no ordinary rain but more like someone was pouring the whole Gulf of Mexico on our heads. The canoe took on bilge at a scary rate just from water falling from the sky. We found a highway bridge for shelter, and when we got out of the rain, Luke pulled his cell phone from a pocket. It was dry enough under his slicker and absolutely safe from water because he kept it in a Ziploc bag. While he messed with the phone, I knocked around under the highway bridge looking for something I could use for a shoe.

And I hit the jackpot: I found a shoe. Maybe not a real shoe, but it was close enough. It was a single thong, one of those cheap jobs that you keep on by wrapping your toes around a plastic strap that's attached near the front. I always hated them because of the way they flap around on my feet. By some miracle it was a thong for the right foot. But there was a problem, in addition to its being about an inch short.

It was bright pink. But I put it on anyway, and I clinched my jaw in thinking how Luke was going to laugh at me for wearing a girly pink shoe.

He noticed immediately, and he snorted out a few semi-mean laughs. "If I had a camera, you wouldn't dare walk around in that prissy shoe. But then I have something better than a camera."

"You have a digital camera in your cell phone." I lifted my foot, put it behind me.

"You going to hop around for the rest of the trip every time I pull out my phone? Then I gotta tell you that it's only a phone. It won't text, won't show me email, won't take pictures."

I put my foot down.

"What I have better than a camera is my memory. I'll never forget your wearing that prissy shoe." He pretended to stifle a laugh.

I ignored his attempt at humor. "The center part," I said, "the part that I wrap my toes around, is loose."

That piece of the shoe pulled through with a popping sound like pulling out a sink plug, and the shoe became useless. When the rain stopped, I hopped back to the canoe, rummaged through one of my bags, and pulled out a roll of tape.

Luke nearly busted a gut laughing. "Duct tape," he said. "You brought duct tape on a canoe trip? How redneck is that?"

I put on my best East Texas drawl. "My daddy tole me a man could fix damn near anything with duct tape. Iffn you can't fix it with duct tape or bailing wire, then it ain't fixable, he tole me."

To prove my point, I had that pink thong wearable in a jiffy—and I covered up some of the pink with gray tape.

As we pushed the canoe back into the water, Luke said, "How did you learn that big word?"

Took him long enough, I thought. "*Anodyne* ain't no two-bit word. It's common enough to them with any smarts. I learned it when I was a kid. Junior high, maybe."

"Bull. You looked it up to impress me."

"Did it?"

"Nah. What impressed me was how you said you got no help from your new girl in getting over your old lady's leaving."

We paddled a mile or two in silence, watching the river ahead since we had learned the hard way it wasn't to be trusted. Finally I said, "She treated me like a dog."

"But she gave you a bone. Or so you sang. I took that to be a boner."

"Maybe. But the price was high, getting chained up."

"Tried to control you, did she?"

"Tried, hell. Tammy was an expert in the control department."

"Tammy," Luke said. "I know a Tammy."

"No you don't."

"I do. The one I know is a regular fishwife."

He did that on purpose, and he knew I knew it, even if I couldn't see his face because he sat in the back of the canoe, and I wasn't about to twist around to look him in the eye. He would see right off that I had no idea what *fishwife* meant.

Before dark the river flung us into another sieve of fallen trees. I grabbed some branches of one of the big ones to slow us so the canoe swung around against the tree trunk, and Luke hopped into the water to steady us so we wouldn't flip again. For an eternity of a minute we held tight against the tree, this one lying longwise with the current instead of trying to be a bridge.

"Hang tight to those branches," Luke said, though the warning was hardly necessary. "No way we're going to get through those trees down-river. We're screwed."

"There's a window though the branches on this tree," I said. "I think the canoe will barely fit through, and look, a shallow wash beside the main channel. It's free of trees. If we can make it through this tight little tunnel, we get another chance at life."

With my tugging on branches and Luke standing on the log, pushing the canoe around, we made it through, and Luke hopped back into the canoe in time for us to paddle out of the river's second death trap.

When evening came we set up camp on the highest river island we could find, a spot just across from a country house perched on a bluff. The work setting up camp on that rocky island proved for me much easier for having two shoes, even if one was a pink thong. Mainly pink, anyway, since the duct tape covered part of it. Luke put up the tent, and I made a quick job with the battery-driven air pump getting our air mattresses ready for the night. Luke climbed to a higher spot on the island so he could use his cell phone again, and I collapsed in the tent, dead tired.

The rain hit again, hard and furious, but I was too sleepy to care. As I drifted off, a woman's voice, shrill and panicky sounding came to me, and at first I thought it was a dream.

Luke scrambled into the tent. "You hear that?" he demanded.

"Sounds like Tammy," I said. The voice droned on.

"Listen. Listen to what she's saying."

". . . drown," the Tammy voice was saying. "There is a flash flood warning. If you stay on that island you will die. Come across the river. My son will help you up the bluff." And she went on and on about a flash flood and how the island would be under ten feet of water.

"Damn," I said.

"You don't believe her?" Luke said.

"Maybe not."

"I just called my uncle, had him check on the web for the weather report in the area of this river. He did. He said there was a flash flood watch."

"A watch. Not the same as a warning. I say we go to sleep."

"A watch can turn into a warning in minutes." Luke's voice was calm, mostly. "Maybe it just did since I got the report from my uncle."

"She sounds like Tammy." I heard a whine in my own voice, a complaining and mean whine, a sound I didn't like.

". . . you will die . . ." the Tammy sound-alike went on.

"Life ain't much fun," I said, "with every danged woman around telling me every move I can make. My wife did that for years, then she up and run off. Then Tammy jumped my bones and got me to believing in women again. But that crap didn't last. I say to hell with them, all of them. I'd a lot rather drown like a rat than be bossed around by women."

"So you did come out here hoping to die."

"Could be." I rolled over on the sleeping bag.

"I say we throw a few things into the canoe and paddle across the river," Luke said.

"In the dark? That could be suicide with the river running so fast."

"Staying here could be suicide. But I guess that's what you want."

It was a statement I had to ponder, so I said nothing.

"You're not a dog," Luke said, "And no woman can make you into a dog. Who wrote that song, anyway?"

"A guy named A. William Hinson."

"Never heard of him."

"He's an Austin songwriter."

"Maybe I have heard of him. Yeah. Writes songs so sad they can make a rock cry, and he writes ones that make me laugh. Like that song you sang about being her dog now. It's funny, even if you make out like it's deep. It ain't deep, just funny. But what the hell are we doing jawing about some song when the river is about to kill us? Not just you. Us."

"You go. I'll get some sleep. You come back in the morning."

"I ain't leaving you here to die alone. You know what would happen if a flash flood hits with us in the tent? We wake up with the tent collapsed all over us, with us zipped up in a bag we can't get out of, and the water tumbling us thirty miles an hour into trees we couldn't fight our way through even if it weren't for the nylon bag of a tent. We would both be dead in minutes."

The idea of being washed away in a bag of a tent got my attention, and I sat up to consider it. "That kind of death wouldn't be like drifting off to sleep from being dog tired, would it?"

"No. We would both be hollering and thrashing around, trying to find a knife to cut the tent away. And it wouldn't be just you dying because you think some woman zapped you into being a dog. It would be me. I don't deserve to die because your old lady ran off and because you think Tammy tried to put a collar around your neck."

"So what happens if we try crossing in the dark and the river spins us around, out of control, maybe into another death trap?"

"Look, you want to take your chance with crossing in the dark or stay here while the river rises? That woman over there lives on the river. She watches it. She knows stuff we got no way of knowing. I say we go across. Now."

The high-pitched wail of a controlling woman seemed to bore into me as the Tammy voice across the river went on about high water and death. Luke's face in the lamplight had more worry on it than it did when we were deep in the death sieves the river dragged us into.

"So you're saying you would stay with me if I didn't get into that canoe?" I asked.

Luke nodded, or I think he did. His eyes, so blue in the daylight, looked mighty dark and sad in the lamplight.

"Okay, then, damn it," I said. "Let's give it a go."

Luke's face brightened with relief, and he handed me my slicker suit.

Shimmerdance

Laura Payne Butler

Laura Payne Butler is Associate Professor of Creative Writing at Sul Ross State University in beautiful Alpine, Texas, where she edits the annual journal *New Texas* and serves as faculty advisor of the award-winning student journal, *The Sage*. Her fiction has most recently appeared in *Night Train*, *Iron Horse*, and *Iconoclast*, been nominated for Pushcart Prizes and Million Writers Awards, and been anthologized in *New Stories from the South* and *CrossRoads*.

Of "Shimmerdance," Payne Butler writes, "I lived away from Texas much in my youth, but I always found myself returning to Texas music as a path back to me, my past, my home. Music helps us make sense of our past experiences and work out our present states and aspire to future dreams. We listen and remember, then hope and long, inspired by melodies, rhythms, lyrics. I found the Flatlanders tape *More a Legend Than a Band* at a flea market in the early 1990s and was struck by its sense of the eerie beauty of our state; I played the cassette so often, all of the songs became as wavy as the saw-blade instrument featured on some of the tracks. So often, Texans are portrayed as belligerent and ego-centric. The Flatlanders manage to bring out a more insecure and complicated existence, the Texas I lived and loved in my core. I wanted to write a story which uncovers how music can influence a life-view, fulfill missing hopes and dreams for a character on the precipice of changing her life."

I've always wanted to visit Dallas—or anywhere in Texas, I suppose. I think about it each time I listen to a Flatlanders cassette Billy Boy gave me once, unthinking—I've listened to the tape so many times, the songs sound wavy, as if the singers are deep under water, strumming their guitars, tapping the saw-blade. The song, "Dallas," speaks of seeing Dallas from an airplane at night, of it being a jewel, light, beautiful.

"I procured this little jewel from some Texans driving down coast." Billy Boy smiles a million-pawnshop-dollars as he tosses the cassette over to me. It arcs in the air, hangs in the dusty sunlight, peeks through wood shade, then drops onto a chair cushion. "Left it in a player they sold right out of their truck." Billy Boy laughs at that one—he looks down on Texans like so much trash—he looks down on just about anyone not him or his people. "Rednecks and their redneck music," he throws back at me walking out the door. "Not enough money to buy gas to the beach—how they expect to live down there. Shit, it costs money just to breathe."

I don't think much about that tape—I scoop it on into a drawer next to where it had lain. Billy Boy is always bringing home useless junk.

Until one day a few years later going through drawers in my study, I find it again. I wonder about the band name—The Flatlanders—and what that can mean. In North Florida, we reside in valleys, under shade of oak and pine. So, I pop the tape in the player, all the while cleaning closets— simplifying my life (an endless job, it seems). Yet I feel as if I owe the tape a playing, as if it would be unfair to chunk it too into the trash bin before giving it a chance to grab me. I do not believe I clean another thing that day—I sit through the afternoon and into dusk playing it over and over again, staring off into shadows like distant dreams falling into vague memories not my own, haunting melodies. I've longed for the West ever since. I sit outside in the evenings and dream of open skies and wind—even of concrete and chrome cities, of flying high above the clouds, seeing Dallas awash below me in light and dreams.

This is years ago—middle age is on me now. I still like to listen to old music, although feelings of longing become complicated. More of loss, I suppose. Like the family house. I've inherited it, and, despite the fact that I scorn it and its veranda, claim it chokes me, I find myself suddenly returning to think through the mess that Quincy has come to be for *me* regardless of marrying Billy Boy, a pawnshop broker nobody from west county. At eighteen, I think for certain he will be the one to break the "old-family" chains, free me to become wild, elusive. But no matter how hard I run with the wind on my trail, along sand roads, through woods toward what I think ought to be a happy ending—or at least some painted-down river on which to float —my past and this house surrounded by its veranda, hold sway.

For years, Mama blames Elder—her own mother—for her frustrations and disappointments. We're all named Louise in one form or another. Elder despises the moniker and renames herself in a style Mama calls, "satanic." I can never fathom how anything may be deemed satanic through the vodka haze Mama lives in, but there you have it. "Satan-incarnate" is Mama's exact name for Elder, but, again, from the cold-hearted perch that is my mother's, that's rich.

They are all dead now, at any rate, and I sit here trying to come to terms with the family, to discover how I can run, run, run—like a nightmare in which I rush through a haze from an indefinable evil yet manage neither to escape nor to discover what's chasing me—in my waking life chasing after Billy Boy Rutledge, Junior, just to realize he proves no answer to the Louises and all that being one means. So, twenty year later, I leave Billy Boy behind in our woods outside of town, safe and pissed off in the air-conditioned monstrosity he builds me when I insist I cannot breathe from the weight and heat of Quincy—yet, once more I find myself stuck here on the veranda of Elder's (and Mama's and now my) house, its choking wisteria, its Spanish moss shadows. Its huge spectre.

I want nothing more than to be alone.

Is this the end-sum of my inheritance?

The Flatlanders call Dallas a woman; the song by the same title calls me as a siren, lures me to become a Texas woman, run west from here and be the kind of woman who walks on Billy Boy, who begs him to be the wild boy he'd been in our youth, all chrome and concrete. I am struck that we are defined by our cities.

In the 1960s, we fly a jet to Atlanta. My grandmother, Elder, is a big-time stock-holder in Coca-Cola. Around the turn-of-the-century, her own parents invest in a then little-known Coca-Cola Bottling Company—an also then suspect idea of the president of First Bank of North Florida: diversify the right folk from their dependence on shade-tree tobacco crops. Coca-Cola pays dividends in return by sending out the jet once a year to bring those self-same right folk over to Atlanta for board meetings.

But flying into Atlanta on a red and white jet isn't the West. Atlanta is deep and forest-green and hidden, like here in Quincy, hidden truths—no light, sun, reflections. I've seen Dallas on television, in pictures. It is a city in which I think no one can hide. Cowboys—honest, unafraid to wear hats and boots, drawl out the truisms and yes'ms. All shining like chromed reflection windows.

Billy Boy diversifies Coca-Cola with huge hot-house tomato farms, becoming richer, even, than Elder's dreams.

Up until she dies, Elder laughs whiskey-spice deep in her throat, gives Mama knowing looks as if to say, "You can never suspect how special I am and I do not know what has happened to you." All she *actually* says is, "I expect it's as cool inside as it is out here," before shuffling her way to the ice bucket and crystal-heavy whiskey decanter, but Mama sits lower over her own iced vodka, peers across the yard, seeks saving shadows into which she might fall.

Later, Elder wanders around, bored, inside the big house and Mama sighs ever deeper into her lungs, lets out the air, purges herself, throws back the rest of her drink, and says simply, "Elder, you're full of crap."

I am sitting in my own spot under the porch, down in the dirt where it's cool and damp in the sand with roly-polies scratching on my thighs. This routine repeats itself as almost my one true memory—three women talking at but not to one another. Elder storms off to the beach, leaving Mama and me alone together—the men in our family always off living in Tallahassee—escaping us. But I do not know this when I am nine, happy when Elder returns to "check up on the house and happenings" in Quincy— and to throw her shade over, smother, my mama.

Even this memory dwindles in a fall breeze when Elder dies. I am thirteen then, past caring about coolness of under-porches, suddenly mortified by roly-polies and dreaming of escaping myself.

Memories dwindle away in the breeze of mother/daughter indifference, I suppose—especially now that Mama too has died and left me the mansion off the square, her final vodka-laced deed: trap me here on her veranda to rock myself into the familial stupor. Mama never forgives me for marrying beneath my raising, for building a new house, for running through the woods, for drinking beer direct from a longneck.

I've tripped on roots and eaten sandy dirt, so now I come home to wind memories around myself like Elder's gold-silk wrap still hanging in the hall wardrobe upstairs. I dance around and around to wavy Flatlanders music, dream of running, of escaping far west of here, of flying to Dallas— perhaps even lighting out to Lubbock. For I've realized who flat-landers are —planted on the plains of Texas, strong and resilient against ever- blowing wind, made steadfast by sunsets which die spectacularly—fiery Phoenixes— each evening.

Elder leaves the silk-wrap behind when she moves down coast. Without her in the house, we all hover, shadows. For all her meanness, she is our sun, peeking out occasionally through Spanish moss when a breeze hits them. For a little girl of eight, her silk shimmers even in the darkness of the wardrobe, and one day, despite Mama's curt instructions to never touch a thing of Elder's—"She will come wanting something some time, Lou.

Elder's memory is like a snarling elephant gone must. Don't get caught on the ugly end of it,"—I snatch it on a rainy Sunday morning when Mama and Daddy travel to Pensacola. I sneak off with it, tip-toe to my room and wrap it around my hair, pretend to be an Arabian princess, or an elephant trainer. It smells of ancient *L'air du Temp* dusting powder, and the smell finally makes me feel queer, like I am losing myself in Elder's old age. I return the wrap, not much wanting to think on it later.

Until now. Like a child again, I grab the scarf, still on its quilted hanger, sneak up another floor to the ballroom—the top floor of the family manse, the one just under the attic—and I hum and dance about, dragging shiny lines and circles across the dusty plank floor, varnish peeking through, given new life.

And in the dust I think of a car sliding over the sand roads of Gadsden County. Boys suspend in cool evening air, fly as they bounce high off rumbling car seats. They breathe deep, whiskey and engine fumes float overhead, hold onto flashy girls who laugh, drunk and abandoned. Girls wear metallic-colored dresses. They are what Elder calls good-time girls, sing squeaky ragtime songs:

> Pack up all my care and woe,
> Here I go, singing low,
> Bye, bye blackbird.

> Where somebody waits for me,
> Sugar sweet, so is he,
> Bye, bye blackbird.

I hum the rest, twirl around. Sometimes this song flies to Dallas in my dream, and I know its story, although Elder never tells it true. I piece it together through years of searching for the shimmer—and then that moment when it expires like lightning bugs drowning in dew, when birds realize they might not make it to Texas, but they'll try anyway.

Jack Sheffield, the boy who will grow up to become my grandfather, travels to the Suwannee Club with Tallahassee boys—from South-Florida families (not as good as North Florida). "It was the fete of the social year in Gadsden County," says Elder—life is a fete to her, although I suppose nothing's wrong with that—and, to believe Elder, it is her emergence into society which drives the power of the evening. I have no reason to disbelieve Elder; the entire town reveres her for her social charm and acumen. Elder wears superiority over all us like a comfortable pair of slacks, her indefinable charm—but with an edge, like the material shouldn't get wrinkled or the fit would be ruined.

In my child-naïve assumptions, Elder lives the life of silk scarves, light and airy, golden. The boys my grandfather brings to her fete are drunk—off-key melodies, all. Jack sits in the back seat, tensed up because it is his father's car becoming quickly dusted from sandy roads, not taking full possession of the trip in which he will crash a society party with drunk friends of south-coast senators—and floozy-girls.

"You come on along, now, boy," his friends assure him. "We'll only borrow the car for this one night. You'll be safe as a bug in a rug, home in bed before first light." They struggle on thin, three-inch-wide, wooden wheels on roads made for mule wagons toward an old-fashioned coming-out party—white silk and uptight mamas.

The boys acquire what New York periodicals have recently proclaimed flappers, girls who laugh and sing loud, harsh, wear rolled-down stockings. Sand road sifts deeper and deeper within the countryside. Somehow, being from Gadsden County, from plantation aristocracy older than the imaginations of his friends, impresses these sons of state legislators who reside in Tallahassee, so they embark on a quest to see for themselves the supposed grandeur of the old ways of Gadsden County. But not without thumbing their noses at tradition by picking up good-time girls in a downtown speak. The girls' eyes sparkle smoke-haze as they slide through the jungle to the Suwannee Club.

"Young ladies from Quincy dressed in white linen and danced with their fathers, indicating good taste and manners, which invited appropriate matches in coming years," Elder sighs over her memories, looking at Mama as a lost cause (Mama marries fine—a doctor—but Elder cannot on principle approve) and then looking at me with some hope for redemption (I marry Billy Boy—not so fine). But this is before, when I am still a girl, sitting so often under the stairs of the veranda, when Elder can still hope.

I listen when I am this little girl and imagine my own prince sliding over to Quincy. Mama almost chokes when I come home at eighteen, tell her I've run off. "Eloped," she corrects, and I shrug my shoulders. "At any rate, it's done. We're happy."

"Where on earth have you dug him up," Mama asks, scared he's someone's gardener. People just aren't nice to one another for the sake of being nice in her world.

"You know his family—the Rutledges," I answer, haughty in my own superiority, feeling good and sticky, sweaty—she, pale, too cold even in the heat of the afternoon. My eyes hold her gaze and watch as realization lays itself over vodka haze.

"Don't they live on the wrong—west, toward Gretna," she stammers, hoping against hope. Georgia crackers would be preferable, this I know—they would allow for some storytelling.

"Just say it, Mama—the wrong side of the tracks," and despite my want for glee, I feel annoyed, pissed off, even. Not that these are my people. None of them are—that is the whole point. I don't feel like I belong here in Mama's world, which isn't anything but a shadow of her own mother's, of Elder's. Elder proves too strong, sucks Mama's life. And with her solitude and coldness, Mama tries in her own way to suck mine, hoping, really, that some miracle will happen for—I'm not certain what.

So, Billy Boy. I meet him at a Seminole powwow. Booker T's there—he disapproves of the Rutledges, too. But I think now it is because he understands people better than any of us, knows Billy Boy for the climber he is. Booker is our gardener and he and old Eleanor mostly raise me. Booker is against Billy Boy from the get-go, thinks I should save myself for fancy dances and white silk: "You can come out and show them that fancy is as fancy does, Lou," Booker once tells me. I reply, "That's rich coming from you, old man—how's the shack by the river treating you?" I know this sounds mean, but Booker and I always talk that way to one another—and I do not realize then what Booker is saying to me.

I have my own coming out in mind, and it involves shadows behind the Bottom Bar, down in the grass with Billy Boy, blissful and bad. I think the world will surround me when Billy Boy strokes my belly with his finger, light. I arch my back toward him, feel him in my blood—hot and shimmering like lightning bugs. I fail to remember that lightening bugs create their own fancy dance in the night, but fade, die away in morning mist.

When I land in Dallas some day, step off that DC-9, the bright lights in the night will draw me to the street. The air will be dry, deep and star-filled. Lights from downtown are eclipsed only by the stars above, and I will fill and become overwhelmed—I will fail to imagine that sunrise could invite disappointment, so full of Dallas lights I will be by then.

Appropriate young ladies to marry—they are not on Jack Sheffield's mind the night of Elder's fete. Jack looks to the bright lights of inappropriate excitement, the kind he has constantly craved since escaping the confines of his rural home, and the excitement he hopes awaits him at the end of the rutted and narrow road on which he speeds with good-time girls, one in particular whose hand crawls up his thigh as wind rushes. Jack cares little for the Suwannee Club or for coming-out parties. Parking in the haze of a field would treat him better, but Tallahassee boys sing and whoop.

Louise Marguerite is Elder's given name. Her mother claims it only proper to retain and use a full name, thus all of the Louises use double names (Mama is Frances Louise, I, Louise Jackson) until I drop it all and go with Lou, forcing my own will. Elder brushes her hair, counting strokes with her name: *Louise Marguerite, Louise Marguerite.* Elder claims she is first given permission to sit in front of her mother's great vanity, mahogany scrolling carved dark and deep, that night and, also for the first time, run fingers over its carved flowers, dull-deep crevasses hiding breathy secrets.

Elder calls the night of her coming out a shimmering triumph. I see her sitting alone for the first time in the great bedroom—in her day as in mine, children do not lollygag around parents' rooms—we have our place and Elder certainly knows hers. The quiet of the ante-bellum room closes around Elder, makes her feel strangely old as she brushes her hair. The silver ornamented brush smooth through the mass of her straight brown hair. It is the only movement other than flame lazing about in scattered oil lamps. Elder dons the silver-white silk evening gown, her mother's dress, which she too wears—I know because the same dress appears in portraits that hang about the house.

In childhood, as in adulthood, Elder claims to take charge of relationships. Looking over at the dress lying on the bed, soft and milky, Elder feels calm, unlike, she imagines, the friends who join her that evening. Elder neither wonders at her serenity nor worries she might not charm in conversation, she will not stumble at her entrance, fail to be asked to dance enough.

Memories are dusty story-telling, and, as I listen to this story a hundred times in my mind, contrary to what Elder consistently proclaims, I see the uncertain want in Louise Marguerite's eyes as they meet with her mother's look. Louise Marguerite (a girl not yet Elder) feels merely insecure, too young, against a mother's serenity. Perhaps she concedes defeat to her mother's ornate silver brush as it trains her hair into a low chignon twined with verbena and baby's-breath. Louise Marguerite will have wanted short hair to flip around her chin. Verbena overwhelms her disappointment, the silver-white silk dress waits, pressed and patient in the flames of oil lamps and candles.

Her mother will present her with pearls, a turn-of-the-century silk dress, elegant slippers for the show of an ankle, white stockings. Louise Marguerite, because she will someday become Elder and I must assume that presence is burgeoning even then, despite Elder proclaiming she is the darling of her papa's eyes, the belle of Gadsden County, will place all of these articles on, and then leave for the Suwannee Club, unhappy, discontented, and snooty. This is where I feel I know the story, wrap the story around me like dust shimmering in sun-drafts, or silk wraps floating across shoulders.

Louise Marguerite walks through the great doors of the Suwannee Club. She holds her head just so, a tilt of the chin, shoulders straight, erect. Her walk is measured—she has practiced this with the family Bible perched on her head, can balance for hours, even up and down staircase. She speaks politely to her friends, the daughters of her parents' friends. She imagines rightly that all eyes drift to her at points during the evening—she is the daughter of wealth and prestige. Louise Marguerite begins to dance with her father, a stiff and formal man in tuxedo. They do not speak; rather, they waltz: one, two, three, one, two, three.

The evening is carnival, theatre. Louise Marguerite dances. The Suwannee Club stands bold and light against the shroud of darkness outside. Cicadas begin their buzz as if in unison with the orchestra. Drivers drink moonshine, shoot dice, chuckle at the spectacle from safe distances outside the great doors.

Jack Sheffield's car brings up dust as its wheels slide from road to woods. Boys and their good-time girls pour out of the car, off rumble seat and up from floorboards, chaotic against the steady beat of a waltz. They whoop and run, some stop to dice, more to drink. Jack, because this is his home and his people, breathes in deep of spring air, cleaner than the air in Tallahassee. Cicadas are old friends; suddenly, he longs to be home on the farm, sitting late with his mother, perhaps smoking a final cigarette before bed—quiet, friendly. Jack panics: his mother might be inside the Suwannee Club; she most assuredly is. Jack makes to grab good-time girl latched to his arm, but she breaks away, enters Suwannee Club with no reverence for occasion, in search of a fast drink—an actress entering stage right, yellow glow of lights lifting her up and up.

Jack, of course, follows swiftly. The lights hit him like an interrogation, but he knows enough of this society—having been born to it—to lift his chin, plaster the measured smile all the dancers wear, and enter, gently taking his good-time girl's elbow to escort her in as if she were a daughter of such occasion.

"I want to dance," she slurs, breathy, low, and boozy. Jack notes the lilt of her voice—slurring, her brazen accent peculiar to the illiterate, a girl unaccustomed to speaking her mind, to free will, until introduced to the speaks of the cities and jukes of the backwoods, to moonshine and backrooms, to sojourning men.

The good-time girl sways heavily, holding out for Jack's arm to steady herself; her heels bend precariously from under her ankles, but she lurches toward the dance floor. A song begins and dancers move swiftly around a circle. Jack makes to stop her, grabs after her arm, but ends with nothing— only a silk-sheer wrap in his hands: "No," she screeches, bleary-eyed. "I want to dance, fine-like, with a gent." She recovers and smiles. "Or ain't you one—a gent, I mean."

Jack can think of nothing to be done so he dances, hoping toward an escape out the back door, or perhaps a stepped upon toe, a broken heel— anything to get her outside before his mother sees him. Music mingles in his ears and it occurs to Jack that his mother's driver would likely have more moonshine to sell and that Jack might bribe her outside, even salvage some time out in the woods with his nameless good-time girl, her Seminole-black hair swinging, shiny in a long bob, rolled down stockings, gold lamé dropped-waist dress shimmering in lamplight. The other dancers— Quincy's society—overshadowed on a lovely brilliant stage.

Louise Marguerite will watch entranced—unknowingly feel the same desires as Jack—to run, escape, lose herself. Although the evening should be her moment, her stage, it is now forgotten.

Billy Boy claims to have been to Dallas, although I doubt him. I make him sit down and give the Flatlanders cassette a chance, a good listen, hope perhaps he will take me in his arms and dance me around the ballroom's dust. I desperately want Billy Boy to feel the depth I gained from the songs, to give him this gift. I hope it might somehow save us if we share the miracle of understanding and hope I have discovered dancing around alone. But Billy Boy just listens calmly, smoking a cigarette, drumming his fingers impatiently, not with the music at all. "I been to Big D," Billy Boy says to me. "Only thing that band gets right is there's a bunch of new money in the Lonestar State—big hats and no ride," he says and swaggers off to fix another drink. I stop the tape, remove it, hide it away, safe and waiting till later when I will again give it my attention, full and true.

Louise Marguerite dances, straight and proper as she has been taught: one, two, three, around and around. She should be secure in everyone's gaze, watched and approved. She might even be struck by the appearance of Jack Sheffield, tall, handsome, older. He might solicit some excitement and she will ponder the possibility that he has driven over with Tallahassee boys to see her, the belle of Gadsden County, feel the tickle of possibility travel over her skin.

But Louise Marguerite locks eyes instead on the good-time girl. The girl twirls swiftly, angles out of Jack's arms, twirling alone around and around to the waltz, willing the music to keep up with her body. Her dress is gold and shines against the lights of the great hall, silk, a drunken dervish of shimmers. Louise Marguerite memorizes each movement, an awakening, until, completely rapt in the shimmerdance, she falls out of step, begs her father to allow her fresh breath. Her father also watches the girl. A mixture of disapproval and male greed fleets across his features. "Yes, we will pause until the fiasco ends—another dance—find your mother." He steers his daughter off the dance floor and strides to the smoking room.

And this is where Louise Marguerite becomes Elder, delighted to steal this moment for strategy. Elder spends a lifetime preparing for an expected evening—now, instead, she faces something alive and fluid, unexpected, exciting. Elder feels the power in the woman's dance, despite now even focusing on the woman's cheap clothing and hard, sad features. These do not matter. What matters is the woman's shimmer, a unique dance amongst all of the staid gentry—and her not giving a damn. What matters is that Jack Sheffield—albeit looking around, horrified, at all his parents' friends—is willing to stumble into the Suwannee Club and let this wild golden phoenix loose to swoop and rise and burn. Now abandoned by him, allowed to complete her ascendancy.

Elder becomes suddenly aware that Jack Sheffield's horrified eyes are now on her. She turns red with the heat of embarrassment that he is aware of her fixed fascination of the good-time girl. He will walk over, touch Elder's hand, bow in the manner which gentlemen from Quincy have bowed to their ladies for generations, and he will say, "I would request a dance, Miss," and they will then dance, off in another direction, to another tune, their backs straight, their touch light, movement synchronous. A shimmering silk wrap held between their hands. Elder will have prevailed, will have won the moment, will have set to always win such moments.

Jack will claim for the rest of his days to have not known this good-time girl, trusting she will find her way back to the jukes from which she has come. Elder will not argue, but she will remain partial to shimmery scarves the rest of her life, a token remembrance. Elder will have a granddaughter who wonders at one scarf hidden in the wardrobe on the third floor, a granddaughter who longs for lost opportunities, who believes she doesn't give a damn about winning only to discover that the life of running from her heritage, this house, and its family is her own attempt at a victory which shimmers brilliantly in the night sky before fading at dawn. Who regrets never flying off to Dallas nor discovering flat lands and skies opening brilliant pinks and oranges, daily Phoenixes. Who remains prisoner under comfortable canopies of North Florida oaks and pines, deep in gullies and ravines, and the society to which she is born. For whom, it becomes finally clear, escape falters and then fades under the weight of it all—the dance, the Suwannee Club, the ornate-silver brush.

These are all just stories: made up, true, some even my own imaginings. The only thing certain is that, even in middle-age, I return up to that third floor wardrobe, pull out the scarf and dance around and around to a an old tape of Texas songs. I know I should simply pick up the phone, call the airline, and book passage on a DC-9 for Dallas, make certain that the flight lands at night, perhaps even book a train to Lubbock and see the Plains for myself. I know I should call Billy Boy and tell him I do not want to live with a man who refuses to dance free, in the middle of a room full of waltzing tuxedos. But I am also afraid that if I move out of the shade of the ballroom, the wash of sunlight which lays itself across the old wooden floor and in which I find one warm moment of shimmer, will break.

The wind might blow me away. Texas flatlanders possess the staidness of spirit to withstand hard, hot Plains winds. But do I?

The Deacon's Horse

Clay Reynolds

Native Texan novelist, essayist, scholar, and literary critic Clay Reynolds is the author about 1,000 publications ranging from scholarly studies to short fiction and poems, essays, critical reviews and fourteen published volumes, including eight works of fiction. He is Professor of Arts and Humanities at the University of Texas at Dallas.

Reynolds explains, "I was driving across country on a winter afternoon the first time I heard 'The Sky Above, the Mud Below,' sung by El Paso balladeer Tom Russell. I was instantly struck by the stark, merciless nature of the ballad, how unredeeming it was, how cruel and final it seemed. As I often do, though, I was more drawn to the idea of what it would have been like to have been a helpless witness to such a thing, someone who is in a position to stop it, but who lacks the courage to act when no one else will. I think this story is about the self-realization that we are seldom as good as we want to believe we are and that maybe our only hope is to come to terms with our limitations and learn to live with them."

The Sandoval brothers come to Groesbeck Creek on one of them raw, windy days that always warned of worse weather on the rise as soon the season could make up its mind. We was stuck between summer and winter, since Texas has no autumn to speak of, and as was usual, we'd get spells of tooth-rattling northers followed by golden sunny days that reminded you of late spring. But as the weeks trailed on, there was more chill than warm, and that would be the story till Jack Frost come to stay a while.

That November morning was cold and planning to get colder. There was icy clouds in the sky and mud freezing in the wagon ruts. The morning sun wasn't warming. It was just there, like a great cold yellow eye looking down on a wore-out whore. It was the kind of day you knew you'd look back on later and wish you'd just pulled up the quilts and slept through. It come a ragged rain the night before, but not enough to settle the dust, then the wind shifted to hard out of the northwest, full of grit and smelling like something with rusty iron in it. If anybody went out of doors, they hurried to get back inside quick. Most felt sorry for any poor son of a bitch who had to stay out there and take it just so he could hear the eagle scream.

A lot of the time, I was one of the poor sons of bitches they felt sorry for. But the cow business was what I'd picked, or what had picked me. So I didn't complain.

This was horse and cow country. Had to be. There wasn't a damn thing else would grow on it. Nothing you could eat. If you didn't have good pasture—and most didn't—and sweet water—and most didn't—cattle come up scrawny. But horses grew fat on the browse. They was the only beasts that seemed to thrive. Still, it was good country in its way and give as much as you had the nerve to yank out of it. A man with gumption could get a toe-hold and make do for a space. Elsewise, it either killed him or he moved on to someplace worse.

So it was here I come to work in the cow trade. And it was here that the Deacon come to set up shop in Groesbeck Creek.

Speaking personally, I wished I'd never heard of Groesbeck Creek.

It wasn't worth a name, truth to tell. Twenty miles from the county seat, and two from the Oklahoma Territory—that was right then trying its damndest to become a state, though there wasn't a white man worth his weight in dog turds who'd live there—Groesbeck Creek might of been a thousand from anywheres else. It was permanent home to no more than a dozen pure-white souls, mostly busted-out saddle tramps, drunks and whores. There was a handful of Negras and a scattering of Mescans here and there, but nobody paid much mind to them till some hard and nasty work was wanted. If you come up on the place, especially on a morning like that November, Groesbeck Creek looked like something that just rose up out of the mud and would probably slide back into it soon as the weather warmed back up and the land crusted over. No drop of paint or straight nail had ever been wasted on it, and half of what windowlights there was was busted out and covered over with pasteboard. You wouldn't think by looking that nobody there had ever heard of a plumb-bob or a carpenter's square.

Nobody ever come to Groesbeck Creek on purpose, especially the county sheriff, so they made the Deacon a justice of the peace for the place, a job he soon widened out to include head lawman, and, as we'd come to

94

learn, judge and, some said, hangman for anybody who didn't meet his mark. I never heard of him hanging nobody from somebody who claimed to of saw it hisself. But one thing I learned in my young life was that damn near anything's possible, if you wait it out.

Word was that The Deacon was crazy as a shit-eating dog, and that might of been about right, but crazy don't trump cunning, and he was about as sly a man as I'd ever run up on. He was once a preacher, some said. Others said he'd been a tycoon back East, ruined in the bust of ninety-three. There was other stories, some believable, some not, most making him out to be a whole lot more than what he was now, which was principally a whiskey peddler and a whoremonger, or such is what my daddy would of called him. My daddy could form a hard opinion of people, though. That was a trait I'd tried not to cultivate in my young self. The last person I ever wanted to monkey-see was my daddy.

Time I come on the scene, the Deacon was just the Deacon. He run The Tabernacle and the whores who worked there. Truth to tell, he run the whole damn town, which, besides The Tabernacle, had a mercantile and a smith and livery, which the Deacon also owned—run by an affable one-eyed, half-wit colored man name of Lee Henry—and not much else.

What kept the place going was cow hands, like me. Honest joes who could do a job of work and didn't have noplace else to be but who kept hoping that one of these days something better would come along. Green as I was, I'd learned that it almost never did, and I'd took the notion that if it did, there wasn't much of a chance that it would linger long around Groesbeck Creek. Most everbody talked about the place as if it wouldn't be there another week, which made you wonder why anybody stayed around. It was better than being on the bum, I guess, but not much if you didn't have a trade. Thanks to my pard, Buster, I did, so that made me a little different. I reckoned I owed Buster for that. I come to owe him for a whole lot more, too, and not all of it was good.

That brings me back to The Tabernacle, the establishment where I spent most all of my time and nearly all of my money. It was a dark and greasy joint, mostly saloon with a zinc-topped bar. Truth to tell, it was no better built than the sorriest nigger shack in town. It tended to lean a little away from the wind and had more droughts than a Mescan shithouse, but it provided everthing we wanted: beer, liquor, hot food, and a whore, if you had the price. There was a barber's chair off to one side, where a full-blood Seminole named Chickenbone would cut your hair for a dime, throw in a shave and a bath in the back room for four bits more. For another twenty cents, he'd do your laundry while you scrubbed down in a galvanized tub.

He also did the cooking on a rusty old stove, and now and then he kept bar when Deke wasn't around.

The rest of the place was nothing to brag on. There was a piano somebody blasted with a shotgun one time or another—so only half the keys worked—a bootblack chair nobody ever used, and there was some ratty greenfelt card tables and a billiard table that was so grooved and cut that it was mostly used by drunks to sleep it off when they was too far gone to stumble outside and lay down in the mud.

The whores lived in the cribs up on the second floor. There was usually five or six girls, and most of them had saw better days. Only one or two was in any danger of being called a "girl," even in polite company. Over time, the number and kind varied some, depending on which might be healthy, which had moved on, or which had died of something or other. Buster said that the thing that killed most of them was that they "was eat up with the dumbass—theirs or somebody else's" and that dying was probably a welcome exit out of the whole thing. It was hard to argue with that, truth to tell. You had to wonder why even a woman who was so down and out that she'd turn to whoring in a cow town would show up in Groesbeck Creek—which had to be the bottom rock in the well, even for a whore—but ever now and then after one or the other would die or run off, a new one would show up. Like everbody else, they was drawn to Groesbeck Creek when there wasn't noplace else to go.

Once in a while, they'd be kind of perky—for a spell—fresh-faced and soft to the touch, but Groesbeck Creek soon broke them down. Before long, the shine wore off and they looked about as rough as a sun-cooked saddle.

That there was always some old boy eager to plunk down a dollar to drop his harrow in one of them crusty furrows was one of the great mysteries of life I sometimes pondered. I also wondered why I, more often than not, was one of them eager old boys. I thought it was just because I was naturally randy, but truth to tell, it was more because I was still a greenstick, and I wanted to be saw as a man, just like everbody else. Poking a dry hole won't make a man a man, I don't expect, but in Groesbeck Creek you took your chances where you found them.

That particular morning, the morning the first bad norther of the year blew in—like I said, the morning the Sandoval brothers rode in—I'd been up in Millie's crib. She was kind of new and had become sort of my favorite, since she was about the only one younger than I was—or so she told me—and I liked to get her early, if I could. She was still fresh in the mornings, didn't feel all wore out and used up, stinking of a bunch of old boys' sweat and pomade. She was a plump, curly-headed little thing with bright brown eyes and a swell laugh that always got me going. She had jet black hair and these pouty little titties with bright red nipples and a firm round bottom and wasn't much to look at otherwise. But her laugh was a jolly thing. She was more than worth the dollar Deke charged for a half hour with her.

When I was with her, I couldn't think of noplace else I'd rather be, truth to tell. I said that to Buster, once, and he said that was about the stupidest thing he'd ever heard in his life. I expect it was. But it was also a fact.

It was near noon when I come downstairs and into the saloon, and I was feeling all strutty. Millie'd been extra sparky that morning, and as sometimes took place, she let me lay around for a spell and get another go-round on the house while she talked about her big plans. They changed a little from time to time, but they always concerned meeting some galoot and hauling off somewhere—usually Abilene—and having a family, a house of her own and a mess of kids. I'm not sure why she lit on Abilene, except maybe that it was the only town of any size she'd ever heard of that wasn't someplace she couldn't go back to. She said she wanted nothing more than to keep a home for a man who'd treat her decent and love her up without having to pay for it.

It never made me skittish for her to talk like that, because she made it plain she was corking for bigger fish than some poor cowboy such as myself. How she planned to catch that kind of a man while working for Deke I didn't know, but I didn't mind her rambling on. Her eyes would light up and her cheeks got all rosy when she talked about it. She got so cute, I couldn't stand it. There was times, truth to tell, when I'd think about maybe making her a little proposition, she made it sound so swell. I could tell she liked me a whole lot more than the average gomer, and that give me kind of the big head. So there was times, I might of considered the matter on the level. But then I'd see the cash tin on her bed table, and I'd recollect where I was and why I was there, and I'd also remember that aside from cowboying, the only thing I knew how to do to earn a living was farming.

I had no notion in the world of ever going back to farming. My daddy seen to that, and it only took him about sixteen years to do it.

Even still, I was a whole lot fonder of her than I should of been, and I expect the feeling was mostly mutual. I'd never been to Abilene and never hoped to go there, but sometimes when the weather was up and I felt myself getting lonely, I'd think of Millie and conjure us living in a regular town and acting like regular folks. It would give me a nice, warm feeling on a cold night. I never had much sense about women, Buster told me, but young as I was, it was a hard lesson to learn.

Buster Milligan was my pard. We come in ahead of the norther before first light that morning to pick up supplies for the line shack where we'd be winter ranging for Mr. Jacob Hadnought, who did have good pasture and who owned about half the county. We also had ten dollars' advance on our found to buy what we needed, plus our left-over wages for the previous payday, so we had some jack in our jeans when we come into The Tabernacle to wait for the store to open up. Or such was our excuse.

Buster was some older than me and a lot more savvy, but we got along good enough, even though he wasn't a big talker and liked to play cards by hisself. He'd invented three or four games of solitary he'd play for hours at a time. I hoped to pick up a book or two or maybe some magazines if there was any on hand. I wasn't much of a reader, but wintertime in a line shack can get long and lonesome. Nothing's worse than being cooped up in a shack with a man who is always occupied when you have nothing to do yourself.

Buster was an admirable soul, and long ago, I decided that he was as good a pattern as I could find to cut myself after. But he was also an odd duck in a lot of ways. He could be fractious, especially when money was tight, and he often said he never figured he'd wind up in a shit-hole like Groesbeck Creek. But he said it seemed that that was where the Almighty wanted him. That was about as close to religious talk as Buster ever got. He wasn't a swell and had no airs, but he liked to be clean and seldom let a week go by without a shave. He never went with Deke's girls. He said he lacked ambition where "professional women," as he called them, was concerned. He'd been in the army during the Cuban War, and he said he learned long ago the foolishness of putting down hard-earned money for something that more often than not would wind up giving you blistering drip. "Day they make it so a piece of ass lasts longer than it takes to earn the geddes to buy it," he said, "maybe I'll reconsider."

Buster never minded putting down quite a bit of scratch for Deke's liquor, though. He also wasn't afraid to risk his wages on a hand of faro or stud poker, if anybody was dealing. Cards was an important part of Buster's life.

We'd rode together since he found me down in Jack County round about five years before. At the time, I was shit out of luck and more than a little puzzled about what I was fixing to do about it. I didn't have two nickels to rub together, and things was looking desperate. Buster come up on me sitting in the mud in an alleyway trying to remember my last meal and unable to conjure my next. He took a look at me and asked if I'd rather work or starve to death. I told him I wasn't afraid of work, but I'd not found any that was both legal and worth my time. He laughed about that. He bought me a chicken dinner, cleaned me up, got me some duds and a kit, and put me on a horse and took me to see Mr. Hadnought about hiring on. He vouched for me, and that was good enough for Mr. Hadnought.

I never was sure why he did it, since he didn't know a thing about me. But I was glad he did. We'd got to know each other pretty good since then, and I'd learned a lot from him, both by watching what he did and listening to what he said. Though I admired him above any man I knew, I didn't always take his advice, but he didn't mind. He always said that a man's got to make his own mistakes so he can be sure. That's sort of how we become partners and friends. Truth to tell, he was the only friend I ever had in Groesbeck Creek, and he was the only man I'd met in my life that I looked up to without shame, at least for a time.

Buster was a lot different from my daddy, who was the kind of man who only saw the right of things and wouldn't brook conversation about any other way. My daddy was a good man but a hard man, and there was times when I wished I could of admired him the way I did Buster. It's just that there was no give to him, and you can't learn much from a man like that. He took stock of things at a glance, and it was damn near impossible for him to change his mind, especially if his first read was a sour one. He wasn't mean, but he was always sure, and among the few things I'd found out about life is that nothing is ever sure. I expect he'd of formed a negative opinion of his eldest boy right off, had he saw me that morning. But I didn't think much about that, especially when I was with Millie. Whenever my daddy intruded into my mind too much, I could always turn my thinking toward her, and somehow, everthing seemed a little brighter in the world.

So I was feeling good when I come down that morning. I was thinking about asking Chickenbone to cook me up a half-dozen eggs or so, if he wasn't busy. I'd always favored a big breakfast. For I and Buster, biscuits and coffee was common fare, but neither of us was much of a cook. Most times, you could use the biscuits for sinkers if you needed to go fishing.

My ambitions for hot grub didn't last long. Early as it was, there was a line at the barber's chair. Some old boys was just in their underwear, since they'd just got up and come down for a shave and a bath. My own duds needed a wash and so did I, but I hadn't thought much about it until right then.

But there was a Saturday morning mood in the place. Even though most of the girls was still asleep, it wouldn't be long before things would pick up as much as they ever did in Groesbeck Creek. I could see that the coffeepot was cold and lonely on a table by the stove, and that was a disappointment, but it was only the first one that day.

I spotted Buster sitting at the faro table where there was a new dealer. He was looking glum, which meant he was losing again. I said morning to him, but he just nodded at me and squinted down at his hand. I seen the stack of greens in front of him wasn't all that big, and I hoped our found money was still in his wallet. The dealer give me a wink and a smirky grin that almost made me mad, because he didn't know me from Adam's off-ox, so I went over to the bar and ordered a beer. Deke was there to pull it for me.

Now, for this and what happened next to make sense, you have to have a good picture of The Deacon. We all called him "Deke," which he'd tolerate to his face from the boys who didn't owe him money. He always wore a black suit and white shirt and always looked clean. He wasn't very tall. I wasn't short—more than six-feet last time I was measured, but lots of old boys had to look down at Deke. I'd guess him to be just over eighteen hands, no more than that, and that was wearing high-heeled boots.

It was hard to tell how old he was. Some said he said he'd never see fifty again. He didn't have a hair on his head. Not even eyebrows. No chin-cabbage or lip-worm, neither. There was ridge that sort of made a shelf that shaded his eyes, and they was nearly scary, dark blue, almost purple, and seemed to fill the whites to the very rim. They was cold, too, like skim ice. When a man that ugly looks at you, you pay attention.

He was also stout. Not blubbery, but thick in the chest and shoulders, and his neck was solid gristle and his hands strong, with short, square fingers. When he made a fist, it looked like a mallet. We always said we could tell he'd be a mean son of a bitch in a fight, but we had trouble seeing him as a scrapper. It might get his shirt dirty, Buster said.

Buster didn't much like the Deacon, and while he never spoke a word directly against him, he seemed to go out of his way to make his opinion clear in other ways.

Deke was always civil, no matter who he was talking to, white or colored. He'd treat the worst kind of trail trash the same as he would the mayor of the seat. He was sort of humble in a way my mama would of admired, but there was always something dark about him, truth to tell, something that made you want to ease away from him if he paid you too close a mind. I reckoned my daddy would of give him the wide part of the road. On the other hand, he might of stared him down, toe-to-toe. Truth to tell, it was a toss-up who I'd rather not tangle with the most, my daddy or the Deacon.

Deke didn't talk much about hisself. Truth to tell, he didn't talk deep about much of nothing but horses. There was no question that whatever else was true about him, Deke knew horses.

He was in a good mood that morning. "How're you keeping yourself?" he asked me when I cracked an egg from the jar on the bar and dropped it into my beer. It sort of caught me off guard for him to jawbone like that, because he'd just saw me earlier that morning and didn't say a word to me. But I checked him, and he was giving me a casual look that showed he wasn't being smart-alecky.

"Fair to middling," I said and drank my beer, swallowing the egg whole.

"That's better than most," he replied and drew me another. I could tell he wanted to call me by name, but he wouldn't. I heard him say once that he didn't like to learn the name of men he might have to hang one of these days. I didn't expect he'd ever have cause to hang me, but I didn't mind that he didn't use my name, either. To answer him, I just nodded and sipped my new beer. My stomach was too empty to hazard too much more on it without some victuals to go with it.

"You still riding that ugly white-spotted nag?"

"You know I'm not," I said. He asked me that question ever time he saw me, because that was the horse I had under me the day I first rode into Groesbeck Creek five years before. It was his idea of a joke, I reckon, for that old paint was about the sorriest horse any man ever put a saddle on, but it was what Buster provided at the outset. Since then, I had a gray gelding that was a better animal than I'd ever hoped to own, truth to tell. Of course, I didn't truly own him. He belonged to Mr. Hadnought.

Joke or not, Deke didn't smile. "I assume Millicent gave you a good ride this morning?" He always called the girls by their full names, never a nickname. Lisa was Elizabeth, Prudy was Prudence, Abby was Abigail, and so forth. So Millie was Millicent to him. The girls sort of liked it, I think. "You were up there long enough," he said. He took a cup from the rinse tub and dried it on a towel he kept draped over his shoulder. "She's still getting the job done?"

I felt myself turning red all over. Not too long ago, my mama would of blistered my hind-end good for even thinking about what I'd done with Millie that morning. Long as it had been since I left home, I still hadn't got much beyond feeling bad about doing it. In a lot of ways, I was still a whelp and hadn't learned how to ride around regret or guilt. For a man my age,

I seemed to have more than my fair share. I liked to act like I was full-grown, but Buster was fond of reminding me that I had a long way to go. He said it took more than acting like a man to be a man. I expect there was wisdom in that.

"She's worth the time."

"She'd better be worth the dollar," Deke replied. "She's a ripe filly. Not much in the udders, but she has a high rump and tight flanks. A curly mane, top and bottom."

That shamed me again. Deke always talked about women like they was horses. I heard that when a girl showed up wanting to work for him, first thing he did was look at her teeth, then at her bare feet. Said he wouldn't hire a woman with bad teeth or twisted toes. I didn't doubt it. But I didn't like to hear him talking about Millie that way. It kind of made me mad. I knew what she was, what she'd always be. But I didn't like the notion that he might kill off her laugh or spoil her dreaming about them plans.

I also didn't like him reminding me that she wasn't no Sunday School teacher and never would be. I was still thinking good things about her, all bed warm and pink up there in her crib. I was half a mind to head right back up there just to show him.

I started to say something back, but of a sudden, he looked at me. He studied my face hard, them dark blue eyes boring into me. "Next time, it'll cost you an extra four bits, you stay over."

I felt myself go steamy all over again. "We was just talking,"

"Talk is the same as time," he said, holding that smile. "Cooze costs."

I wasn't going to get the best of him, and there wasn't no percentage in getting all head-up, so I just nodded to show I heard him, then went over to watch Buster play out another losing hand. He *was* in a sour mood, I could tell now, and it wasn't apt to get any sweeter if he was losing big, which he often did. The only good thing I could see was that Buster was sober. I was about to tell him we ought to pack it in and get our necessaries and hightail it back out to the line shack before the weather got worse. That was when the Sandovals come in.

* * *

Of course, we didn't know they was the Sandovals. To this day, I couldn't *swear* that they was, truth to tell. But I'm sure I wasn't the only one who set up a wonder about these two when they come in. After all, it wasn't ever day that a couple of strange Mexes just come right into Deke's. But they come in, anyway, like they was blown right through the door by that whipping wind that chilled everbody the second it hit them.

102

Everybody just stopped what they was doing and looked at them.

They was worth the look. There was a Mescan word I had heard—
"*hombre*"—which meant sort of a man's notion of a man, or so I took it. If
anybody looked like a couple of *hombres,* these two greasers did. They was
big men, and both had on real tight pants that fanned out at the cuffs over
their high-heeled boots. They wore these big spurs with rowels that looked
like little bitty windmills with sharp blades. Even though it was coming on
to freezing outside and the wind was howling, neither one had on an
overcoat coat of any kind. One had on a short vest that had these four big
conchos on it, but the other one just wore a plain flannel shirt. Their hats
was like small versions of the *sombreros* that some of the local Mexes wore
in the summertime, and like most everthing else about them, they was
stained nearly black with old sweat and dirt.

"*Vaqueros,*" I heard Buster say. His voice was real soft, and nobody
but me heard it, I don't reckon. I glanced down at him, but he kept his back
to them and his eyes on his cards. "Goddamn it," he breathed out in a near
whisper. Buster had spent a lot of time down around San Antone, and he
spoke some Mescan, so I reckoned he knew what he was talking about. I
also knew that when it come to Mexes, Buster was like everbody else. He
had no real use for them. Meanwhile, the two stood there for a spell, letting
their eyes adjust to the dim.

When they began to move, everbody went back to what they was
doing, but there was now a new feeling in the room, something heavy that
hadn't been there before, like the air you feel right before a thunderburst.
There had been some hubbub before, joshing around and hoorahing from
the men in line at the barber's chair. But now it was real quiet. You could
hear that high-pitched whine the wind makes when it finds a piece of loose
stripping someplace and blows through it. Somewhere far off, I could hear
something being banged, like a board that hadn't been nailed down good.

Now, I don't want to give you the wrong notion. Mescans wasn't
routinely kept out of Deke's place, at least the local ones wasn't. One man's
money spends as good as another's, truth to tell. I personally never paid
much mind to any of them. They tended to hang together and palavered in
their own lingo more often than not. Only them with hard money ever
come to The Tabernacle, though. Deke wouldn't give credit to a preacher.
These two didn't seem that jaked, but they looked like they knew what
work was, which could of meant they likely had some cash to spend. But I
was wrong about that. And that was too bad for them, too bad for all of us,
in a way.

They come up to the bar and stood there, then turned around and looked at the room, like they was taking our measure and letting us size them up at the same time. There wasn't a scrap of humble in them. They hadn't been shaved in a while, and the shorter of the two had a big set of mustaches hanging down, almost past his chin. It made him look kind of comical. The taller one was cockier. He was better looking, too, and more serious. I reckoned him to be older.

Neither was wearing side-iron, something I always notice on a man when it's there. We didn't usually carry handguns around, and if a man does, then you figure he either knows how to use it or he wants people to think he does. Either way makes him dangerous. Each one had a frog-gigger in his belt, and I noticed that the small one had another blade in his boot. I then saw that the large one had a leather string around his neck. It looped down and went inside his shirt, and I figured there might be a hogleg on the other end of it.

They grinned at the room like we was a bunch of pards about to jump up and buy them a drink, but most of us was trying hard to watch them without actually looking at them. They was different from the usual Mex, and that was a truth to tell. For the longest time, they just stood there smiling and friendly, bold as sunrise. There was a lot of stirring and shuffling around in the room, but not much talking, and nobody looked right at them, especially Buster, who was taking a close interest in the cards in his fist.

Finally, the bigger one reached into a cornmeal sack he had looped on his belt behind him and pulled out a bridle. He held it up high so we could all see what it was, then he put it on the bar. "We trade this for whiskey drink," he said, nodding at Deke, who hadn't moved a muscle since they come in but just stood behind the bar and watched them straight on. He didn't care if they saw that he was looking at them or not.

The bigger one slapped the bridle on the bar again. "One bridle, hand-made. One bottle, *auguadente*," he said. "Fair and square, okay?" Then he looked around the room and grinned. This time, I saw he had a silver tooth right in front. He was a little buck-toothed and that made it stick out some. The other one, Mustaches, just stood there and kept on grinning right along with the other.

"Bob's your uncle," Buster said real low and threw down his cards. I heard him whistle out through his teeth, though. "God*damn* it," he whispered. I could tell something was eating him. I reckoned it was his usual bad luck. "You gonna deal or just sit there?" he asked the dealer, who give him a grin and started up a new game.

"I deal in hard currency," Deke said.

"That bridle, she's worth the cash dollars," the big one said.

Deke took another long look at them, then he picked up the bridle and looked at it. He turned it over in his hands a couple of times, then held it up to the light from a lamp. From all the way across the room, I could see that it was thick and plaited tight, and it shone in the light with a dark red tint. But what made it special was that running right through the middle of the braiding was a white line, so bright against the blood-red color that it seemed to shine.

"Where'd you get this?" Deke asked.

"We make him," the big one said, nodding to the short one, who grinned and nodded back. "We braid him. Bridles, halters, quirts, *todos*," he said. He turned around the room to see if anybody might have something to say about that, but nobody did.

Deke didn't say nothing, neither. He laid the bridle down on the bar, smoothed it out like it was a cat he was petting. His eyes stayed on them while he put a bottle of toenail juice and two glasses up on the bar. I seen it was the cheap stuff, mostly raw alcohol with a dose of camphor, a little old coffee for color and whatever else he might find lying around that would give it some punch. He never served that to us local boys since Homer McGillicutty, a busted-up saddle bum with a bottle problem, drank too much of it one night and went blind. While they pulled over the glasses and poured, Deke picked up the bridle again and run it through his fingers over and over again. The men drank off their round and watched him for a spell, then looked at one another and shrugged and poured again.

Now, all of us knew that horses was important to Deke. There was no question that, next to Mr. Hadnought, he owned about the best saddle stock in that part of the country. But there was one horse that was special to him. It was a big red stallion, and he claimed he was the fastest horse he ever seen. I was never straight on whether he bred it or bought it, but it was clear that he prized it higher than springtime. He raced that horse against all comers, and it always won. Deke refused to stud him out, saying he was waiting for the right mare to come along. He said he wanted any colt to come out of him to be better than the sire. He didn't put him out to the pasture but kept him corralled behind the livery barn, so he could take people down to look at him if he was a mind to.

Buster, who knew horses, too, said he was the prettiest horse he'd ever saw. He said it was the best horse that he'd ever saw in Texas, bar none. Fact of the business was that Buster coveted that horse. He tried to buy him off Deke one time, he said, but Deke wouldn't sell for love nor money. Buster said it showed Deke didn't have good sense, that it was a pure waste to keep a horse like that penned up when he needed to be outside, running free. But I got the notion, truth to tell, that turning the horse loose wasn't what Buster had in mind. He just saw something in that red horse that he hadn't saw anywheres else. He talked about that horse ever time we come into Groesbeck Creek, and we always had to stop by the corral and have a look at him.

And I reckon he *was* pretty. He was long-legged, deep in the withers, with slender pasterns and a high top line. Buster thought he was a cross between a true bay and a true sorrel. The bay part, I guess, give him a pure blood-red color, darker in his mane and tail, and he'd shine crimson in the sun. But what set him apart more than anything was what he might of got from the sorrel side. He had this one white streak of hair just over an inch wide that started about half way up the middle of his rump and then run right down through his tail, all the way out to the tip. It was like a stripe of some kind—the sort of thing you'd see on a polecat—stark-white and razor-sharp against his red coat—and it was so bright that the first time you seen it, you'd think somebody used a straight-rule and painted it on him. It was odd, and it made him special. Buster said that a mark like that could also make him worth a pile of money. I soon had reason to reckon that Buster wasn't the only one who thought so.

One evening about a year before, I was hanging around The Tabernacle, waiting on Buster to come back from a cattle buying trip down to Bosque County, trying to figure out how to make five dollars stretch into five days. It wasn't ordinary for Buster to go off like that on his own, but he said Mr. Hadnought—who was known to be tighter than Dick's hatband—wouldn't buy but one ticket, so I had to just cool my heels till he got back. A norther just like the one that was blowing outside that morning was howling out of the northwest, and everbody was hunkered down inside, which was going to make the money a lot thinner to spread. Then word come that Deke's big red horse was stole. He'd been turned out into the corral that morning about daybreak, before the norther hit. The corral gate was wide open and tied back. Four other horses—good horses—had got out and was milling around back of the barn, but the red horse was flat gone.

I was in The Tabernacle when Lee Henry come helling in and give Deke the word. He stood there for a heartbeat or two, and I swear the temperature, which was already icy in the room, dropped ten degrees. His eyes went dead black, then they flared into that deep blue, and he breathed out a long sigh. He stomped down to the corral in the high north wind, looked at the open gate and then at the prints leading off to the north, out of town. Then he took off in his shirtsleeves on foot, tracking the thief. It come a bad storm that afternoon, and there was ice all over, and everbody thought he'd be back in an hour or so and at least get hisself a mount and some winter duds, but he didn't. Truth to tell, it was near a week before Deke come back. He was still afoot. Some claimed he walked all the way to Kansas before he give it up, but I don't know how they knew that. All that everbody agreed on was that he come stumbling back into town half-starved and near naked, covered with Red River mud. His face was dark as a thunderhead, and nobody would look him in the eye. I don't reckon anybody had ever had the gall to steal nothing from him before, especially nothing as special as that horse.

He didn't say nothing to nobody, just locked hisself in a back room behind the bar and sulled up. After a couple of days, he come out, took a shave, ordered up a bath and fresh laundry, and went back to work, like nothing ever happened. But he was different, somehow or other. Quieter. Harder. It was like he was in some far off place, looking at you from a distance.

Buster come back two days overdue with his wallet stuffed with folding bills. He said the calves he went to buy wasn't worth the trip, but he'd got lucky in a three-day poker game down in Mineral Wells and cleaned up. We all give him the news, which he took in without much notice—and that surprised me, given his notions about that horse—then he went inside and sat down at the faro table, fixing to lose ever cent of the winnings he'd brought back, which he did. After he cleaned Buster out, the dealer said something about what a shame it was about the red horse, then give a little laugh. The Deacon stopped what he was doing and stared at him with a hard-eyed look that could freeze hell. He stared at him so hard the galoot gathered up his derby hat and left. He never come back, neither. Nobody else, not even Buster, ever mentioned that horse again, even when Deke wasn't around.

I'd saw this sort of thing before. Once a bunch of hobos come through our part of the county and stole two shoats we'd been fattening for Easter Dinner. It was Good Friday, and my mama pitched a hissy fit. Daddy grabbed up his 8-gauge and put me in tow and went looking for them. I didn't know what to expect, he was so mad. We found them in a kind of ditch down by the rail yard, cooking them shoats on spits over a fire they built in a sixty-gallon drum. They was a sorry-looking bunch, mostly dressed in rags and floppy moth-eaten hats, and half starved. They was so forlorn and lost, I felt nothing but sorry for them. They was looking at them two little pigs like they was manna from heaven. I didn't know but what my daddy'd run right down there and give them ten kinds of hell, maybe even shoot one or two of them. He went right up to them, and they all backed away, figuring this big man was fixing to blast them to Kingdom Come. But he didn't. He run finger over one of them shoats and tasted it. "This is my pig," he said, turning that scattergun on them. "And you're all thieves."

That set up a scaredy hubub in the group and made them shuffle around in a nervous way. Then one of them, a big one, stepped forward and doffed his hat and said, "Mister, we was hungry."

My daddy held that old shotgun steady and looked at him for a breath or two. Then he looked at me and said, "There's worse things than that to be." The man wadded up his hat and stared at the ground and nodded. Then my daddy said, "You boys watch yourselves," then turned around and led me away. When we got back home, he said to my mama, "We can have chicken for Easter." And that was an end on it. He never mentioned them shoats again, and I knew better than to remind him.

* * *

The two Mexes started another round, and Deke took the bridle over by a windowlight. His movements was kind of jerky, like he was having trouble making his hands work. He held it up and studied it. I saw him sniff it, then bite it, and run his tongue over his teeth, like he was tasting it.

The boys was drinking that bottle fast and talking low to one another in their own lingo, laughing a little now and then. But they was the only ones in the room doing any talking at all. Except for Buster and the dealer—who was paying little attention to the game—the rest of us was watching Deke. He started yanking the bridle, pulling it between his hands like a latigo. He stopped of a sudden and run one finger down that white line. Then he lifted up them dark blue eyes and give them two Mexes a hard stare. It was cold enough to frost breath in that room, but that look chilled me down to my crotch.

I looked down to catch Buster's eye, but he was focused on the table in front of him. "You gonna play or not?" he asked the dealer, who give him a grin and took up the game again.

"This is an unusual design," the Deacon said, his voice low and calm. He stepped over toward them a ways, holding that bridle out in front of him, like it was a snake that might bite him.

Mustaches, the short one, turned and hooked an elbow on the bar and smiled at Deke. He had a glass in his hand, tilted it up the way you might see a fancy-goods drummer do, with his little finger stuck out. He was kind of a comical cuss. Then he swallowed the whiskey down in a gulp, run a finger down each end of his mustache, and smiled. "*Muchas gracias.*"

"We trade *los caballos*," the taller one said and smiled. "The horses. We buy. We sell. Maybe you has some you want to trade?"

"Shit." Buster breathed out the word in a whisper and picked up the new hand.

"Trade," Deke said.

The men looked at one another quickly, then nodded. "We know . . . horses," the taller one said.

Deke slapped the bridle down on the bar, making everbody jump. "What kind of horse did *this* come from?" he asked, then stepped to the end of the bar where he had a rolltop desk full of papers.

The tall one shrugged and looked around the room, noticing, I guess, that everbody was looking at him. "A horse. Like another."

"Like another?" Deke said, but it was near a hiss.

His leg, it got broke." The tall one smiled sadly and shook his head. "We used him up."

"Used him up?" Deke asked, but in a way that made me think he was only half listening. He had the desk open now and was going through some papers. The men looked at one another, and then Mustaches shrugged, poured hisself another shot from the bottle. "You et him?" Deke asked.

The tall one shrugged. "Meat is meat. *Mejor que nada.*" He smiled.

"You didn't eat the tail," Deke said.

The tall one laughed—too loud, truth to tell. "No, *señor*. We *braid* the tail, you bet." He nodded at the bridle in Deke's hand. "She is the best bridle. *Muy . . .*" he trailed off, looking for the right word in American. Nobody helped him find it. He shrugged and poured hisself another drink. "Beautiful?" he said all at once. "*¡Ah, sí!* Very beautiful." You could tell by the way he said it that he getting some worried, but he wanted to be agreeable. "Very beautiful," he said again. He grinned big.

Deke turned around, the piece of paper in his hand, looking at them from under that brim of skin over his eyes. "And where did low-down prairie trash like you come up with a 'very beautiful' horse like that?" His voice was low and steady. The tall one's head snapped back a mite, as if he'd been slapped. He shifted his feet a little, trying to soak up the insult and decide what to do with it, I reckoned. I felt myself growing a little hollow in my gut. I noticed a lot of old boys was clearing their throats, of a sudden. I heard Buster sigh again.

Mustaches' eyes flicked around the room quickly. He was trying to take the measure of what was going on, I expect. They stood there like they was thinking the question over, then the tall one downed his shot, poured another and flashed that silver-toothed smile again. "We buy him."

"You're a liar," Deke said quietly.

I felt something drop inside me from my throat down to the pit of my stomach. I'd never heard a man called a liar before, not straight-out and just like that.

The tall one swallowed hard. Of a sudden and cold as it was, large globs of sweat run out from under that greasy hat and into his shirt. Mustaches was lost, though. He was trying to follow what was going on, but it was passing him by. He started to pour another drink, but the tall one's hand come out and stopped him. They traded hard looks, then, and I could see pure scared growing in their eyes.

Everyone was staring hard at the pair. It was so quiet, I could hear somebody's watch ticking. Then I heard Buster clear his throat the way a man does when he really don't have to. I looked down, but his eyes was still on his cards.

The tall one opened his hands, like he was expecting to catch something. "*Señor—*"

"I might believe you bought that horse, or that you came into him in an honest swap," Deke said, stopping him. He looked down quickly, then his eyes come up again, sharp on the pair. "He might have stepped in a gopher hole and broke his leg," Deke went on. "And I might believe you shot him out of pity." He held the paper up, backside to all of us. "I might believe you sat around and ate the steaks you cut off him while you plaited up the tail and thanked God for the bounty of good fortune." He nodded, and his smile was almost friendly. "I might believe all of that," Deke said. "But I don't."

Then he turned the paper around. It was a circular, a wanted poster such as I'd saw in the post office at the seat. It was for the Sandoval Brothers: Horse Thieves." Deke said, "I don't believe one goddamn word of it."

Before I could blink, Deke had filled his hands with a sawed-off scattergun he kept behind the bar. Both hammers was back, and it was pointing right at the two Mexes, who stood gaping at them twin barrels pointing at them. "You think I'd stand for two sorry, thieving, sons of a bitches to steal my horse and then sell him back to me one piece at a time?"

"*Señor*," the tall one whispered, his eyes wide.

"You don't have a bill of sale for that horse, do you?" Deke asked.

"*Señor*," he repeated, but Deke raised the scattergun a hair, and he just swallowed hard and said nothing more.

"That's what I thought," Deke said. "I find you guilty. Somebody go dig a ditch. We're about to have a hanging."

* * *

Now, I'd never saw a man hung, and I wasn't anxious to. Fact of the business was that I'd only ever saw one dead man in my life, and that was a galoot they'd mummified and was toting around in a circus side-show. So this was a whole new step for me, and not one I wanted to take. Like everbody else in the room, I stayed still as time and stared at Deke. But he was serious. I could hear men breathing around me and the wind howling outside, but nothing else. Buster was the first to move. He threw down his cards, raked in what little money he had left and stood up. "Lex," he said to get my attention away from what was going on over at the bar, "let's go."

"You stand where you are," Deke said when he seen Buster herding me toward the door.

"I ain't digging no graves," Buster said and kept walking.

"I need you," Deke said. He put his deep blue eyes on us and stared, like that would hold us.

"We're heading out," Buster pulled his hat low on his head.

"Justice will be served," Deke said like Buster hadn't said a thing.

"Like hell," Buster said and give me a push to hurry me along.

"I mean it, Clarence," Deke said. That stopped Buster. Clarence was his real name, and he hated it. The only person I ever heard use it was Mr. Hadnought. Since he paid our wages, Buster tolerated it from him, but from none other, not even me.

He looked at Deke, and I could see the muscles of his jaw working underneath his whiskers. "You can go to hell, Deacon."

Now, Buster wasn't a big man, but like ever other man in the joint, he was a lot taller than Deke. And he wasn't unformidable. He set his legs and bowed his neck, and doubled up his fists, and I couldn't see reason in any man who'd stand against him. But Deke wasn't your normal man. He didn't move a muscle and just stared at him. Neither one moved.

What did move, though, was the Sandovals. The taller one was talking a long, hard look at Buster, and I saw something familiar in his stare. It was near spooky. He looked down at the short one, and he also looked through the gloom over to Buster and nodded, then he stepped toward him. "*Señor—*" he said, but that broke the spell. Deke's head swiveled around and he raised the shotgun right to the man's nose. He was close enough that if he had pulled either barrel, he'd take his whole head off.

"Be still," he said. "I'll hear no more from you."

The tall one looked at Buster, then at his pard. Both of them was sweating rivers. Mustaches was shifting his weight back and forth, and I started thinking he might just fall down.

"*Por favor,*" the tall one said, but the Deacon lifted up the barrel and knocked off his hat. His long, greasy hair fell down around his shoulders.

"I'll hear a prayer, but nothing more," he said in a low voice. "Make your peace with God. May He have mercy on your soul. I sure as hell won't."

Buster held right where he was, with me sort of behind him. "You think everbody's just going to stand by and watch you hang these men?" he asked.

Deke looked around. "Who would stop me?"

I looked around the room. Most there was saddle tramps and odd-jobbers, waddies and dollar-a-day men who managed to scrape up enough money for a cleanup and a top-off at The Tabernacle, but who didn't have enough pocket jingle to get over to the seat for a bona fide day off. There wasn't any regular men there but I and Buster. The dealer at the table had only been in town near a week or so. Since he was a gambler, he probably wasn't reliable.

"I'm the law here," Deke said. "Besides, it was my horse."

I glanced at Buster, wondering what to do. But he still hadn't moved. I couldn't imagine that Deke would actually hurt these two, not on such skinny proof as a horsehair bridle. But then, with a man like the Deacon, you never know, and I wasn't eager to find out.

"Well, Clarence?" Deke asked, looking again at the Sandovals, who was looking at him and at Buster, like they expected somebody to say this was all a mistake, a joke of some kind, break out laughing or something, like somebody would jump up and put things right. But nobody did. "It's your move," Deke said. "Yours and his." He turned his head and looked right at me, his dark blue eyes boring right through me. "What about you," he said to me. "What are you going to put on the line?"

Of a sudden, I got that sick feeling you get when you wake up early of a morning and have a miserable job of work to do that day and know in your heart you just don't want to do it but there's no way around it. I'd felt that many a time. It was a dread I always connected up with memories of my daddy. But this was worse. I felt it was my place to step up, to do something to make this right. And much as I didn't want to, I thought about my daddy and what he would do, and I could see that Buster, for all he might want to do, couldn't do it by hisself. But I also knew right then I didn't have the sand to stand up to the Deacon, with or without Buster beside me.

Deke was not a man you said no to. Buster must of thought the same thing, for I saw his shoulders relax, his neck draw back into his coat collar.

"Well?" Deke asked.

Buster looked at the two Mexes, who was staring at him like he was their only hope. "Let's go," he said, giving me a push.

"That's what I thought," Deke said. "Get the hell out of here. You make me sick, the two of you. He looked them up and down. "Chickenbone!" he said in a loud voice. "Shear them. We'll see if they can plait a noose." Then he put the shotgun down, took the bridle and went back to the far end of the bar. Chickenbone didn't hesitate a blink. He was like that, quick and easy on his feet. He started toward them, and the tall one glanced at Deke, who had his back to them, then his hand moved quick to the inside of his shirt. He was slick, truth to tell. He jerked his hand out and, sure enough, he had a pretty nice little *pistola* in it. It was nickel-plated and looked to be a caliber .36 with a short barrel and ivory grips. We all took a step back when it come out and of a sudden was pointed right at Chickenbone. He put up his hands in front of his face and shouted, "No!" I almost dove under a table before I caught myself. Buster was froze where he stood.

For a breath or two everthing was still as a picture. I could hear the wind moaning outside, that board off somewhere banging, but all else was quiet. Nobody was breathing. Chickenbone crouched down with his palms open, like they might stop a bullet from hitting him in the eye. The tall one said something sharp in Mescan to Mustaches, but of a sudden, there was a noise behind them. They turned around and looked again down the twin barrels of Deke's shotgun. I never saw Deke move, and he was fifteen feet from where he put down that corkpopper, but somehow or other, he got back to it and picked it up without nobody noticing.

"I'm very fond of that man," he said. "He seldom talks much, and that's a quality I admire. Lay that down and be still."

Everyone stood quiet as a breath, and I could see that the Sandovals was thinking things over. Even if they got off a shot, Deke would cut them both in two and all they'd have to show for their trouble would be a dead Seminole. Besides, Chickenbone wasn't their problem. Deke was. Finally, the tall put the *pistola* down on the bar, and then he turned and looked Buster in the eye. "We don't *steal* no horses," he said. Buster tugged his hat down low, turned away from him, nudged me again, and we slid out the front door.

* * *

The wind hit us full in the teeth. Even though it was past noon, by now, the weather was red-raw, the sun making no dent in the wind's bite. It cut through our clothes and made our skin sore. Frozen and muddy as it was, dust and dirt blew in from somewhere, swirled in the street and got into our eyes, and on the horizon, if you could stand to look out that way, long, dark clouds was coming on fast. It looked like a big old mountain was marching right at us. Sleet, maybe snow, would be here quick.

"You think Deke's really going to do that?" I asked—or really yelled, because the wind was so high, Buster wouldn't hear me, elsewise. Buster give me a narrow look, then stared off to the north at the building clouds. "You think he'll truly hang them?" I asked. But Buster just kept looking into the wind toward the north sky and didn't say nothing. He pulled out makings and tried to roll a smoke, but I could see that he wasn't going to have no luck in the wind. "You think them old boys stole that horse?" I yelled across the wind at him.

He give up on the cigarette and stared at The Tabernacle's front door, his jaw working hard. For a second, I thought maybe he was going back inside. "I don't think nothing," he said. He looked again at the door, stared hard at it with his fists clenched. "They're just a couple of damn fool Mescans. Should never of come here." He wiped his mouth with his hand. "Goddamn it," he said. "Let's get shed of this." He stepped off, and I was right behind him. We was both holding our hats down on heads with both hands when we crossed to the store and stood for a moment in the lee side of the building, panting like we'd run a mile.

"I don't think we can take the horses out in this wind," I said when I caught my breath. "It's colder'n hell out here." And it was. It was that kind of cold only Texas knows, the kind that won't let you find any comfort with it, no way of keeping it off you. It would be this way till the wind lay down. Then snow would come, for sure. But I knew that wind and cold or otherwise, we'd be heading out right into it.

"I'm hungry as hell," I said. I wished I'd gone ahead and ordered up that breakfast. I hadn't eaten a bite of hot food since yesterday noon, and that wasn't much. "Want to try to find some grub somewhere?"

Buster looked out into the street and the prairie beyond and shook his head. "Need to go," he said. "This ain't going to get no better." I didn't know if he was talking about the weather or what was about to happen over in The Tabernacle, but it didn't matter. Either way, he was right. I looked down at The Tabernacle, but it was tombstone quiet. I saw the Mexes' horses—or I guessed that's who they belonged to—tied to the post in front. They was mustangs, a black stud and a yellow mare, but apart from their size and the usual wildness mustangs have, they wasn't nothing special.

114

They already had their winter coats and was shaggy, which meant they'd come in from the north. I had to admire their bridles and saddles, though. Mescans or not, them galoots knew their tack. That was sure.

"You don't think he'll really hang them boys?" I asked again, and that bothered me, as it made me sound stupid.

"I reckon he'll do what he says he'll do," Buster said, then tugged his hat down over his eyes.

"So you reckon they stole that horse?"

"I told you, I don't reckon nothing," he much as growled at me, then, of a sudden, he grabbed me by the lapel of my jumper and jerked my face up close to his. I could smell stale beer on his breath and see a flaw in the pupil of his eye. "What makes you think I know one damn thing about it?" He give me a kind of a shake. "Hell, you don't know shit from squat."

That kind of rocked me back. In all the time I'd known him Buster'd never laid a hand on me or even give me the sharp side of his tongue. I'd always figured I had his respect, even if I wasn't the man he was. "I was just asking," I said and tried to squirm out of his grip.

He pushed me back a little and let me go, making me go tangle-foot, which caused me to feel more foolish. "Don't ask," he said. "Don't say nothing more about it. Get the goddamn horses. I'll get the goods." He went on into the store and left me standing on the porch, wind whipping through me like a knife. I was all trembly, and I didn't know why. All I knew was that I didn't feel right, but there was nothing for it. I stumbled across the street to get the horses.

* * *

It was warm in the livery. Lee Henry had the fire going and was in a good mood. I could tell he wanted to jawbone a spell, and it was my habit to pass the time of day with him whenever I come by. That frosty morning, he had a rabbit stew working on the forge, and truth to tell, it smelled better than anything I'd ever put a lip around, but I held my teeth in a clench and didn't accept his offer to stay around for dinner. I paid him a half-dollar for the livery and started putting on my chaps while he saddled up our animals.

I started to tell him what was going on over to The Tabernacle, but I couldn't decide if that was the right thing to do. He might think he needed to be there, and I couldn't see that would do nobody no good. Then a thought hit me. "Lee Henry," I asked, "you remember the morning when the Deacon's red horse got stole?"

He stopped cinching up Buster's saddle, and looked at me out of his one good eye. "Lord, I surely do, Mr. Lex," he said. "I don't expect I'll ever forget that day."

"That morning," I asked, "you see any Mescans lurking about?"

"Mescans?" Lee Henry said, then rubbed his eye.

"Yeah. Couple of hard licks with fancy tack."

He rubbed the gray stubble on his chin and thought for a second or two. "Naw. Can't say that. Didn't see nobody extra-ordinary," he said. "Just the usual folks." He finished saddling Buster's paint mare. "Why you asking?"

"No reason," I said. "I was here that day. I didn't see nobody, neither."

"I seen *you*," he said, pulling our mule out of a stall and leading him over. "And Mr. Buster."

"You seen Buster?"

"Sure I did," lee Henry said, "And I seen—"

"Obliged, Lee Henry," I said, cutting him off. I decided he didn't remember right. Buster wasn't in town that day. He was down in Bosque County. Lee Henry was only about half there, anyhow. Nothing he could say was going to do them two Mexes any good. I flipped him a nickel tip then I led our mounts and the mule back over to the store. Of a sudden, I felt all antsy to get the hell out of Groesbeck Creek.

* * *

The horses was balky in the wind and didn't take to the cold. By the time I got them back to the store, the sun was all gone and the sky was near black. The wind was blistering and sleet was already pecking away at my hat. Buster was waiting out on the porch with our goods tied up in flour sacks. He'd managed to roll a cigarette and was trying to smoke it in the wind. When I come up, he worked quick, strapping down our goods and tying them tight to the packsaddle on the mule. He handed me one sack that had peaches and tomatoes and pickled cucumbers and another with some roasting ears and a sack of Arbuckle's.

"You carry these," he said, again giving me a growl and a hard look. "They're too heavy for this animal."

I started to say something smart-alecky, like how the gray I was riding was an animal, too, and it already had to carry me, but I could tell he wasn't in the mood for sass, even if I'd been joshing. I remembered the feel of his hand on my coat, the hot stink of his breath, the flame in his eyes. I didn't much like it, I expect. Time I got the sack tied down, he was in the saddle and leading the mule into the wind and the dark sky to the northwest. He was never a talky man, but I could tell something toothy was eating at him, and of a sudden, I had a good notion of what it was. I jumped up and fell in behind him, the collar on my jumper pulled up and my kerchief around my mouth and my hat bent against the blowing sand and ice.

About then, something hit me harder than the sleet that was pecking away at my hat. I thought about what Lee Henry had said. I remembered the money Buster had in his pocket when he showed up two days late from Bosque County. I also remembered what the tall Mex had said. He was talking to us all, in a way, but mostly, he was talking to Buster. That old boy wasn't lying. They might be the Sandovals, they might be horse thieves, but they didn't steal the Deacon's red horse. That much I was sure of. I kept turning the whole thing over in my head.

We rode for a bit, out past the edge of town, fighting the wind and sleet ever step of the way, but my mind wasn't on the wind or the weather. I now saw what had happened the day that horse was stole, clear as a blue sky. I also knew that Deke would hang them men. Once he said he'd do it, especially in front of all them gomers in The Tabnernacle, he didn't have much choice.

I wrestled with all of it for a long time. It took me near an hour to make up my mind. I expected whatever was going to happen back in Groesbeck Creek had already happened, and I told myself that nothing I could of done would of stopped it. I couldn't really conjure it, but I knew I'd be dreaming about it, and for a long time. As I looked at Buster's shoulders, bent over and hunched against the wind, I knew he *could* of stopped it. But he didn't. It would of cost him too much. Even with me backing him—useless though I likely would have been—he just wouldn't take the chance. I wasn't eager to scrap with Deke by my lonesome, but I'd of stood with Buster, Katie bar the door. Besides, I didn't know for certain then, not like I did now, but Buster did. He knew the right of things and he didn't do nothing. Of a sudden, looking at his back, I reckoned Buster for what he was. Right then, I figured I couldn't spend a whole winter looking at that man, watching him play solitary and humming to hisself the way he did, like he had no care in the world. I owed him, I expect. He might of been my pard, and my friend, and in a way, he might of been the one to save me when I was so far down I couldn't see the Devil's hindquarters, but all of that was off to one side, now. It wasn't so much that he stole the Deacon's red horse—anybody might of been tempted to do that, even me. It was that he'd let them two boys hang for it. They might just be Mexes, and they might of been the Sandovals with more stole horses to their name than there was stars in the sky. But this was wrong, and it was one pile of regret and guilt that I just couldn't ride around.

I pushed the gray up ahead, reined up and pulled down my kerchief. "I'm going back," I yelled over the wind.

What?" he asked, staring at me over the top of his bandana. Ice was all over his eyebrows and eyelids. "Back where?" He looked off to the southeast. "Back there?"

"I can't go with you."

He pulled down his kerchief and yelled at me, "Are you crazy?"

"I'm done," I yelled back, then repeated, "I'm done."

He looked off to the direction of Groesbeck Creek. There was lead in his eyes, but then I saw it melt away. "You can't save'em, Lex," he said. "What's done's done."

"I can't go with you," I said again. I pulled my bandana up and turned my gray. "I'm done." I didn't know no other way to put it.

"Don't be a damn fool," Buster said, reaching out and grabbing my mount's bridle. "There ain't nothing you can do."

"Tell Mr. Hadnought I'll leave his horse at the livery," I said. He didn't move or let go. I took my quirt and slapped the back of his hand, and none too gently. He jerked it back to his chest and sidestepped his pinto toward me.

"What're you going to tell Deke?" he asked.

"I'm getting Millie, and we're going to Abilene," I said. I hadn't had that notion at all, not until that very minute, but of a sudden, it seemed right. I had all I wanted of this country. And Millie was the best thing I'd run up on in my life. She made me feel good. I expect I made her feel good, too. I had no idea if it would work—or even if she'd go. But I reckoned it couldn't be the worst thing that ever happened to either one of us.

"Millie!? You're just a damn fool kid!" Buster yelled. "She's a whore." I let that hit me and bounce off. "Have some sense, Lex. She's just a whore!"

My daddy's face flickered across my memory. "There's worse things than that to be," I said in as even a voice as I could muster.

"What about me?" he asked. Truth to tell, he looked forlorn and a little bit lost.

"You watch yourself," I said, and I spurred the gray hard back toward Groesbeck Creek. After a bit, I turned and saw Buster still sitting in the icy wind, watching me go from under the brim of his hat. So far as I know, he's still there.

How to Listen to Country Music

Laurie Champion

Professor of English at San Diego State University, Laurie Champion specializes in contemporary American literature. She has published scholarly essays, reviews, and short stories in distinguished journals such as *Southern Quarterly*, *American Literature*, *Texas Review*, and *Journal of the Short Story in English*. Currently, she is working on a novel, *All In*, a romantic comedy set in a small Texas town.

Champion says of her story, "As I was listening to my husband playing Pat Green's 'Songs About Texas' on the guitar over a two-week time span, it occurred to me that the act of playing the song over and over would make a good country song. Because 'Songs About Texas' is a song about songs, I began to ponder ways music can be meta-music like stories can be metafiction. This notion inspired me to consider ways songs become stories and then to think of ways stories might become songs. I first set out to focus on country western Texas songs in a short story but soon expanded the piece to include country western songs in general. It was a fun piece to write."

There's a lot more to listening to country music than simply loading your iPod with country tunes or watching country western videos on TV. Anyone can pretend to like country music when they only know one or two songs. But these wanna-bes only know the songs that somehow make their way to pop stations. Or by some fluke, they hear a Willie Nelson song on an elevator or memorize a few lines from "I'd Waltz Across Texas With You." No, that doesn't count.

There's a real art to becoming a true country music fan. To learn quickly, re-set all your car radio buttons to country stations. Dress in comfortable jeans, pull your hair back in a pony tail, and put on your vintage Levi's jacket. Then cruise around town while you punch the radio

119

buttons. Try to figure out what songs are played most often and listen closely to the singers' names. If you want, you can get a six-pack of beer, preferably Lone Star. But don't drink too much—the songs won't make sense. Face it, lines like "I miss you already, and you're not even gone," "Let's quit before we start," "If your phone doesn't ring, it's me," or "Is forever longer than always?" don't make a whole lot of sense even when you're sober.

Plus, you could get a DWI, but that's not all bad—it sort of goes along with the whole country music lifestyle. You're also sure to meet country music fans in jail and can get a pretty quick education. In fact, going to jail, or even better, prison, is one of the most efficient ways to learn first-hand what country music is all about.

It's best if you study country music before you fall in love. The lyrics won't make a bit of sense, but you can at least get a feel for the rhythm and the beat. Then you can sort of work your way backwards and learn the oldies. Hank Williams, Ernest Tubb, Bob Wills, Johnny Horton, Loretta Lynn, Patsy Cline—all the classics. That way, when newer artists refer to their forefathers, you don't have to sit there like an imbecile—you'll know who they're talking about. Besides, you can't completely understand songs like "Achy-Breaky Heart," unless you know their predecessors—songs like "Your Cheating Heart."

Listening to this stuff takes a little getting used to. You'll hear some really strange lyrics that may sound a little weird at first. Maybe you'll hear something like "If I don't love you, grits ain't groceries," "Old King Kong was just a little monkey compared to my love for you," or "How come your dog don't bite nobody but me?" Don't panic—you get used to it after a while.

It won't take long before you'll come to recognize the songs' main ideas. For example, they sing about walking and shoes a lot. There's familiar lyrics such as "I'm walking the floor over you" or "These boots were made for walking" and not so well known lines like "My shoes keep walking back to you" or "I bought the shoes that just walked out on me." Then there's cutesy lines like "She can put her shoes under my bed any time," "I wish I was walking out of your shoes tonight," and "With my boots on, he's gonna take me home."

While you're in phase one, try to keep a low profile. You're not ready to go public yet. Shouldn't take more than a couple months till you start to become familiar with the songs. When you feel like you're starting to figure out what it's all about, get a "I Love Taylor Swift" bumper sticker and a Tim McGraw tee-shirt.

Warning: This is a turning point, the place where your life starts to change. You'll get honked at, waved at, winked at, and even flipped off more often than ever before.

Next, you need to fall in love. That first-in-love feeling adds a lot of meaning to the songs. So you've got to find someone to fall in love with. The best way to accomplish this goal and to increase your country music listening skills is to hang out at country-western bars. Pick a place with a name like *Cowboys* or *Billy Bob's*. Make sure you wear the right clothes. No lycra tights or ruffled skirts. Get you some Rocky Mountain jeans, the ultimate kicker denim. Then you need some Justin lace-up ropers. Preferably red or maybe black. Either way, make sure to get black laces.

Always get a matching belt. Trust me. If you just get the boots, you may never get around to buying the belt and the outfit won't look right. Add don't forget a belt buckle. You can't go wrong with silver-plated, heart-shaped.

Note: If you want to go all the way, engrave your name across the middle of the heart like a tattoo.

Next, you'll need a kicker blouse, one that buttons down the front and ties in the center. Don't get a cowboy hat. You'll look like a tourist or the amateur that you are. You can only wear the hat once you're confident and after you get all the rules down real good.

It's essential that you look semi-rodeo-queen when you go to these bars. Curl your hair—make it real puffy on top and swirl down the sides—all North-Dallas like. Paint your nails, spread good-smelling lotion all over your body, and spend extra time getting your make-up just right—all that girly-girl stuff. And perfume, spray on lots of perfume. Get some samples from the cosmetics counter at Nordies and put them in your purse. Make sure to put on lip liner and always, always carry a small comb and travel-sized hairspray.

Until you feel comfortable in country-western bars, it's best to go with a group of girls so you won't look so out of place. The first time, go real late, around eleven. That way most people will be drunk, and they won't notice that you're a newbie. Prance right into that bar like you've been there a million times. You'll easily pass for a pro, especially in those tight Rockies and that shiny belt buckle.

First thing, get situated at your table. Sit next to the men's restroom, so they'll be a steady stream of men walking past you.

Note: If it's *really* late, they may stumble past you.

When the waitress takes your order, say, "Lone Star, please." Say it like you love the taste of Lone Star and remember to let her know that you're a native Texan.

> *Note*: If you're not from Texas, make sure one of the girlfriends you bring along is. Make sure she was *born* in Texas. Helps if her parents and grandparents were also born in Texas.

You might want to remind the waitress not to bring you a Lone Star Lite. Sometimes waitresses confuse the two.

Don't just drink the beer. You've got to do this right, too, or everyone will know you're an amateur. Whatever you do, don't pour it in a glass. Drink it out of the bottle. If someone at your table asks for a glass, roll your eyes. If you want, and this is *totally* optional, you can squeeze a little lime in the bottle and around the rim, then sprinkle salt on the top.

Observe the couples who sit near your table. Watch the girls and take tips from the ones who look natural. Notice what they do with their hands during conversation. Watch them fold cocktail napkins or touch their earrings. Look at them as they approach the dance floor.

Pay attention to the way the men usually walk behind the women. Look at the way the women stand alone on the dance floor for a second, waiting for their partners to arrange their arms. At first glance, it all looks so natural, but believe me, someone out there's doing some counting. Only the couples who are real good at it can dance and talk at the same time. Take written notes if you need to, and save what you've learned for future reference.

You'll have to learn to two-step pretty early in your training. Sorry, there's no way around it. You can hold off on the popular line dances and the Cotton-Eyed Joe. For now.

As you're learning to listen to country music, go to some bars where you can still smoke. Even if you don't smoke, it's good practice in case you find yourself in a smoke-filled bar one day. Take a cigarette out of your purse and light it with a friend's lighter. Never, never bring your own lighter. Sooner or later some cowboy will walk by. If he looks like your type, ask him for a light. He'll give you one, then he'll kind of hang around your table. "Wanta dance?" he'll eventually stutter. Say no. But you got to say it in real nice way. Believe me on this one. Bat your eyes and flip your hair and say, "No, but thanks for asking. I never really learned how to dance. Want to talk?" If he says, "Up yours. I never really learned how to talk," you're out of luck. Most likely he's a smart ass who was potty-trained too early or something. Or an abuser, and we've all seen enough of Dr. Phil to know to stay away from that type. Say, "Excuse me" and go to the restroom. Put fresh lipstick on. Buy some mints from the woman who sits by the door and sells bar-hopping essentials. Tip her.

Return to your seat and wait for another cowboy to approach. Ask him for a light. This time, say it this way: "Excuse me, do you have any matches?" He'll say "yes" or "no" and eventually get around to the dancing question. Answer accordingly, but change it a little to entertain yourself. Be a little more simple. It's getting late—people don't want to mess around. Just say, "No thanks. I can't dance. Want to talk?" If he just says, "I can't talk," you're in luck. He's got a sense of humor. If he smiles real big and adds, "but I think I can talk to you, darling," you're in double luck. He's also charming.

Go for this guy. Say, "Well, you're talking just fine. You can talk." Try to say it with a Texas accent. Don't say something real hip like "I bet you can really psychobabble."

> *Warning*: The music will be so loud, you'll barely be able to hear him. You can't carry on a real conversation in these places.

Just nod and say "uh-huh" a lot. Smile and act all fluttered. If he's your type, you'll really feel fluttered. If this is the case, try not to flirt *too* much. Act like you don't care one way or another. You don't want to come across as desperate. Look up at the ceiling or watch people dance. Say, "Man, I sure do wish I could dance like them." Then look around and pretend you're staring at some of the other cowboys.

Here's where your hard-earned knowledge of country tunes and singers comes in handy. Wait until the band plays a George Strait song. Say, "I sure do like George." He'll think you're on a first-name basis with these people. If he says, "Yeah, me too. You know, 'that wasn't my chair after all,'" you're in triple-ripple luck. This guy is into entertaining you, and apparently he's done some studying too. Laugh. Laugh and say, "That's funny, but I *meant* Jones. George Jones." He'll grin from ear to ear. Maybe he'll quote George Jones. Maybe not.

> *Note*: If the guy sitting beside you is named George, pick another singer. One with a less common name like Garth Brooks. If you use his name, he might think you're talking about him and feel uncomfortable.

If you get nervous, re-tie your boots. These boots really come in handy when you need something to do with your hands. Say, "Excuse me, my boot came untied." Then bend down and act like you're tying it. Don't look up and say something like "Isn't that strange? I was just sitting here. Sitting here minding my own business. And my boot came untied." Try not to make a big deal out of it. Act like your boot really did come untied.

Immediately after you tie your boot, while your hands are still under the table, elbow your girlfriend's leg, then quickly sit up straight. If she

doesn't react, nudge her again and wink at her. Hopefully, she'll understand you're giving her the universal secret code. If not, she'll say, "Who's
kicking me?" Glance at the table beside you. Pretend you don't know what's
going on at your own table. Wait a few seconds and then make eye contact
with her. This time, make sure she's looking you straight in the eyes.
Nudge her again, clear your throat, then point your eyes to the women's
restroom. Look at the cowboy, and say, "Excuse me." Now she'll get the
message and follow you to the restroom.

Inside the restroom, tell her you think the guy standing beside you is
cute. She might be drunk. Or she could be sober. Most likely, somewhere
in-between. In any case, she'll most likely agree with you. Unless, of
course, she's still in shock because the guy she's been dancing with all night
turned out to be married. Try to act like you understand. Then say, "Watch
him . . . the guy beside me. See if you think he likes me." She'll say, "Okay."
Actually, she'll say it like this: "God, okay, for Christ's sake."

Don't remind her that she did her laundry at your house for the last
three weeks and borrowed your car the day before yesterday. After all,
she's a good friend. But she can't help herself at the moment. Just smile
and say, "Thanks, I need all the help I can get." Offer to let her use your lip
liner, then when she asks if she looks all right, say, "Yeah. You look great."
She'll stand in front of the full-length mirror, bend her head way down
between her knees, and run her fingers through her hair. Ask her what
she's doing. "Fluffing my hair," she'll answer.

Take more notes. This is an important lesson. Stand beside her, and
do the same to your hair. Gaze at her through your knees, cut your eyes,
and ask yourself, "Is this what my life has come to?" Look at her and smile.
Ignore the woman in the second stall who keeps complaining that her
husband looks at other women. When your friend says, "They all look at
other women," laugh. Follow her out of the restroom and nonchalantly
return to your table.

Try not to get too drunk. Look at it like a first date. Drink water or
Coke in-between the Lone Stars. If the guy you're eyeing has "Lone" or
"Star" for a last name, make a joke. If not, make a joke about something
else. Don't talk about anything too serious. Remember, he can't hear you
anyway.

If the band plays a song by Reba McEntire, make up a story about
something that happened to you a long time ago while you were listening
to Reba on a CD. Use your imagination. On the longshot he *can* hear you,
he's probably drunk, and there's a good chance he won't remember what
you said. If he appears really drunk, just move your lips. Move your lips

and smile a lot. And giggle.

Stay until the bar closes. He'll walk you to your friend's car. Give him your phone number, but don't, under any circumstances, kiss him. First kisses are important, and you want to make sure it's one he'll remember.

Open the passenger car door and take your seat. After your friend backs out of the parking lot, look out the window and wave goodbye with your right hand.

On the way home, tell your girlfriends that you like him. Say, "I really, really like him. I hope he calls me." Be thankful you gave him your correct phone number. Thank God you could even remember your phone number. Hope to God you *did* give him your correct number. Say, "What's my phone number?" out loud to your girlfriends. They'll look at you like you're crazy. Quote your number and ask them if it's right.

"Of course it is," one of them will say. "What's the matter with you?"

Breathe a sigh of relief and say, "I don't know. I think I'm a little tipsy." Giggle.

When he calls you, make light conversation. There's no doubt he can hear you, and there's a good chance he's sober. You are now accountable for what you say. Tell him you're busy Friday, but you'd be happy to go out with him Saturday night. Remember, you are not desperate. Pretend he's just one of many men you see on weekends.

On the first date, you get your chance to make the all important, first sober impression. Make mental lists of the things you'll talk about. Absolutely do not mention your dating history. Don't tell him your former boyfriend dumped you for his first ex-wife.

If the lyrics, "I wish I was a teddy bear, and I wish I hadn't have fallen in love with you" come over the radio, don't comment. Just laugh. He'll say the song doesn't make much sense. Agree with him, then laugh again.

Enjoy your dinner, then let him take you to a country-western club for a few drinks. Don't tell him you spend your weekends riding around town listening to country music. Pretend you're a regular at the bar scene. Act at home.

By the third date, you can go ahead and start falling in love with him. But always, always, keep your *real* goal in mind: understanding country music. It has little to do with the guy.

Go out with him on Friday and Saturday nights. Talk to him on the phone frequently. Dance with him a lot. Remember, continue to listen carefully to the country lyrics. Keep up with the new songs and listen for singers you don't recognize. Wait a couple months before you sleep with him, but wait much longer before you tell him you love him.

Note: No matter what else you do or don't do, absolutely *do not* tell him you love him for the first time while you're in a bar. Make sure he's sober. Make sure you're sober. Make sure he can hear you. Don't laugh. Most likely, he'll say he loves you too. Believe him.

Now you've got things rolling. You're just a two-step away from knowing what country music is all about.

Note: "They ought to put warning labels on sad country songs."

You're really in luck when he sends you flowers and cards and buys you CDs. Keep telling him you love him. Convince him. Convince yourself. He'll take you out and say witty lines and caress you and sing country songs to you. "I love you, and that's all I know," he'll sing.

Dedicate country songs to him over the radio. Start with safe songs with lyrics like "If I had only one friend left, I'd want it to be you." You can even fax or text dedications. Fax or text the radio host a dedication for him every night. Every night for two weeks straight. Tell him you will *always* love him. Later, have Tammy Wynette sing "Stand by Your Man" for him over the local radio station. Don't cheat—stick to country tunes. Most likely, some man will call the radio host and say, "Boy, he's a lucky man." Tell him other men think he's lucky.

On his birthday, sing to him: "Happy birthday, Darling, I don't have anything to give you, but I'd like to take a few things away . . . doubt." On the anniversary of the day you met him, buy him a Hank Williams CD boxed-collection. Hank Sr., of course. Wrap it. Quote Willie: "Pretty paper, pretty ribbon, of blue. Wrap your present to your darling from you."

A few months later, out of nowhere, he may start to act strange. But when he forgets to call you or acts less anxious to take you to country bars, assume it's your imagination. Blow it off when he tells you that he doesn't like the way you light your cigarette, the way you fluff your hair, or your shade of lipstick. Presume that his nights out late are job related and remind yourself that he's under a lot of stress at work.

Confirm your presumptions when he tells you he's moving to an apartment closer to work. Whatever you do, don't wonder why he doesn't suggest you move in with him. Assume he doesn't believe in living together before marriage. Wonder if perhaps he doesn't believe in marriage, but never, never suspect that he doesn't believe in you. Remind yourself that at the end of the day, or night in this case, it doesn't matter anyway because you're only in it for the country music.

Don't take it personally when he calls three weekends in a row and says that he's going out with the guys. Remember, he was out with the guys when you met him. No, don't remember that. You'll start thinking about the night you met him and you might get all teary-eyed. Instead, convince yourself he won't even be thinking about going to a bar, much less lighting anyone else's cigarette.

When he finally decides to give you a call and you agree to go out with him, don't act surprised when he shows up go get you in a new pick-up. Punch the buttons on his new stereo and act as if everything's peachy creamy.

When you notice an earring hanging over the volume control, pull it off and hold it near his face. "What's this?" say loudly.

"An earring," he'll say.

Even though his sense of humor first attracted you to him, absolutely do not laugh. Whether or not he is kidding is beside the point. In a straight-forward, informative tone, say, "Did I ever tell you I don't have pierced ears?"

"Uhhh," he'll say, "I don't guess you did."

"Isn't that strange? I mean, everyone thinks it's weird that I don't have pierced ears." Put in the Hank Williams CD that's sitting on the dash. Punch the number for "Your Cheating Heart," then just sit back in silence. Sooner or later, the silence will get to him. It may take a few songs, but eventually he'll fidget with the rear-view mirror or open and shut the console. Until he does, continue to sit silently. Cut your eyes toward him every once in a while. But keep on dangling that earring in mid-air. Then pretend you're examining it. Hold it real close to your face, and ask him to turn the light on. While the light's on, look at the CD case and study the songs. As you recite the titles out loud, use the earring for a pointer.

When he stops at a red light, while "I'm So Lonesome I could Cry" plays, scream at him. Cuss him out. Lose control.

> *Note*: Consider this another pivotal point in your country music
> education.

He'll mumble something about black-cowboy-hat night at some bar near his new apartment. Wednesday. Yeah, it will all start to make sense. The night you usually have dinner with your mom or do laundry. Say, "I thought you just didn't want to meet my mom." He'll either nod or try to defend himself. "I get nervous," he might say.

Don't start pumping him. Don't ask him her name or how long he's been seeing her. Sing along with Hank: "If you've got the money, honey, I've got the time." Tell him to take you home. When he pulls in your driveway, he'll turn off the car. Ask him to turn on the ignition so you can hear the music. Eventually, he'll start talking. They always do. And over Hank Williams, he'll explain how he needs his space and thinks you both should date other people.

This is where it gets hard, but you've got to do it. Remember your dignity. Agree with him. Say, "Well, yeah, I was thinking the same thing." Don't insist he see only you. Don't beg. Don't crawl. No matter what, do not become a whining character out of some country-western song.

A month later, when he calls you and says he's doing okay, hanging out with his friends, just say, "Yeah, well, that's funny. I'm going out with the girls a lot lately. Nothing like perfect timing. Perfect timing, that's what we've got, isn't it?"

"Uh, huh," he'll say.

Don't admit that you lie awake at night thinking about him or that you've had a couple of bum dates with guys you met at country-western bars in another county. In fact, don't admit much of anything. Hopefully, he'll get around to saying that he just called to see how you were doing these days. If he doesn't say it, say it yourself. Say, "I just answered the phone to see how you were doing these days."

If he says it, don't pretend you didn't hear him. And don't make a joke. Instead, say, "Oh, okay, I guess. Yeah, I'm doing all right." Wait a few seconds, then tell him goodbye. Say it nicely. Don't try to get fancy by saying something like "So long, or *adieu*, or it was fun while it lasted, or we'll always have Midland." No, a simple "Goodbye" will suffice.

But don't go out with the girls. Don't go out with anyone. Dress in some comfortable jeans, pull your hair back in a pony tail, and put on your vintage Levi's jacket. Then cruise around town while you punch the radio buttons.

Fill your car up with gas. Treat yourself. Get full service, and ask the attendant to check your oil. Buy a six-pack of Lone Star and keep on cruising. Sing with Wynonna: "How did you get to me?"

Crack your window and smoke a lot. After two beers and seven cigarettes, slip the Patsy Cline he bought you for your birthday in the CD player.

When Patsy sings "Crazy for thinking that my love could hold you," light another cigarette and drink another beer. Whatever you do, don't cry. Do anything to keep from crying. Take Patsy out and turn the radio down real low. Sing to yourself: "Where there's a cloud don't mean there's rain. Tears in my eyes don't mean there's pain." Fidget with the cruise control. Reach under your car seat and feel for loose change. Find a quarter and sing: "Here's a quarter, call someone who cares." Re-tie your boots.

Take a couple deep breaths, then turn the radio back up.

Warning: If you play the music too loudly, you'll bust your speakers.

If Merle Haggard starts belting out "Today I started loving you again," punch the buttons. Maybe George Jones sings "He quit loving her today" on the next station. If so, punch the buttons again. When you hear "I can't help it if I'm still in love with you," hum along. Keep humming until you can't hum anymore.

Now you can cry. You've earned it. Cry and cry and cry.

Pull into a 7-11 parking lot and cry some more. Buy more Lone Stars. Don't forget the lime and salt. If the checker asks you if you're okay, don't try to talk at first. Just nod. Keep nodding, while he rings you up. Before he finishes, set a new cigarette lighter on the counter. A red Bic.

Take your change and say, "Thanks. Yeah, I'm okay. I'm just having a bad day." Don't, under any circumstances, cry while you stand inside 7-11. Wait until you get back in the car. Start the car and cry some more. Sing "Funny face, I love you. Funny face, I need you."

Light a cigarette with your new lighter, and start on another Lone Star. Drink slowly at first, while you continue to listen to the songs. Turn up the volume. If you feel like you're going to start crying, turn down the radio and guzzle a beer or two. Then open another and drink more slowly.

Don't worry about drinking too much. Drink all you want—the songs will still make sense. The songs will always, always make perfect sense.

Massage Therapy

Jim Sanderson

Jim Sanderson has published two collections of short stories, *Semi-Private Rooms* (1994, winner of the 1992 Kenneth Patchen award and published by Pig Iron Press) and *Faded Love* (2010, Finalist for 2010 Texas Institute of Letters' Jesse Jones award for best fiction of the year by a Texan or about a Texas, and published by Ink Brush Press); an essay collection, *A West Texas Soap-box (*1998, Texas A & M University Press); four novels—*El Camino del Rio* (1998, Winner of the 1997 Frank Waters Award, published by The University of New Mexico Press), *Safe Delivery* (2000, finalist for Writers' League of Texas 2000 Violet Crown Award, published by the University of New Mexico Press), *La Mordida* (2002, published by the University of New Mexico Press), and *Nevin's History: A Novel of Texas* (2004 published by Texas Tech University Press); and a composition textbook written specifically for Lamar University, *Ways of Writing; A Writer's Way* (2007 published by Kendall Hunt). In addition, he has published over sixty short stories, essays, and scholarly articles. Sanderson is the 2002 Distinguished Faculty Lecturer and 2006 University Scholar Award at Lamar University, and he is currently serving as Writing Director for Lamar University.

Jim's website: http://sites.google.com/site/jim2sanderson

Sanderson explains, "A Texas songwriter, in this case Guy Clark, didn't inspire me or create 'Massage Therapy'; rather, he rode to the rescue. Several years ago, as reported in Texas newspapers and eventually in *Texas Monthly,* the owner of a massage parlor in Odessa used it as cover for prostitution. The prostitutes met their clients at the massage parlor and then 'delivered,' so to speak, at a motel or hotel in town. The woman who ran the operation was not prosecuted for a long time, and the case was hushed because so many prominent men were clients. Similarly, a year or so ago, several Beaumont policemen, went under-cover and infiltrated a massage parlor in Beaumont. There, they contracted with the masseuses for services beyond a rub down and actually had sex with the massaging prostitutes. After the shakedown, both cops and prostitutes faced trial—the cops for ethical violations.

"I wanted to steal these episodes for my own. I first thought about placing the story in West Texas, but I wanted to give something back to my East Texas home, Beaumont, and I already had an unpublished character inhabiting other stories and living in Beaumont. So I gave him a girlfriend, and I made her a student and practicing masseuse and prostitute. The fun part was busting her and her client in a motel in the opening scene. But then her lover, my often used but seldom published character, bails her out.

"I wanted to show what happened when they got home and then what would happen over time. So I put them in his kitchen because these tense scenes always seem to take place in the kitchen. I needed one of those scenes between a male and female character in which both want an explanation, but neither can give one. I've written such scenes before. At that point, in rode Guy Clark with the dusty, West Texas lyrics and his mournful warbling in 'The Instant Coffee Blues': 'Time was of the essence so they both did their best, /to meet up in the kitchen feelin' fully dressed.'

"To me this song is the best rendition I've heard that deals with a silence that no one wants to puncture for fear of saying too much or not enough. I wanted to add dialog. So these lyrics and the tune to the song buzzed around in my head in two scenes, where I tried to bring this man and his lover into his kitchen to try to patch up their lives."

Haley heard the pounding at the door and the word *police*. Her mind blotted out all the other sounds. She looked from the bed to the window and remembered that they were on the second floor of the Economy Motel. As her mind raced ahead then jumped back, then forward, it stuck for a moment on a number: her lawyer's cell phone. Then another number kept her mind from racing: Roger's cell.

She knew this moment could come. Everyone at the Golden Day Massage Parlor knew that this could happen. Haley looked toward the door and saw her lawyer, naked except for his underwear and socks, trying to pull his pants, shirts, and jacket from the closet. Like so many others, Frank had kept his socks on during the whole session. She chuckled. But maybe she ought to call him. She imagined his phone ringing in his slacks' pocket, adding to his panic; while he struggled to put his legs into his pants, he could dig through his knotted pockets to retrieve his cell phone, answer it, and she could ask: "Frank, what would your legal advice be?" Haley knew that this could happen, perhaps was bound to happen. Yet, she couldn't make it upset her. She couldn't get concerned, so she chuckled.

"Just a moment," Frank Longley yelled toward the door. But the door slammed open, and a petite woman police officer was the first in the room. Haley pulled the bed sheet up to her chest and looked squarely at the lady cop whose eyes under the police cap visor darted like a robot's to follow the barrel of her pistol. Haley continued to laugh. And while the police woman's fellow officers filed in behind her and the housekeeper who had let them in eyed the scene from the hallway, the police woman's eyes settled on Haley. Haley could not stop her laughing. Obviously, with Haley's solid laughter floating around the room, infecting Frank so that he stared shaking from suppressing his chuckle, no one would start shooting. The housekeeper laughed. The police woman lowered her pistol, but the officer kept her eyes on Haley. The lady tilted her head to get her cap's brim out of her line of sight and smiled, and then, in some sort of communion or recognition with Haley, started laughing along with Haley. No matter what the moralists said, this scene, though played a thousand times a day across the country, was funny. And Haley could not get the funniness of it out of her head.

Frank had gotten his pants on but not his shirt, and he held his tie, in a loosened knot so that he could slip it over his head, in his left hand. "This isn't what it looks like," he said. Haley laughed some more. It was exactly what it looked like.

"It never is," the soft-faced cop said. Haley laughed harder. The woman cop laughed.

"Officer Henderson," a male police officer said to scold the lady cop. But the lady kept laughing, holstered her pistol, and stepped toward Haley.

"You have the right to remain silent . . ." another cop began to intone.

When the cop had finished telling Frank and Haley their rights, Haley said, "Do you think that I could get dressed?"

"Do you have anything to put on?" Officer Henderson asked.

Haley, with her hands still holding her sheet to the tops of her shoulders, motioned with her hand to the closet.

"You better start dressing," Officer Henderson said. "We can't turn our backs."

Haley, thinking that her laughter and amusement had made this a performance, folded her sheet off her, stood, stretched, slowly walked to the closet, then just as slowly reached to the hanger for her clothes. "Excuse me," Henderson said. Then added, "Mam," and gestured toward the bathroom. Without slipping into panties or bra, Haley took exaggerated, long steps toward the bathroom. She wanted to show the males what Frank had paid for. When she stepped inside, Henderson closed the door. Now, backstage in her dressing room, Haley looked at her dresser, pulled her strapless bra in place, and turned her back to Henderson who hooked it closed for her. "New job?" Haley asked Henderson over her shoulder.

"Six months full time. I was lucky to get this assignment," Henderson said.

Haley turned to face the woman and stepped into her panties.

Henderson couldn't help herself, "You?"

"I've been doing this one way or another for years," Haley said. "Wait, that could be held against me."

"Yes, Mam. It could."

"But I meant it to be funny. As women, I mean, we all do this. You ought to know, *Officer Henderson*."

Officer Henderson gritted her teeth, "That'll be enough, Mam. No reason to insult the uniform."

"But I'm not meaning to insult . . ." Haley tsked. "I just mean none of this is real. This is a comedy, not a drama."

"Mam, your sentence will be real, and it won't be funny."

* * *

The Golden Day was a legitimate massage therapy business. And Haley, who had studied massage, as well as a great many other things, primarily gave massages to old people with their muscles in knots. With warm oil spread on her hands and her client's backs, Haley could manipulate and push the old folks doughy fat to get underneath to the muscles and stretch them. When she got that deep, an older client would usually clinch her teeth and moan, but then, with the loosening muscle relaxing into a limp rope, the client would melt. From that point on, it was a pleasure to do her job. Then the massage was like kneading dough. And when the elderly clients would leave with the tingle of the massage still in their backs or limbs, they would work a shoulder or jiggle a hip and smile in appreciation. But no masseuse could make that much money from these loosened, appreciative older folks.

A female masseuse would inevitably get a lewd comment or an offer from the men she massaged. Most virile men just couldn't let loose of the idea of a "massage parlor," the type that used to appear out on interstates and cater to truckers. So Barbara Koons, who managed the Golden Day Massage Therapy, and Haley talked and thought and calculated and came up with the idea of making a counter-offer to the lewd comments made by virile or even the unvirile men. Innuendo led to method. So a gentleman could call and arrange an appointment. And if he asked in the right code, the masseuse or Barbara met him at motel for an afternoon or early evening massage. Word spread, reputation grew, and Haley was soon meeting the needs of some of the more prominent male citizens of Beaumont, Texas. She met male doctors, lawyers, bankers, judges, and professors. In the process, she made enough to pay her university tuition and put some money in the bank. She also got lots of legal, medical, financial, and some academic advice. Haley was nine hours short of a degree and had the grades and brains to get into law school. Many of her clients could help her.

As the cops led her out of the motel—dressed in her tie-behind, cotton and Tencel blouse with the plunging neckline, off-white twill jeans, and high-heeled flip-flops, but handcuffed—Haley felt the August humidity seize her. She felt beads of sweat form on her face and felt sogginess under her arms and across the strap of her bra, and the cop's hand on the underside of her bicep felt clammy and wet. As Haley and the cops stepped in unison down the metal stairs of the Economy 8 Motel, Haley cussed August Beaumont, just as Roger always did.

Salesmen, a few families with kids, and some motel housekeepers, drifted out of rooms and into the heat, working up their own sweats, to watch Haley being escorted by the cops. Haley had stopped laughing but kept smiling. She had this audience, but with her walk, her head held high, her smile, her blonde hair glowing, her outfit showing she had prepared for this heat, this occasion, she showed them that she was not mortified, not ashamed. And in fact, looking at huffing Henderson with the beads of sweat running off her face, she felt sorry for the officers, who were dressed in black synthetic and cotton uniforms. They must have baked.

Then, feeling self-absorbed, she twisted slightly from the policeman's grip on her upper arm, pulled her head around to see Frank handcuffed, head hanging, shuffling into the story of the defeat of his life and ambitions. Haley shouted. "Are you okay?"

Frank looked up from his escort cop. "Why no. Of course not," he answered.

"Frank, good luck," Haley shouted as she got close to the police car. And as Henderson gently folded her head forward, Haley felt that she was taking a bow to her audience.

* * *

"What tipped us off, Haley, was that there *weren't* cars at the Golden Day," Henderson said to Haley as she was getting fingerprinted. "I'm Gwen Henderson, by the way," she said. "We won't have a bail bondsman come around for some time yet, so unless you know someone, you've got a long wait."

"Thank you for your kindness," Haley said. And she paused to look down at the petite Gwen Henderson, who could in Haley's imagination very easily have been a masseuse, and deliberately smiled, just as she had for her attractive mug shot.

"Is that a real smile," Gwen asked.

"Of course, thank you."

"I've had whores try to knife me," Gwen said. "You're confusing."

"This doesn't have to be ugly or humiliating," Haley said.

"But how can it not be?"

Gwen's question required a long answer, and Haley wanted to give it. But the jailers pulled her away from Gwen, and over her shoulder, Haley saw Gwen form a shrug with her body, and Gwen's face drooped into a frown.

In the holding tank, with just one other woman sleeping in a corner, Haley sat on the folding chair and gazed out the plexi-glass wall at the wall beyond. She could wait for the bail bondsman to come, but if she waited that long, Roger would worry. Still, she did not want to call him, not yet. She wanted to sit in the quiet holding cell and think before she made her phone call.

Haley thought that Roger, of all people, would surely understand, for Roger was a specialist in human infidelities. He made his living on them. Before he retired to part-time work, Roger made a living taking photos of cheating spouses. Three years before, when she was called to testify at a divorce hearing as the "other woman," the unshaven man, wearing a polo shirt, who had ducked his eyes from her as he testified about what he had seen, stopped her and apologized for bringing her into the nastiness.

He held his head down as he mumbled his apology to her. He said that he had been doing this for some time and that the view from his digital camera gave him just part of story. So he wanted to try to make something right.

What Haley did not tell him three years before, what she still had never said to Roger, was that the good husband with her was not having a torrid affair with her but was paying her. The enjoyment or enthusiasm or joy or willingness or maneuvers that that good husband couldn't get from his wife, he got from Haley. He still loved his wife, didn't want to lose her, but Roger's photo of Haley and him ended that gentleman's marriage. And this silly man divorced his wife, leaving her to think that he had found another lover, not just someone to give him some loving.

Back, three years before, as Roger mumbled his apology to her, Haley found herself wondering about this late fifty-ish man who had not shaved that morning. Despite his stubble, he was very well spoken, illustrated his points with examples, did not talk with a discern-able Texas accent. He could be charming. So Haley asked for a dinner, then another, and then moved in with Roger. She had done more than move in with him. She had taken his money. She let him buy her a life. And she thought that she had given him more than simple loving.

The person sleeping on a cot at the other side of her holding cell sat up. It was Dolores. When Dolores saw Haley, she dropped her head into her hands, and Haley heard her say, "Oh, shit." Dolores was a Filipino who worked at the Golden Day also. "You too?" Dolores asked.

"Less than an hour ago."

"My appointment was earlier."

Dolores pushed herself up. She wore very tight shorts and a T-shirt with a plunging V-neck. "You wore those expensive clothes?" Dolores asked.

"Why not? I wasn't going to massage anyone."

"How am I ever going to get my nursing degree now?" Dolores asked.

"Arrests don't get you kicked out of school or the program."

"I mean how am I going to afford it?"

Haley began thinking about the same thing. "Maybe, we should have met them outside of town, or at least in south county."

"So what are you going to do?"

"Maybe there are some openings giving massages just to women."

"So you think somebody would hire us? After this?"

"It was good, quick money. We should have saved more."

The door to the tank opened, and another afternoon criminal joined them, Barbara Koons, the owner of the Golden Day Massage Therapy. "Hello, ladies," Barbra said.

Barbara had a slight cut along the brow of her left eye, and her right eye was puffy. "Barbara, did you fight them?" Haley asked.

"The sons of bitches," Barbara said. "It was a fucking sting. They'd been watching us for several months." Barbara sat beside Haley. She was trying to keep her chin from quivering. "It smells like pee in here," she said.

"You ain't been in here too many times, huh?" Dolores said. "Probably is pee."

"What are you going to do?" Haley asked Barbara.

"I'll take the hardest fall for procurement. I guess I'll lose the business and go broke."

"Wha, wha," Dolores said. "All you worried about is you."

Haley put her arm around Barbara's shoulders. "We'll all just become trash," Barbara said. She looked at Haley, "I'll bet they looked at you like trash. To them, we'll just be whores."

"Ain't that kind of what we are?" Dolores asked. Dolores stared at the floor and muttered, "I pray every morning and every night. So why is my life so fucked up?"

Haley had been above average in intelligence and looks but poor when she was growing up in East Texas. She sensed that she could do something different with either looks or intelligence, but she had no script; no one had written one for her. So before she ever got out of high school, she developed a certain resignation toward what waited for her and those girls like her. She resisted the usual clichés: an early marriage and/or kid. But she found herself stuck in other clichés—dead-end jobs, several semesters of flunked community college courses, and a reputation for being easy. Before Roger, men were fun but not very interesting. So she figured that she might as well get paid for what she saw as giving nothing away. And the money she got for what she did not give away, she reinvested in herself: a good dentist, a touched up nose, a gym membership, massage classes.

Then she met Roger. He encouraged her to go to school and then on to a law degree, like his, only she, he said, could make hers into something. He paid her tuition, and this time with Roger's concern and appreciation as well as her own intelligence, Haley excelled at school. With the money she earned at the Golden Day, before their attempts at adult entertainment, she began paying Roger back, by giving him money, by getting herself close to a degree, and by allowing him to become the first man she truly, really cared for. She realized that helping her truly gave Roger pleasure. He had been too long without someone close to him. And the closer she physically got to him, the closer she got to him, becoming a part of life, knocking away at shared concerns about living in his small, rented A-frame house out on Tram Road, on the verge of the piney woods, surrounded by pot-growing neighbors. She filled his house with herself so that it became their house. Ironically, the closer she got to him within the house, within his life, the less she needed to physically rub up against him.

And she felt it unfair that ultimately she would have to leave if she was going to ever get on with her life. He said, when the subject came up, that he understood.

"What's Roger said?" Barbara asked.

"I don't know," Haley said. "I haven't called him yet."

"You know you owe him that much," Barbara said.

"What do you owe a sugar daddy?" Dolores said.

Haley appreciated Barbara for glaring at Dolores and saying, "He is not just a sugar daddy. There's something there. Haley knows the difference. That's why she makes more money than you."

Because Barbara was beside her, Haley said, "We can sleep together."

"I bet you can," Dolores said.

"No, I mean that I can lay down with the man and literally sleep. He is there in that little house. And even when I don't try, I think about him."

"So you think he's going to be pissed?" Barbara asked.

"How can he not be," Dolores said.

"I've got to call him," Haley said. "He has to know." Then she caught herself, "Who are you going to call?"

"I *was* going to call your lawyer, Frank what's his name. But now I got nobody."

"Maybe Roger can help."

* * *

When Haley called to tell him that she was in jail on a prostitution charge, Roger went out the backdoor of his house to check on his dog. Harry was slobbering, moaning, and throwing himself against the gate of the picket fence that Roger had had built just for him. Harry could wag his tail and cry at the same time. He'd bark like a normal dog, but when he was happy and wanted someone to pay attention to him, he would moan. He craved attention more than food, so he moaned a lot. And what Harry wanted most was Roger petting him or just talking to him.

Roger pushed through the wall of humidity and heat and started sweating even before he got to Harry's gate. Roger reached over the gate to cradle Harry's jaw in his hand and then to rub his head. When Roger pulled his hand away, Harry raced around inside of his fence, wagging his tail. He was always happy, and though he liked everyone and would follow people, Harry preferred Roger. Roger pulled his now stinky hand away with Harry's slobber on it.

Harry was something of a freak. He had the short, stubby legs of a basset hound and the demeanor and head of a lab. From a distance, he looked like a furry, long-eared lab on his knees. He was fast, but his short legs made him clumsy. He was sort of like a slow torpedo. He had a thick chest and powerful hindquarters. With a head start, he would run to Roger and just throw himself at Roger, a couple of times knocking Roger over. When he found water, he scooted toward it like and amphibious landing craft. Roger once told Haley, "Harry's daddy was the guy who always said, 'I'll do her.'"

Besides the heart-worm treatments, the shots, and the grooming, Roger paid for Harry's fence. Roger was not even sure that all the property that fence surrounded was what he rented. But the land gave Harry a shady, grassy playground. And Roger even had an awning stretched out from the house to give Harry a place to stay out of the rain and sun. When Roger let Harry out of his fence, his tongue lolling around outside his open mouth, no two feet hitting the ground in unison, Harry burrowed through the woods. Roger and Haley could track him by the shaking palms and tallow trees.

Harry had a habit of standing in front of a car to make it stop. And then, if the car was low enough and stopped, he would rest his front paws on the hood of the car, wag his tail, and moan. Out on Tram road, in the rain, Harry had stood in front of Haley's car and stopped her. She didn't know what to do with him, so she brought him home to Roger, as a joke and a gift. Roger named Harry after a man whom he had once spied upon, Harry Krammer. Harry later got murdered. After two weeks with Harry, with Haley laughing at Harry, Roger just couldn't get rid of *his* dog.

Now, twice a day, Roger took Harry for a walk, and at five-thirty, when he went for his drinks at the Nothing Left to Lose bar, right down Tram, even though he could have walked, he put Harry's leash on him, put him in the cab of the truck, and drove to the bar. Before he went in, Roger would park under a tree, put a large bowl of water in the bed of his pickup, and chain Harry to the bed. Even though Roger was his favorite, Harry had no attention span; he might desert Roger for anybody. The patrons and the owners of The Nothing Left to Lose Bar didn't like Harry because he stunk and, despite Roger's lessons at house training, couldn't be trusted not to pee inside. The reason why he went through the trouble that Harry demanded and what made Harry important to Roger was Haley.

As Roger turned his back to the moaning Harry and walked to his pickup, he finally felt something like heartburn making its way up from his chest. He kicked at the fender of his Toyota pickup. Maybe he had grown too old, too worn down, too burned out to respond to the fact that the woman living with him was involved in a prostitution ring. Maybe he was just neutered, like Harry. Maybe he had adopted Harry's demeanor. Maybe Harry had adopted his. He wondered, if at the jail, he would give just one long mournful moan like Harry's and then wag his tail and lick and nudge Haley when she came back to him.

In his truck driving through Beaumont, Roger rehearsed how he would talk and what he would say when he bailed Haley out of the new jail facility out on 69 near mid-county. The typical response was the redneck one: screaming, yelling, accusations. Or he could simply hug her. They could try a heart-to-heart talk with confessions and pleas for forgiveness.

But what plagued Roger was why Haley was soliciting men in the first place. Mid-evenings, after coming home from the Nothing to Lose, the beer and bourbon spreading throughout his body and making him feel relaxed, Roger would make himself one more drink so that he felt a definite buzz. And he would wait for Haley to get home from school or work. This waiting, with just a touch of anticipation, was so much more pleasant than sitting at the Nothing to Lose as was his habit before meeting Haley. Roger would hear her pull up and then hear Harry moan, and she would come through the backdoor with a smile, and maybe some dinner, and they would kiss. Then after dinner, some TV, one last visit to Harry, then lying in bed, usually reading and chatting, rarely much sex—since that was saved for special weekends or celebrations—then drifting off to sleep and getting up early and getting started on another day of light work for him, heavy work and study for her, and then his routines: lunch, a long walk-and-jog, shower, Harry, bar, and so on. This was what he would have called, along with so many other people, *boredom*. But to Roger's surprise, since meeting Haley, he liked this boredom: the common, the ordinary, the mundane, the ritualistic ways we go spinning out our lives to fill up our time so as not to face any deep, annoying, ultimately destructive questions. Maybe, it was like Harry's life. Roger enjoyed his life with Haley because it was easy, so as he pulled into the new jail, he wondered if he should have been trying harder.

The jailers recognized him, for he often accompanied the bail bondmen or visited clients or witnesses. As they let him into the halls that led to the cells, he thought that this was his world, not hers. He was the one with a life to hide, not her.

* * *

When they let her out of the holding tank and she walked down the hall to be released, Haley thought she could hear the snickers of the cops and jailers. When she got to the lobby, in front of her, in his shorts and t-shirt, grown shabbier and fatter since his knees started bothering him and he had to quit jogging, was her—her what: her lover, her partner, her live-in, her roommate—Roger Jackson. His experience, his nights hiding out and taking pictures of cheating spouses had sculpted his face into its latest form. His brows were furrowed. Wrinkles spread out from the outer corners of his eyes and did not go away when he stopped smiling. His chin had started to droop, and maybe, if he kept gaining weight, a double chin was not far away.

The moneyed-men she massaged spent a lot to arrest aging: tucks, pulls, gym memberships—massages, hell, her massages, the ones that got her arrested. But not Roger, he had surrendered to age or made truce with it or didn't notice it.

As she got closer to him, he opened his arms, and that gesture just sucked her right into him, and she wrapped her arms around him and pushed her head up under his chin and held him as tightly as she could.

Later that night, after dinner out, several drinks, happy hour at the Nothing To Lose Bar, they went through their usual rituals. They went out in the yard together, each with a drink, to feed Harry and to pet and pamper him one last time for the day, and they felt the slight drop in temperature and the rise in humidity that pressed in on Roger's A-Frame from out of the trees; and then after the TV nightly news and late shows, they climbed into bed, and Haley lay her head on Roger's chest to listen to his heart thump and waited for one or both of them to drift off to sleep. But neither one could sleep. "So do you want to talk about it?" Haley asked.

"I don't know what to say," Roger said.

Haley pulled her ear from Roger's chest, leaned to the other side of the bed and pushed the switch to the lamp. With both of them circled by the glow of the weak lamplight, Roger rolled over, away from Haley. "Eventually, we need to talk."

"I read somewhere that as a man gets older, rather than fight, he flees. Fighting could kill him. It could give him a heart attack."

"We're not fighting. We're talking."

"Right now, talking seems like fighting. You want to kill me?"

"Well, you're not sleeping."

"I'm thinking."

"So why don't you tell me what you are thinking."

"I'm not thinking very well."

Her arrest and humiliation had been performance. But once she had seen Roger, Haley had dropped all performance. In her mind, there was nothing to explain, she had simply been caught; now, perhaps, her plans might have to change. She could have gone to sleep with these facts, but seemingly, Roger could not. "This is nothing to be concerned about."

"Well, it does answer some things," Roger muttered.

"What does it answer?"

"We sleep. We just sleep. So you've found what you need with other people."

"What I needed was a financial arrangement."

"So you found my financial betters. You have your pick of moneyed people. And money buys time, and it buys looks. Hell, it buys right and wrong. So why wouldn't you be attracted to them? So no wonder you come home tired."

"Roger, why do you have to twist this like this."

"I know I'm older than you. I'm older than most people. I know I drink too much. I may not be what you're used to. Hell, I'm not what I'm used to."

"I don't like where you're taking this."

"So why are you even here?"

"I can do something with you, though, that I can't do with them."

"What's that?"

"Sleep."

There was a time when Haley would not have needed to explain at all. Instead, he said, "A person can sleep by himself."

Haley put her hand to her forehead to hold her thoughts in her forehead. "Excuse the cliché, but I'm not *just* fucking with you."

"No, you're not *fucking* with me at all. You're fucking them."

"Roger, don't. Please don't. Don't be the smart-assed you. Smart-ass you can be cruel."

"You mean don't be me."

"Roger, Roger. Oh God. Be you. But don't be mean. You aren't mean. You don't mean to be mean. So don't."

"So you're telling me, I have no cause to be mean to you? Couldn't I try being mean just a little to see if that helps?"

"So then go ahead and be mean."

"I don't feel like it anymore."

Despite her grades, despite her skill in writing, she could not make the right sentences for Roger. The more she tried, the more his quick responses confused her. So Haley squeezed her forehead so tightly that she was sure she left pink fingerprints. She muzzled herself and rolled on her side away from Roger because she feared that if either of them said anymore, the other would start yelling. She waited for two hours before she heard Roger snoring.

* * *

Afterwards, for several months, they settled into a quiet truce with only occasional bouts of Roger's frustration, when Roger, not knowing what else to do, would make the first smart-assed comment that would come to his mind. What he wanted to do was yell. When he got frustrated, Haley could tell and would leave him to himself in his cabin while she went out for a drink or ice cream or a burger. And Roger would sit by himself and wonder why he had to say anything at all. He didn't mean what he said to her; the smart-assing was just something to do. So instead of relaxing, they were just quiet. They slept warily together.

So they discussed the weather, homework, TV shows. Sex was completely gone. They could have confused themselves for a tolerant if estranged father and daughter. Partially, they were waiting for Haley's trial.

The trial wasn't a problem. They didn't even need that good of a lawyer. For, in Texas, cops were indiscriminate about prostitution charges, and defense attorneys and judges knew it. So while Haley was convicted, her sentence was light: the crime classified as a misdemeanor so she wouldn't have a life penalized with a felony. She got a $1500 fine, and no jail time. So she returned to Roger. On a January night, with the rain falling through the trees to plink on the tin roof and with Harry moaning at intervals because he wanted inside for a treat and a few minutes lying at Roger's feet, Haley told Roger that she was going to prove to him why they should be thankful for each other.

Haley made Roger stretch out naked the length of a long portable, folding table set up in the kitchen. His toes stretched out over the edge, and he rested his head on his folded arms. "Look at me," she said. Roger rolled his head to the side in the direction of Haley's voice and squinted through the red haze of their dining room. Haley had replaced the three regular light bulbs with muted, low-wattage red ones, she had filled the room with sticks of old incense that gave off a cinnamon smell but left little clouds of smoke wafting around the dining room. When he located her in the dark, Haley pulled one then the other bow holding her shoulder to thigh length terry cloth shift in place, wriggled, and then straightened as the shift settled around her feet. She was completely naked, not even make up, no paint on her finger or toe nails. "Look at me," Haley told him.

"I'm looking," Roger said.

"Look longer. Study me." Roger looked and noted that she had captured her own specific beauty.

"Now roll back over," Haley told Roger.

He did as he was told to peer over the edge of the table at his dirty floor. Then he felt Haley's greased elbows poking into his shoulders. He grunted and looked back over his shoulder at her. He saw just her face, straining but concentrating, just above his ear, as she pushed her weight on to her elbows. "Turn back around," she commanded. Roger did as he was told. "Look at me." Roger felt what must have been a drop of her warm sweat splatter on his back. She was working hard. "Now, turn over again."

Roger turned around, then felt the points of her elbows work slowly from his shoulders to his mid-back, then to his butt. The hurt turned soothing. And he felt his muscles stop resisting so that he felt the pressure down beneath his muscles and into his organs. He grunted. Then the pressure was gone. He missed it. So he turned his head to see Haley, through the red haze, rubbing oil all over her naked body. She slowly stepped to him, then took his head in her hands, turned it back so that he was looking at the floor, and straddled him. Then the tips of her thumbs began to work their way through the same territory softened by her elbows. She must have been trying to show him what she gave to her customers. He liked it.

By the time she started digging into Roger's back with the heels of her palms, the pressure had lost all pain. Roger turned into a puddle. Then Haley rubbed with her flat palms, and Roger lost track of time, calculating it only by Harry's intermittent moans. She stepped off him again. Then she rubbed a lotion on him that felt like peppermint tasted, and then she piled smooth rocks heated in the oven over the length of his body. Slowly, she picked each rock off his back.

Now a sizzling puddle, Roger moaned with pleasure. Then, Haley rolled him over so that he was back-down on the table, then she straddled him again, this time just with her hips and thighs, guiding him into her. And she didn't move so much as undulate, contract and compress her every organ. More than aroused, Harry felt alive.

Then with the sweat and oil on both them, she slid from off him and lay on top of him, writhing, only internally, through the contractions of muscles. Within a few moments, she started to cry. And then Roger quietly cried. Harry moaned.

For awhile they lay on each other, an exhausted puddle that had once been two distinct puddles. And when Roger got some presence of mind, he saw a clock. This had taken an hour and half. Since he was aware, Roger stepped off of the table, walked through the kitchen, opened the door, and let Harry in. Some of the cloud of humidity, cold, and rain followed Harry in to mix with the warm red, sweat and lotion filled haze. "What the hell," Roger said to Haley and shrugged.

Harry charged through the house dripping and banging into furniture like a malfunctioning, clumsy torpedo. Haley chuckled, "he stinks." She started laughing. "So I just give you the best massage I'm capable of and you let him in. What are you thinking?"

Naked Roger sat in his recliner in his living room and now yelled at Harry. Harry curled, as best the thick, long dog could, at Roger's feet. Oily, shivering, Haley stepped in front of Roger and laughed uncontrollably. He stared at naked, laughing Haley. She stared back at his nakedness and hugged herself to make herself stop laughing. "What do you feel now?"

"Disorientation, confusion . . . ecstasy."

"I feel the same way."

Roger rose from his recliner and stepped toward her. Harry twisted to look a the two of them.

"I could give my clients only half of that. And I couldn't let Harry in afterwards." Roger felt drained. "It was a performance for them, Roger."

"It was still fucking them," Roger said, but he didn't mean that to be a mean comment.

"That was all I did. But look at what we can do. Why have we wasted a minute of our time? Eventually I'll leave because I'll just run out of what I can do here. We've always known that. But until then . . . "

In the red light, Roger could see Haley pleading with her eyes. A person was lucky to find an hour and half like he had just had. Then Roger felt Harry's rough tongue gently scrape up his ankle. Without Harry, without this A-Frame on the edge of the woods, without the pot growing neighbors and the broken down bar, The Nothing To Lose, that hour wouldn't be possible and wouldn't be repeatable. He had been lucky and yet he had worked at this luck too. What he hadn't been was aware of what he had stumbled upon and what he had done to keep it and how it was temporary and fragile. And here he had been squandering time when he should have been aware of it. "What do you say, Roger?" Haley asked.

Roger, after being away from himself too long, came back to himself, "If Harry weren't so long, he'd be able to lick his own ass. That's one of a dog's biggest pleasures. It's what makes a dog a dog. He ought to be miserable. But look at him. You think he minds?" Haley took a tentative step toward him. Harry ran through the house, banging into the furniture. "And you gave him to me," Roger said. Then he looked at naked, oily Haley. "I no longer mind," he said.

Jelvis

Andrew Geyer

Andrew Geyer's books are *Siren Songs from the Heart of Austin* (Ink Brush Press 2010), *Meeting the Dead* (UNMP 2007), and *Whispers in Dust and Bone* (TTUP 2003), which won the silver medal for short fiction in the *Foreword Magazine* Book of the Year Awards. Geyer's stories have appeared in numerous literary magazines and won many awards, including the Spur Award from the Western Writers of America for best work of short fiction published in 2003. A native Texan, he currently serves as Assistant Professor of English at the University of South Carolina Aiken.

Geyer explains, "Growing up as I did in and around Frio County, George Strait was always the 300-pound gorilla in the room. He was the local boy who made it big. I've never written a story about that—in fact, I've never written a story that involved George Strait or his music in any way. When I got the invitation to submit a story for possible inclusion in the *Texas Soundtrack* anthology, I realized that the time had come.

"The two songs that are so important to 'Jelvis,' 'Amarillo by Morning' and 'Let's Fall to Pieces Together,' are two of my favorite songs by George Strait. I grew up on a working cattle ranch, riding horses and working cattle and doing all the things a ranch kid does. George Strait's version of 'Amarillo by Morning' came out when I was about to finish high school, and it seemed to capture the hopeless financial situation that all those ranch folks I grew up with were in, and the crazy optimism they seemed to have about the future despite that situation. 'Let's Fall to Pieces Together' came out the next year. It was one of those songs that got covered at every rodeo dance, and one that all the girls wanted to dance to. If you couldn't find a partner for 'Let's Fall to Pieces Together,' you ought not to have been at the dance to begin with. That alone made the song popular with most of the guys I grew up with, including my two-left-footed self.

147

"As for the Jesus and Elvis part of the story, it was something I just couldn't resist."

According to Wanda Mulebach, the high school secretary's desk —which she had occupied for the past five years—was shaped like a capital J. It was beyond May Belle why Wanda was so insistent on this point, particularly since the desk was really shaped like an L; but this was May Belle's first day at the high school, and she thought it best not to argue. Wanda, the outgoing high school secretary, was training May Belle to take over.

Massive, made of solid oak, the secretary's desk served as a barricade between the students who came in from the main hall and what Wanda called "the sacred heart of the principal's office." The only way for the students to get at the office's sacred heart—which, according to Wanda, was the master clock—was to get past the secretary at her desk, which Wanda reminded May Belle once again was shaped like a capital J. Hung high up on the wall that divided the office from the main hall, the master clock controlled the bell system, which in turn controlled everything else at Carlotta High. The master clock currently read 6:30 a.m. The first bell, which would send all of the students scurrying for their homerooms, would not ring until 8:05. Underneath the master clock, Wanda had hung two pictures. One of them was of Jesus. The second was of Elvis. Jesus was blonde, blue-eyed, and pale-skinned. Elvis was dark-haired, dark-eyed, and dark-complexioned.

"When you come in every morning, just remember *J for Jesus*," Wanda said. "*J for Jesus* is step one." Then she ducked under the desk.

L for loony, May Belle thought but didn't say. Instead, she silently studied the broad backside of Wanda Mulebach and wondered what the front side of Wanda was up to under the desk.

"We don't have to unlock the doors until 6:45," Wanda said, her voice muffled by a half-ton of solid oak. "So the first step in your day should be to crawl under the desk and turn on the computer. That way, it has time to load while we make the coffee."

Sure enough, May Belle saw the monitor on the desk flash as the computer went into the start-up sequence. Then Wanda's ample bottom was replaced by her tanned, makeup-caked face.

"When you crawl out from under the desk, just remember *J.C.*" Wanda fluttered turquoise eyelids at the picture of Jesus. "Those are steps one and two in your day. But instead of *Jesus Christ*, think *J-shaped desk* and *coffee*."

May Belle nodded. At least she knew now why Wanda was so insistent about the desk being shaped like a capital J. "What about Elvis?" May Belle asked.

"E is for *e-mail*, of course. But that is step three. We'll get to step three after we make the coffee."

Wanda led May Belle into a little shelf-lined room off the main office that was filled from floor to ceiling with supplies—notebooks, binders, paperclips, boxes of paper, cans of coffee, bandages, pens, pencils, chalk, markers, paper towels, toilet paper, a seemingly endless array—along with a sink and a small refrigerator. A big stainless steel coffee urn sat in the middle of the floor. Wanda filled the urn from the sink, scooped coffee into the grounds basket, then carried the urn out into the main office and set it on the corner of the desk farthest from the hallway door.

"Everyone who drinks coffee comes to the office and shares." Wanda plunged under the desk again, this time with the coffeemaker cord, and then reappeared. "But when we get to step four, which is doors, the first thing we have to do is lock up the supply room. No one is allowed in there but me, and now you."

"What if they need supplies?" May Belle asked.

"They have to buy them. I have a price list in the desk."

May Belle glanced at the picture of Jesus on the wall behind the desk. "What about Christian charity?"

"That's what the coffee is for. Everything else must be paid for in cash."

The luscious aroma of coffee brewing filled the office as Wanda led May Belle on to step three. "Like we talked about before," Wanda said, "E is step three." She nodded at the picture of Elvis. "But instead of *Elvis*, think *e-mail* instead."

May Belle was thinking about coffee. She'd had her customary single cup, scalding black, on her back porch an hour ago; along with her customary single Camel unfiltered cigarette. Normally, that was all she allowed herself until afternoon. But training with Wanda had May Belle aching for seconds on both. Since the campus was smoke-free, coffee would have to do.

But the coffee was still brewing. And Wanda was still talking about e-mail.

Seated at the desk now, she showed May Belle how to open the online e-mail program—despite the fact that May Belle had been using the exact same e-mail program for the past year in her job as the superintendant's personal secretary—and then showed her how to prioritize the messages: principal not showing up, teachers not showing up, no-show teacher lesson plans, and then everything else. "Remember that all voice-mail messages are converted to e-mails," Wanda said. "If the high school principal calls in sick, you'll have to call the junior high principal later for all the discipline issues that arise. We'll have plenty of chances to talk about discipline issues after the first bell. If a teacher calls in sick, you have to call a sub immediately. You can only call subs from the list of approved substitutes, which is in the desk. The no-show teachers are required to e-mail their lesson plans for the sub."

"What happens if they don't?" May Belle asked.

"Sodom and Gomorrah," Wanda said. "Teenagers nowadays are full of lust. Without a lesson plan, the sub walks into a roomful of sex-crazed adolescents with nothing to occupy their minds but each other's private parts." Wanda shuddered. "If the no-shows don't e-mail a lesson plan, you have to call them up and make them send one. There is a list of teacher phone numbers in the desk. Remind them that a written reprimand will go into their permanent file if they don't send that lesson plan. Three written reprimands and they're out of a job. Got it?"

If lust was such a terrible thing, May Belle found herself wondering, why did Wanda go to the trouble of tanning and slathering on makeup? This question led in turn to another that was becoming more and more pressing: How long could it possibly take for the brew cycle to finish on that coffee urn?

But what May Belle said was, "I think I've got it."

"Good. It doesn't look like we have any no-shows today. That means it's time to move on to step four," Wanda said. "When you get done with e-mail, just remember *J.C.* and *E.D.*" She nodded at the supply room door. "D is for doors. And now it's time for a little pop quiz. What is the first thing you have to do when you get to step four?"

"Lock up the supply room."

"Excellent! When Superintendant Sumps told me that you were taking over the high school secretary's job, I thought to myself: May Belle Folds has certainly got the *cajones* for it. Now I see you've got the *cabeza* as well." Wanda pulled a ring of keys from the top desk drawer and handed it to May Belle. "The key with the gold jacket is to the supply room. The key with the green jacket opens the outside doors. The key with the maroon jacket is the master classroom key. If there are any no-shows, you have to unlock their classroom doors so the subs can get in. But today it's just the supply room and the outside doors. Do you feel like you're ready to do this step yourself?"

Still stuck someplace between her *cajones* and her *cabeza*, May Belle managed to reply in the affirmative.

"I'll tag along just in case you have any questions," Wanda said.

May Belle tried to clear her mind of everything but coffee, which she told herself should certainly be ready by the time she finished step four. Then she locked the supply room and walked into the main hall on her way to unlock the four sets of outside doors. The mascot for Carlotta was the Cowboys, and the school colors were maroon and white. All of these elements had been incorporated into the interior design of the high school building: the lockers were painted maroon, the walls were painted off-white, and maroon-colored cardboard cut-outs engaged in various cowboy activities—bull-riding, bronco-busting, calf-roping—covered the walls between the banks of lockers. It struck May Belle that her dear departed husband Horace, who everyone had called Rooster, would have loved the cut-outs. Rooster had been a cowboy's cowboy—a horse breaker and competition roper by trade, a bare-knuckled scrapper by disposition, and the best two-stepper who ever lived. The thought of Rooster reminded May Belle about Wanda's *cajones* comment. May Belle had never met anyone with more *cajones* than Rooster.

"Actually, I do have a question," May Belle said. She turned to face Wanda, who had been following May Belle around the hallways and watching her every move. "What did you mean about my having the *cajones* to do the high school secretary job?"

"Are you kidding me?" Wanda's turquoise-shadowed eyelids fluttered and her perfectly-plucked eyebrows arched. "You're a legend. The way you beat the snot out of that boy who assaulted you in the breakfast line? The one they used to call Boxer? Everybody in Carlotta knows about it. You've got *cajones* alright. The kids are scared to death of you."

"Bobby," May Belle said. "The boy's name was Bobby Lindell."

"Whatever. I heard his mama went in front of the school board to personally thank you for beating some respect into that boy, and setting him back on the straight and narrow path. Sometimes the only thing that will set a body straight is a good thrashing. It's just like Proverbs says: 'He that spareth his rod hateth his son: but he that loveth him chasteneth him betimes.' The day they took corporal punishment out of this school was the day this school started to go downhill."

May Belle hoped she didn't look as stunned as she felt. Being a legend was not something she had ever aspired to. That had been Rooster's department; and he'd had a good deal of success, both as a competition roper and a bare-knuckled scrapper. The dancing had been just for May Belle. The fact that she'd become a legend for beating up Bobby Lindell was deeply disturbing to her. As May Belle finished unlocking the outside doors and headed back to the office, she remembered her altercation with Bobby Lindell. It had happened more than a year ago, back when she was still working as a lunch lady in the cafetorium. She'd been serving food on the breakfast line when Bobby—who all the lunch ladies had called Boxer because of his belligerent attitude and this habit of punching the air when he talked—had come through the line and insulted the food, hurled the worst possible insult at May Belle that a man could use to stain a woman's honor, and then hit her upside the head with a handful of scrambled eggs. She had reached across the serving line, grabbed the boy by his shirt, and beaten him until blood from his nose and mouth was spattered all over the eggs and sausage. Despite the legend, and what Bobby's mother had said to the school board, *cajones* had nothing to do with it. May Belle had lost control.

When they got back to the desk, the coffee had finished brewing. The smell was irresistible. "Could I have a cup of that?" May Belle asked.

"Of course," Wanda said. "Where is your cup?"

"I didn't bring one."

"There are Styrofoam coffee cups in the office. They cost ten cents."

"I didn't bring any money, either. I didn't think I would need any."

"I'll buy you a cup, and even fill it with coffee for you, if you'll answer a question for me," Wanda said. "That's a penny for your thoughts, times ten."

"Sold," May Belle said. "As long as I get the cup of coffee before I have to answer the question."

While Wanda took the keys and headed into the supply room, May Belle took a seat in the secretary's chair and looked around the office. The master clock now read 7:05 a.m. That meant she still had a whole hour left until the first bell—an hour she would have to spend training with Wanda. May Belle hoped those Styrofoam cups were jumbo-sized. Her eyes wandered down from the clock and onto Wanda's pictures. Both Jesus and Elvis had maroon plastic frames that, in the fluorescent light of the office, looked to May Belle as though they were blood-colored.

"What do you think of my pictures?" Wanda asked.

Startled, May Belle turned to see Wanda reaching a tiny Styrofoam cup of steaming-hot coffee across the desk. "Is that the ten-cent question?" May Belle asked. She took the cup, savoring the rich aroma that wafted up with the steam and wishing she had an unfiltered Camel to go with it.

"You said you wanted to have some coffee before we got to that. I thought we might warm up with the pictures before we move on to the harder stuff."

"Harder than Jesus and Elvis?" May Belle asked. "Are you sure you really want to hear my thoughts?"

"I want to hear the legend speak."

"Alright then." May Belle took a cautious sip of the coffee, which she found to be surprisingly strong and good. "Truth be told, I've never been much into Jesus. My parents, God rest their souls, raised me Southern Baptist. They dragged me to Sunday School and Sunday sermons, both. But I guess it just didn't take. And my dear departed Rooster never believed in much of anything besides rodeo and country music." May Belle took another slow sip of coffee. "I've never cared all that much for Elvis, either. I've always been more into Texas singers like Willie and Jerry Jeff, and of course George Strait. King George grew up right here in Southwest Texas. He was a rancher and a competition roper before he ever became a singer. Rooster roped against him a couple of times, back in the day. And Rooster and me used to follow his Ace in the Hole Band around to the dancehalls. Of course, that was back before he became a big country music star."

"But what about Elvis's movies?" Wanda persisted, apparently having abandoned the Jesus angle for the present. "Don't you like any of them?"

"Well, I liked that one real Western Elvis did. *Flaming Star*. That was a good one. It was set not too far from here, on the Texas frontier."

"You mean the one where Elvis is Pacer Burton, half-Kiowa and half-white, persecuted by the white settlers that he lives among until he dies to save them when the Kiowas go on the warpath?"

"That's the one. Elvis was always a little too pretty for me. That is, before he got so fat. I like my men to look, well, manly. And Elvis sure enough looks the part in *Flaming Star*."

"You know, May Belle, Jesus was persecuted by the very folks he died to save the same way as Pacer Burton. So Jesus and Elvis had something in common."

May Belle shifted uncomfortably in the secretary's chair. "So what's the ten-cent question?" she asked.

"Does beating somebody up, somebody who really deserves it I mean, make you feel better? I know a good thrashing can set a body back on the straight and narrow. You proved that when you beat up that Boxer kid. But did it help you find peace within yourself?"

"No," May Belle said after another slow sip of coffee. "Since that day in the breakfast line, I've come a long way. But not because I beat up Bobby Lindell. After it happened, I became secretary to Superintendant Sumps—who should have fired me, but gave me another chance instead. Dr. Sumps handles things with his heart and his head, not with his fists. He always does whatever is best for the person he's dealing with, and he's always smart in the way that he does it. He only uses his power when he has no other choice. That's the reason I agreed to come over here to the high school with him this semester while he fills in for Principal Toston. Truth be told, I used to be a little bit afraid of kids. Now I'm not afraid of anything. But that's because I've learned to use my heart and my head, and not my fists. Those are the three steps I always remember when I have to handle a problem: *Corazon* first, *cabeza* second, and *cajones* last."

"Some legend you are!" Wanda pressed her lips so tightly together that furrows of bright red lipstick formed in the corners of her mouth. "Let's just focus on the steps you need to learn to handle your job as high school secretary," she said through clenched teeth. "I believe we were up to step five, which is entering the previous day's absentees into the computer. To show you this step, I need my chair."

May Belle vacated the secretary's chair and stepped back as Wanda huffed her way into a sitting position. May Belle had no idea what to think of Wanda, of whom all that was currently visible was a ramrod stiff back and equally stiff blonde bouffant hair. In fact, May Belle was only sure of two things at this moment: she had certainly earned her ten-cent Styrofoam cup, and she needed an unfiltered Camel like she needed breath.

"Each absence has to be listed as excused or unexcused," Wanda snapped, rapid-fire. "To be excused for an absence, a student must bring a note. Enter E for excused; enter U for unexcused; enter A when they have a verbal excuse, but no note. An A automatically turns into a U after three days, if the student doesn't bring a note. If the student does bring a note, you have to go back and change the A to an E. T equals tardy. Three tardies in one day means In School Suspension. Five tardies in one week also means a trip to ISS. All ISS trips get entered into the Discipline module of the computer. Got it?"

The whole time Wanda was talking, her fingers were flying so fast that May Belle couldn't follow what Wanda was doing. "Could you slow down a little bit?" May Belle asked.

"Attendance is done every period," Wanda continued, her back ramrod stiff and her face still buried in the computer screen as though May Belle hadn't spoken a word. "There are eight periods, so you have to keep

154

a running total throughout the day. If a student misses a period, the secretary calls the room the student is supposed to be in next; if the student isn't there, then the secretary calls the student's home; if the student isn't there, then the secretary calls the Constable. Calls to the Constable must be documented in the Discipline section under LGP, which means *left grounds without permission*. Got it?"

"Not exactly."

"What part didn't you get?" Wanda asked without turning her head.

"Well . . ."

But before May Belle could gather the confused state of her thoughts into actual words, students and teachers started trickling into the high school. The kids headed straight to their lockers; but the teachers came into the office, coffee cups in hand. After hitting the coffee urn, they stopped to visit. All the teachers welcomed May Belle to the high school, and the ones May Belle didn't know introduced themselves. The ones she did know kept saying things like: "There's a new sheriff in town," and "Whoa, take 'er easy there, Pilgrim." Then everyone in the office would laugh—except for Wanda and May Belle.

Finally, the first bell rang. The teachers who had gathered in the office sauntered off to their classrooms, and the students who had gathered in the hall scurried off in the same direction. May Belle and Wanda were alone in the office. But by this time, May Belle had framed her confused thoughts into words.

"If I said something to offend you, I apologize," May Belle said. "You can have your ten cents back, if you want it."

"I don't want my ten cents back," Wanda sniffed. "I want my husband back." She looked up from the computer screen, streaks of mascara running down her rouged cheeks. "I was hoping you could help with that, you being a legend and all."

It struck May Belle that Wanda hadn't looked up from the computer since she huffed her way down into the chair. It looked as though she'd been crying the whole time May Belle had been visiting with the teachers.

"I want my husband back, too," May Belle said gently. "But for me, that is impossible. Let's see what we can do for you."

"Really?"

"If you'll walk me back through all that data entry, slow and easy, I'll do what I can to help you figure out this husband thing. But first, I need to know what the problem is. And second, I need to be back in that chair."

As they switched places, Wanda pulled her handbag out of the desk. "To tell the truth, I was just hoping you could teach me enough about fist-fighting so I could beat the snot out of Beau." She pulled a handkerchief and compact out of the handbag, wiped the mascara off of her cheeks, then started to reapply the makeup that her tears had washed off. "Beau is my husband. I don't want to hurt him, just to get his attention. He's been acting like a kid, and I think a good thrashing might set him back on the straight and narrow."

"Do you remember what I told you about the three steps that I always take to handle my problems?"

"*Corazon, cabeza, cajones*?"

"Exactly," May Belle said. "Why don't we take a look at steps one and two before we move on to step three?"

"Okay, okay. I do love Beau. But Beau is a total TV sports junkie. His favorite is football, but he'll watch anything that involves competition. He's also hooked on reality TV. He's got more than a dozen television sets spread around our new house. There are a half-dozen in the living room alone, all tuned into separate channels. Then there's one in the kitchen, one in both bathrooms, one in the master bedroom, one each in the other two bedrooms, one at the end of the hall, and one in the family room. He's even got a TV in the garage and one on the screened-in porch. They are on all the time, and it's driving me crazy. Worse, it's ruining our marriage."

"I don't mean to overstep," May Belle said, "but it sounds to me like you need to turn off those TV's and spend some serious alone time with your husband."

"Alone time?"

"You know, sex. Physical intimacy with the man you love. Doesn't the Bible say to be fruitful and multiply?"

"We're not . . . fruitful . . . anymore. We used to be. That was back when there were only two TV's in the house, one in the living room and one in the bedroom."

"Why in the bedroom?" Wanda asked. "Do you have trouble sleeping? Just then, the tardy bell rang. The high school suddenly went silent.

"This is just between you and me." Wanda lowered her voice to a breathy whisper. "But back when Beau and me used to . . . well, you know . . . really often, sometimes I would get him to put on an Elvis movie first. While Beau was getting busy, I was fantasizing that he was Elvis."

"I guess that explains the TV in the bedroom. Did you fantasize about Elvis the singer, or Elvis the movie actor?"

"Both. Sometimes it was Elvis in *Jailhouse Rock*. That striped shirt and those little black pants with the white stitching over his . . . man parts . . . made him look like a bad boy alright. And sometimes it was the Elvis of the *68 Comeback Special* in that black leather suit. But even the husky Elvis of the later years, in that white sequin jumpsuit with the cape, was enough to send me into . . . well, you know."

A batch of e-mails came pouring in, interrupting Wanda's Elvis fantasies and May Belle's attempts at data entry. The e-mails were all from the teachers that May Belle had visited with earlier, and they all had spreadsheet attachments.

"What's all this?" May Belle asked.

"We covered this earlier," Wanda said. "Don't you remember? Each teacher takes the roll every period, then delivers it via e-mail to the office. The secretary compiles it on a daily attendance summary sheet, then in the morning it gets entered on the computer during step five."

"Well, should we do that now? Or should we keep entering yesterday's absences? It seemed like we were making some progress there, both with the data entry stuff and the husband thing."

"There's not really a separate step for the running roll. It's all a part of step five, which kind of goes on throughout the day. Since we can't start looking for the class-cutters until second period, there's really no rush. So I guess it's your call. Which would you rather do?"

"Why don't we keep up what we were doing?" May Belle said. "That Elvis stuff was getting mighty—"

May Belle was cut off by the entrance of a boy with shaggy red hair, a black leather jacket, and a patch of peach fuzz under his lower lip. He walked up and placed a slip of paper onto the secretary's desk. Then he took a long, measuring look at May Belle and stepped back.

"You'll have to excuse me, May Belle," Wanda said. "This looks like a write-up slip, and that looks like Quentin March. We've got our first discipline problem of the day. What is it this time, Quentin?" Wanda took the slip of paper from the desk and scanned its contents. "You called Miss Gurr a *what?*"

Quentin mumbled something unintelligible and looked up at the master clock.

"Don't you look up at that clock," Wanda said. "You look down here." She pointed at the picture of Jesus. "Don't you think Jesus is sad about what you said? Don't you think He is just heartbroken?"

Instead of Jesus, Quentin's eyes were on May Belle. "Yes ma'am," he said.

"All the write-ups, along with the punishments, must be entered into the computer under the Discipline section," Wanda said. "If it's something minor, the secretary either gives a verbal warning or assigns ISS, especially if it's a talking-back thing. Anything more serious, like calling Miss Gurr a *stuck-up* ..." instead of saying the word, Wanda showed the write-up slip to May Belle, "... gets referred to the principal."

May Belle glanced at the slip, saw the word *BITCH* written on it in capital letters, and glared up at Quentin March. "What gives you the right to say something like this to Ms. Gurr?" May Belle snapped.

"Well, I ... I mean she—"

"It doesn't matter why," Wanda cut in. "It only matters that he did. What we've got to do now is call the principal. Well, I guess in this case, it would be the acting principal. May Belle, could you please call Dr. Sumps?"

"Superintendant Sumps is spending the morning at his main office," May Belle said. "That's why he's not here now. In fact, Dr. Sumps plans to use his own office as much as he can while Principal Toston is recovering from his nervous breakdown. Dr. Sumps said that he wanted me to handle everything except emergencies myself. Here in this office."

"This boy has put his immortal soul at risk." Wanda cut her eyes back and forth between Quentin March and the picture of Jesus. "Wouldn't you say that qualifies as an emergency?"

"Truth be told, I'd say that calling his teacher a *bitch* in class qualifies Mr. March here for a week in ISS." May Belle gave the boy a long, hard stare. "Starting right now. Move!"

Quentin sidled along the wall toward the main hall, then turned and fled when he reached the office door.

"If the Rapture came right now," Wanda called after his retreating form, "would you be ready? We are living in the End Times, young man! Just like it says in Matthew: 'But of that day and that hour knoweth no man, no, not the angels which are in heaven, neither the Son, but the Father.'"

"Being a legend has its uses," May Belle said when Wanda had finished and Quentin March had disappeared down the hall. "If really you want me to help you, I need to ask you something now. I don't want you to take it the wrong way. But have you always been this religious?"

"No. I used to be a Jezebel."

"What happened?"

"A miracle," Wanda said in a dreamy voice, her turquoise eyelids fluttering at Jesus.

"What do you mean?"

"I mean just that. About this time last year, Beau and me were on our way home from Graceland. Right outside of Dallas, traffic was backed up. We stopped just over a hill. All of a sudden there was a scream of brakes.

Then a Mack truck slammed into the back of our car and rolled over on top of us. As we were laying there in that wreckage waiting to be rescued, I promised Jesus that if He would save Beau and me, I'd dedicate my life to Him. Not only did Beau and me get saved, but we got a big cash settlement because that trucker had been driving seventeen hours without taking a break. That settlement is what built our new house, and the reason I don't have to work at the high school anymore. It was a miracle all right. And ever since then, I've kept my promise to God."

May Belle sat quiet for a long moment, looking up at the blonde, blue-eyed Jesus on the wall underneath the master clock. She had never put much stock in miracles. To her, what other people called miracles seemed more like accidents. Sometimes the causes of those accidents could be explained by the laws of science, and sometimes they couldn't. But if human ignorance was the source of divine power, May Belle would pass.

"Don't you believe in miracles?" Wanda asked at last.

"For both our sakes, let's just agree to disagree about miracles." May Belle shifted her gaze firmly from Jesus to Elvis. "That way, instead of spending the rest of our morning arguing, maybe we can work our way through this husband thing."

"Okay," Wanda said. "How?"

"By being fruitful. You can't make fruit without pollinating a flower. You don't need to beat the snot out of Beau. You need to get his attention another way."

"What way is that?"

"Take him out dancing," May Belle said. "It always worked for Rooster and me. For the two of us, George Strait was an aphrodisiac. Whether we were two-stepping to something upbeat, or waltzing to something slow, pressing our bodies together at a rodeo dance to the music of the Ace in the Hole Band—or to covers of George's big hits later on—was enough to make Rooster and me fruitful in spades. All you need to do is take Beau out to a rodeo dance, and the rest will take care of itself."

"He'll never go. Beau wasn't much on dancing before the miracle. And since then, about the only time he leaves the house is to buy another TV."

"Then dance at home," Wanda said. "And not to Elvis, either. Put on some George Strait. 'Amarillo by Morning' is a good one. It was Rooster's favorite. Mine was 'Let's Fall to Pieces Together.' I guess it still is. I don't have any settlement money to wager, but I'll bet my bottom dollar that one of those songs will work for you and Beau."

"What if we don't have any George Strait?"

"Can you cover the desk a minute while I run out to my car?" May

Belle asked. "And while you're at it, can you write me up a list of the steps in the high school secretary's day that we haven't gone over yet?"

Without waiting for an answer, May Belle bolted out of the office and into the parking lot. As she jogged across the pea gravel, she was almost as glad for the crisp January air as she was that she'd worn flats instead of heels for her first day as high school secretary. When she got to her car, she rustled through the trash on the passenger side floorboard until she found her *George Strait Greatest Hits* CD. Then she headed back to the secretary's desk.

"What on earth are you up to?" Wanda asked as May Belle burst back into the office, out of breath and about to die for a cigarette.

"Giving you a gift." May Belle handed Wanda the CD. "Play this for Beau the minute you get home. Turn off all those TV's, and make him dance with you. Go right now."

"I can't leave you here alone on your first day."

"How many steps are left?"

"Six," Wanda said. She handed May Belle the list she'd made. "But the last one is just G for *go home*."

"I think I can handle it," May Belle said. "And if not, I'll give Dr. Sumps a call. He was high school principal for six years before he took over as Superintendant."

"But—"

"Go!" May Belle said firmly. "But answer me a question first."

"Anything."

"I don't believe in an afterlife," May Belle said slowly. "I think all the life we get is the life we have now. Then the lights go out. But if you're right, what do you think Jesus will look like?"

"Honestly? I've always believed that there is a strong resemblance between Jesus and Elvis." She pointed up at the two pictures under the master clock. "They have the same chin. See? And the same bone structure around the eyes. I don't think that's a coincidence. I mean, think about it: The Holy Land? Graceland? Pilgrims going to both places? It can't be an accident."

"Hmm . . ." Gazing up at the pictures, May Belle found herself imagining Jesus coming back dressed like Elvis in his later years: the jumpsuit, the cape, the pompadour. "Jelvis?" she asked at last. "It does have kind of a ring to it."

"It kind of does."

"Now go home! Before something else comes up," May Belle said. "Put on George Strait, turn off those TV's, and don't take no for an answer. But this time, don't pretend Beau is Elvis. Just let Beau be Beau. And make that be okay. Let Beau send you into . . . well, you know."

"I know," Wanda said. She put the CD into her handbag and headed out of the office.

May Belle watched Wanda disappear down the main hall, then looked back up at the pictures. She wondered what Rooster would do if he met Jelvis come again. Maybe, she thought, give him a cowboy hat and invite him to a rodeo.

Bigger Wheel

Wayne Nichols

Wayne Nichols is a Lead Content Teacher in the Fort Worth Independent School District. He is also a screenwriter and filmmaker, having written and produced four short films and is currently in the process of shooting his first feature film, Texas Tango. Another script, entitled Far Enough, is in pre-production. It features numerous Texas independent musicians in acting roles, including Jimmy LaFave, Patrice Pike, and Guy Forsyth. Nichols is also a songwriter and musician, having produced a CD with 16 original songs, entitled The Lost Episodes.

Nichols says, "Stephen Bruton was always a big inspiration for me. Stephen's legacy as a Texas singer/songwriter extends far beyond his work in *Crazy Heart*, for which he is well-known. I knew his father and his brother, who were customers of mine when I was a record rep at Warner Brothers in the 70's. Sumpter Bruton Jr and Sr ran the Record Town across the street from the TCU campus. Stephen was a Fort Worth native, whom I saw play many times. His song 'Bigger Wheel' touched me in much the same way as another song of his,'One More Trip Around the Sun.' He seemed to be looking for answers to questions that were bigger than himself. The protagonist in my story follows a journey that was inspired by the song, not necessarily literally, but spiritually, as he tries to redeem himself by solving his father's murder."

As I lay bleeding, certain that my next breath would be my last, I had the curious thought that I had not yet seen my life flash before my eyes. I was looking forward to that bit of entertainment to be the very least that I could expect from an unanticipated gun shot to the chest. Did that mean I was still alive? Or instead, perhaps, that I was already gone.

I still had enough of my faculties to know that the bullet had hit very near the heart, not an encouraging proposition, and that I clearly was not alone out here in the desert, as I had originally thought.

I also knew that no one was coming to save me. Lying on one's back in a makeshift grave, miles from nowhere, outside a New Mexican ghost town near midnight, is a bad place to expect the cavalry to come storming in. In fact, the pair of us were quite likely the only two-legged creatures within miles.

Then, as I heard the footsteps of my presumed assailant approach, my breath became more labored, my eyesight more fuzzy, before a numbness and a quiet overtook me. I tried to keep my wits about me long enough to see who had killed me, but to no avail. I dove off into the deep end of that black pool. And at that moment, that life-flashing thing, there it was.

I guess I should clarify, having experienced this first-hand, that it is not your entire life that flashes before your eyes. That would require an extreme fast-motion mental camera, and the picture would be too blurry to see at that speed, particularly when you have 24 years of film to scan, as I did. But it is still quite amazing how very much you can think of in a short amount of time.

My first thought was to recall how I got into this unenviable position to begin with. So, instead of flashing back to my youth as a young child on a jungle gym or an embarrassing moment in the third grade, I went back three days to what had turned out to be a life-changing, and apparently life-ending, event.

I was a graduate student of English literature at the University of Texas in Austin. I liked, but certainly did not love, this path that I had chosen. For the most part, I didn't feel that it was so much a choice at all, but an inevitability, a destiny if you will.

I had earned my bachelor's degree in five years, and because I loved Austin and the college life, I took advantage of my Dad's vicarious desire for me to follow in his footsteps and went on to begin my post-grad studies, with the implicit understanding that I would choose the teaching profession, just as my father had.

My father, Dr. Herbert Green, was a history professor at New Mexico State University in Las Cruces. I grew up around colleges and universities. My father had taught at two small schools in the Texas Hill Country area since before I was born. He and my mother met in college, got married and had me, their only child, soon after. But when my mom succumbed to cancer on my tenth birthday, my dad was left to raise me alone. I spent many a day in his office at the college, or in the library while he conducted his research, or just hanging around when his students would come over for the occasional study group or cookout.

There was never a doubt that I would be a good student and go to college, too. My dad and I were very close, but as I grew older, I came to feel that his support was becoming more of a burden than a gift. Like many teenagers, I balked at what I felt were his suffocating expectations, but I could not bring myself to openly rebel against someone who had given me so much. I suppose my only real attempt at any form of adolescent insurgence was to choose to study literature instead of history, which in retrospect must have been quite a blow to him.

You see, my dad had just three loves in his life. First, of course, was his family. He worshipped his wife, and when she passed, he transferred all of that attention to me, his son Daniel. His other great passion was history. He lived and breathed history. His fascination with the past was unrivalled among people I had known. He loved teaching it, and when I graduated high school and went to Austin, he accepted a position at NMSU and took his talents and passion to Las Cruces. And in the Indian pueblos and cattle trails and old Spanish ruins, he found a true home. Even among the more modern historical sites like the White Sands Missile Range, he was more like a kid at a circus than a dry academician gathering evidence and artifacts.

His third big love was metal detecting. He loved to go out and explore the mountains and ghost towns around Las Cruces. His historical background helped him locate the best areas for his searches, and he could spend entire weekends with his headphones on, walking and moving his high-powered detector in circles around the barren ground. He would find old mining caves and campsites in which to wield his instrument. Sometimes, he would hear that beep and start to dig. His loot was often nothing more than bottlecaps and old iron shards from a cowboys' spurs. But once in a while, he would find cap and ball bullets or brass soldiers's buttons or even silver items and old coins. He loved to research the legends of lost treasure near the old silver mines in Shakespeare and Chloride.

My pursuits, however, while centered around the university, were hardly primarily of a scholarly nature. I was smart enough to make the grades and keep my good academic standing alive, but it was all a means to an end. My real passion was for the parties, the women, and my fledgling rock band, the Wild Ideas.

I shared a house off campus with what one might call an eclectic group of Austin denizens. The bumper sticker expression "Keep Austin Weird" was child's play for this bunch. Mike was a 27 year-old filmmaker who specialized in bizarre short films about women in bondage being seduced by cigar-smoking clowns and octogenarian cowboys. Not my cup of tea, or maybe anyone else's but Mike's, but let's just say that art is in the eye of the beholder. And Mike was truly a nice guy without a camera in his hand. His best qualification as a roommate was an ability to score the best weed in the state.

One of my other roommates was Jeff, bass player in the Wild Ideas (I played guitar and sang.) Jeff had a day job at Staples and a predilection for getting his heart broken at least monthly, and twice recently by actresses in Mike's short films.

And finally there was Maurice, or Momo as he was called. Momo was a six-and-a-half foot African-American of Haitian descent, who studied law and worked nights at one of Austin's best restaurants as a cook. He cooked for all of us on the nights he didn't work, and brought food home from the restaurant on the nights he did.

Needless to say, between Mike's awesome smoke and Momo's food, it's a wonder we weren't all three hundred pounds. But a daily early morning bike ride around Town Lake and some late night study sessions (when there wasn't a band practice or a party,) kept me relatively fit, and the lifestyle kept me happy.

But back to three days ago. My father had called to report that he had found something important in his research on a detectorist trip that he couldn't wait for me to see. We had planned for a couple of months for me to visit him over the spring break, and he was really excited that he had cracked the case in the old Padre La Rue hidden treasure legend of the Organ mountains. My dad was prone to that kind of excitement and hyperbole. At any rate, over the last year or two, my visits had grown fewer and further between, and a certain distance, for which I knew I was solely responsible, had grown between us. The upcoming visit would be my first in months.

But I had also promised the band that we would get in an extra rehearsal or two in advance of a rare gig at the Cactus a couple of weeks hence, and there was one of our famous house parties on the docket as well. So I made up a really lame excuse about a paper or two I had to write and bowed out of my visit to see my dad. The rejection and hurt in his voice was palpable. I got off the phone feeling as guilty as a prodigal son should.

But not half as guilty as I felt when I received the call that night, around midnight, in the midst of an epic revelry, that my father had been murdered.

A quick check of the airlines revealed that driving would get me there an hour or two quicker than catching the earliest morning flight to El Paso, deplaning, renting a car and driving an hour on to Las Cruces. So in less than an hour, I was on the road, with nine hours to think about my dad. I could not subdue the guilt I felt, but these feelings were interspersed with thoughts of happier times, and of the lessons that my father had taught me, even as I had lately been in denial about the obvious positive influences he had imbued in me.

I listened to some CDs and some radio programs to give my grief a break, but nothing worked. In the middle of the night on the lonely highways of west Texas, most of the radio programming was either sad country songs, talk shows from the lunatic fringe, or bible thumpers extolling the need to seek a higher power to take charge of my life. Frankly, none of these provided any comfort. The one thought that kept nagging at me, more even than the guilt, was the question of what had caused this gentle sixty year old professor, who to my knowledge had never made an enemy, to be shot in cold blood. Three times, the police said, with a handgun at close range, at ten pm in his office on the campus.

I arrived at the scene at 9:00 am, having flown most of the way after all, albeit on wheels. I was exhausted, but not sleepy. Most of the forensic evidence had already been collected when I walked in to meet Detective Rodriguez, who was heading up the case. I tiptoed around a lot of blood and the chalk outline of my father to shake the Detective's hand.

"You made good time," he said, casting an eye toward the floor. "I'm sorry for your loss."

"Thank you. Not a lot of traffic at three in the morning on I-10 to El Paso. Do you know what happened here?"

"Looks like a robbery homicide, but not sure why here. Did your dad keep any valuables in his office? It seems that someone was looking for something," he noted as he gestured around the room. Books had been torn down from the shelves, artifacts lay in pieces on the floor, and the desk was ransacked, with drawers opened and papers scattered about.

"No idea. He said something on the phone about a big discovery he had made, something about a local treasure legend. But he was always on to something like that."

"Would you know if anything was missing?"
I looked around the room, but had trouble focusing on anything but the blood.

"I'm sorry, I can't tell."

Rodriguez said, "If you think of anything, here's my card. Officer

Darnell will take you down to ID the body."

That unpleasant thought had not even entered my head, but I followed, as if in a daze, as the officer led me away. Once outside in the hall, I was vaguely aware of a young woman, crying inconsolably as she sat on a bench with another policeman. As I walked by, she looked up at me and sobbed, "Are you Daniel Green?"

I was startled out of my trance and must have looked somewhat confused, but I mustered a half-hearted "Yes." I noticed that she was quite attractive, in a girl-next-door kind of way. She stood and offered her hand.

"I'm Emily Elliott. I was Dr. Green's graduate teaching assistant. He was such a fine man. I'm so sorry."

"Did you know him well?" I asked.

"Yes, I suppose. I just started working with him last term, but I took two classes with him before that. Everyone loved his classes."

"That's nice to hear. Do you have any idea what happened? Why was he here so late?"

"He worked late a lot. I left about seven last night, and he was making notes and pouring over his journal. I don't even think he heard me say goodbye."

Just then, it hit me. His journal.

"Excuse me a minute."

I walked quickly back into the office and interrupted Detective Rodriguez, who was on the phone.

"May I check something? It may be important."

Without waiting for an answer, I went to my father's desk and looked at the mess and searched the open drawers. The journal wasn't there. Which meant one of two things. Either the murderer took it, or. . . . I glanced up at the bookshelf and noticed that many of the books were still in place. Including the one I hoped to see. I debated whether to tell the officers, and in retrospect, maybe that would have been the right thing to do. But I just said, "Sorry, I just had a thought. It was nothing. I'll call you later if I think of something," and walked out before he could even get off the call.

As I walked back outside, I paused.

"Ms. Elliott?"

"Emily."

"Emily, may I get in touch with you later. I'd love to sit and talk with you about my dad."

"Of course," she said, as she took a card from her purse. She wrote her number on the back of the card, which read "Jerry's Automotive – Tow it in, Drive it out." She rallied a little, with a weak smile, "It's the only thing I could find to write on. Call me anytime."

I stood over my father's body at the morgue and held his hand for what seemed like an hour, but was probably just a couple of minutes. It was cold, and I knew he wasn't really there, but I said "I love you, Dad," and wished I had said it 1,000 more times before. I received his personal effects, signed some papers, and drove to his house in the desert to reflect.

Looking around the place, though I had been here many times before, I felt as if I was seeing it for the first time. So many reminders of happier days, but taken as a whole under the circumstances, still almost pitifully sad. There were pictures of us as a family, before Mom died, and more of just him and me. In a glass case were some of his trophies from his metal detecting, many of which he found while I searched with him, and a few, including a group of three Morgan silver dollars, that I found myself when we had visited Shakespeare. I remembered vividly how excited I was, as a thirteen year old boy, just to be hunting in a ghost town with the man who was at that time my best friend in the world.

In a special place on the top shelf of the case was Dad's prize possession, a Brown Mfg. Southerner, a small derringer-like pistol that he found near an old campsite. He was especially proud of the fact that his diligent research had led him to this find. The gun was in excellent condition for its age, which a collector had estimated to be circa 1870. Dad had the whole thing restored, grips and firing pin and all, to the point where it could be discharged, and even bought some special ammunition from a mail-order house to test it. He had fired it once at a tin can in the back yard, and then put it on the shelf. To my knowledge, it was the only time he had ever fired a gun in his life.

As I moved through the house, it seemed like there was a memory around every corner, and when I looked in the garage and saw the two metal detectors, standing there as if waiting for us, I sat down and cried for an hour.

I was actually able to sleep, albeit fitfully, having been awake for nearly thirty-six hours. I didn't get out of bed until 10:00 am. I knew that I needed to get back into my father's office, but I also knew that would be difficult for another day or so, with the police still guarding the entrance. I called Detective Rodriguez and asked if I might go in and retrieve some of my dad's personal items. He said that I could go in later in the afternoon, with an officer present, but since what I needed to get was a secret, I told him it could wait until tomorrow.

I called Emily and asked her to meet me for lunch, which she agreed to do, and after spending the morning at the funeral home making arrangements, I met her at a little place called Nellie's Café. She came in wearing a short yellow sundress with boots, her hair tied up in a bun, with a little ponytail. Her wholesomeness was utterly charming. I suppressed the urge to blurt out, "Hey, I'm in a band," or "Ever been to Austin?" and simply said hello.

We ate and talked for close to two hours. We even had a few laughs, as we both recounted stories about my father. I told her about my college experiences and she shared hers. She gossiped a bit about the faculty at NMSU. Apparently, there was a clandestine affair between one of the teachers and a staff member, which, of course, everyone knew about.

Emily recommended that I stop and talk to the chairman of the department, Dr. Henry Rose, who had been one of my father's best friends. He and my dad shared a number of intellectual interests, including local history. They had hung out together for years, she said, since both were bachelors and more or less introverts. Dr. Rose's wife had left him several years prior and taken their son and moved away, and my father had helped him through that dark period.

I decided to find out if Emily could help shed some light on what had transpired.

"Do you know what my father was working on? He called me a couple of days ago, pretty fired up about some hidden treasure."

"All I know is that he was on one of his metal detecting binges lately, and he had me do some research on the Padre La Rue legend, one of many stories that circulate in this part of the country."

"Do you think he was on to something? Could that have been a motive in this?"

"I don't know how close he actually was to finding anything. Most of these legends have been around forever. Not much ever comes of them."

"What about this one?"

"It dates back to 1797, when this Father La Rue supposedly left seven silver bars in a cavern in the Organ Mountains with symbols and directions to seven caches of gold and silver. A man named Noss was said to have found a document relating to this treasure, and his wife spent her life searching for it after he left her."

"Wow!"

"The legend goes that Noss actually found one of the caches, or perhaps a hideout for outlaws, and that it had sixty pound gold bars and hundreds of silver bars."

"But not confirmed, right?"

She smiled. "Nothing's ever confirmed. Except that Noss was shot by a partner who was helping him search."

"That's very Treasure of Sierra Madre."

"What?" she said.

"Never mind," I replied. "At any rate, if Dad really knew something about this, that would be enough to get him killed."

"Highly unlikely, though," Emily said. "It was probably just a break in, and whoever it was didn't expect Dr. Green to be there at that time of night."

"Maybe. By the way, do you know where his journal is? The police didn't find it. He kept these little journals from the time I was young enough to know better. He was always scribbling in them."

Emily laughed as she said, "That was part of his charm. He was always reading or taking notes in that thing. But he never let anyone read them. It was like a diary."

We talked some more. I found out in a sneaky way that she was sans boyfriend at the time. It may have just been me, but I felt a connection to her, and maybe a spark or two. Then, it seemed like just as both of us realized this, the situation kind of horned in again, and we became more solemn and reserved. Eventually, our conversation ran out of steam altogether, so I picked up the check and told Emily that I had some errands to run.

"Thank you so much for your time. It's nice to know that my dad had friends and was well thought of here."

"He was the best. I miss him already," she replied.

"I've made arrangements for a service at the university chapel tomorrow. Will you be there?"

"Of course."

"His wishes were for a cremation. I believe I'll scatter some of his ashes in these hills he loved so much, and take the rest back to Texas."

"It's all so sad. I hope they get whoever did this. Please call if there's anything I can do."

"You've been great. Thanks again."

And with that, I watched her walk away. I couldn't help thinking, another time, another place.

I went to the University and walked past my dad's office on the way to see Dr. Rose. There were no police, but the room was locked and the police tape was on the door.

I wasn't sure how I would manage it, but I needed to get in there.

My conversation with Henry Rose was much the same as with Emily, except for the flirtation. He had nothing but great things to say about Dad, and had a lot of questions for me as well, telling me that he felt like he knew me, from all that my father had said about me. Apparently, my dad was quite proud of me, but I can't say I felt worthy of it.

Later that night, it dawned on me that among the personal effects I was given at the morgue were my Dad's keys. I had used my own key that he had given me some time back to get into the house, but I realized that his would have an office key among them.

I parked several blocks away from the History Building, and found a side door open. There were a few lights on in the building, and as I snuck up the stairs, I noticed a custodian on the first floor with a cart. He had his back to me and didn't see me. I quietly slipped down the hallway on the second floor, and was surprised to find that there were no new padlocks on the door to my dad's office. I quietly tried two or three keys before finding the right one, unlocked the door, ducked under the police tape, and went in.

It was so much easier than I expected. My breaking and entering career was off to a flying start, or maybe it was just beginner's luck.

I knew what I was looking for and I didn't want to linger. I closed and locked the door behind me and flipped on a small flashlight application on my cell phone as I made my way to the bookshelves. I reached up on a head-high shelf filled with genealogy and other large research volumes and pulled down the oversized Texas Almanac 1949-1950 (which was the year my father was born.) I opened it and discovered exactly what I had come to find. The book had a hollowed-out center, which housed the leather bound journal I had purchased for him at Christmas some seven years ago when I went to college.

My heart was already pounding, but it hit warp speed when I heard footsteps in the hall. Not the clip-clop kind, like someone who is just trying to get where they are going, but the stealth, quiet kind, like someone creeping up on you. I pocketed my phone, so I was in the dark. Whoever was outside the door stood there for a moment. And then I heard the door handle turning and the door shake gently as if someone were pushing on it. I crouched and waited, but the person on the other side must not have had a key, so after a minute or less, I could hear the footsteps retreat. Man or woman, I could not tell. Nor did I know if they knew someone was inside. I waited in the dark for about thirty minutes before I dared to venture out.

When I peered through a crack in the door and saw no one, I crept out, and as soon as I hit the outside door, I sprinted to my car. I felt as if someone was watching me. As I drove back to my dad's house, my fears eased and I chalked up the feeling to paranoia. Still, I knew I would be sleeping with one eye open that night.

What I found in the journal astonished me. Dad had made copious notes, diagrams and maps, which seemed to indicate that he believed he had stumbled upon a treasure. There was a photo of some skeletal remains, the disembodied hand of some poor soul, with index finger outstretched and pointing. A gold ring was still on the bony ring finger. The hand was in a hole, perhaps two feet deep, and there was my dad's metal detector on the ground near the hole in the photo. Folded inside the journal was a very old, weathered piece of paper, a handwritten letter, which told an amazing story of Indian slaves and mines and hoards of silver. The writing was faded and hard to read and the directions in the letter were fairly non-specific, alluding to caves and mountain peaks in certain shapes, noting other physical landmarks, with paces for distances and stars for directions. And a cryptic, now confirmed, allusion to a hand to point the way.

I couldn't believe what I was seeing. Had my dad actually put it all together? And who else knew? The mystery of his murder still had no suspect, but I had no doubt now of the motive. I reached for the phone to call Detective Rodriguez, but something stopped me. I thought of my father's phone call and of his excitement about my visit, and his obvious wish to bring me in on this. I felt a sudden opportunity to redeem myself and fulfill his destiny and perhaps even find out who had killed him. But my own investigation would have to wait.

The next day the chapel was literally standing room only, with many people spilling on to the street. Dad not only had scores of admiring former students and friends, but the murder had touched off a wave of emotion and a sense of loss for the whole campus, even among those who had never met him. Local news crews were there to chronicle the event, which had struck a nerve in the entire area.

But as I sat beside Emily for the service, I felt such a deep, personal loss that I barely noticed the crowds, and I left the service as soon as I could to go back to the house and plan my next move. I told Emily I was leaving the next day to head back to Austin, taking Dad's ashes with me. She gave me a warm embrace and asked me to look her up when I came back to deal with Dad's property and the rest of his business.

That night, I recreated from the notes in his journal the exact location of the buried hand. I felt that if someone was watching me, as I had sensed, then I might be able to lure them out. I tried to subdue thoughts of the certain danger that such a scheme presented. After all, what I was setting out to find could very well have cost my dad his life.

I packed some tools, a shovel and a metal detector and followed a hand-drawn map in the journal to drive out to the outskirts of a ghost town known as Chloride. You know you are in the absolute middle of nowhere when you are on the outskirts of a ghost town. It was a cool night, so I put on a jacket and measured the paces from a landmark rock formation that was noted, using a compass to show the direction. Thirty paces due east of the rocks stood a juniper tree, and when I had taken fifteen more paces to the north, I flipped on the metal detector. The ruins of an old stone building lay just a few yards away.

My father had been smart enough to leave the gold ring on the bony finger of his grisly discovery in order to be able to find it easily again. And sure enough, after no more than twenty minutes, the beeper indicated a strike. I turned my headlights on to the spot and dug for a while, creating a hole a couple of feet deep and several feet wide. I wasn't as good at pinpointing a find as Dad had been, and after forty minutes of digging, I was just about to give up. And then, I saw it, at first a glimmer of gold from the ring.

As I bent down to look closer, I felt first, then heard, the shot to my chest, and tumbled into the shallow grave I had inadvertently dug for myself. My last thoughts were of my father and the events I have recounted as I heard the footsteps approach and slipped into darkness.

I don't know how long I was dead, or in the state where I assumed I was dead, but it couldn't have been long. I was vaguely aware of someone digging around beside me and going through my pockets. My first thought was "Please, not Emily."

I was barely conscious and could not make out the person's face in the low light. But when I heard a man's voice say, "Where is it, damn you?" I must say I was relieved. I remembered then what my Dad had told me about that little prize derringer he had found. He had done research on it and learned that these small handguns, like the Brown Southerner and the Remington .41, though quite popular in their day, were of little use in the Wild West, because they packed so little punch and were so inaccurate. He had told me that one needed to be at point blank range and hit in a vulnerable area to do any damage. He said that in the old West, you were about as well off throwing a rock.

Well, I didn't have a rock handy, so the little derringer would have to do. I had carried it in my jacket pocket just in case. While my assailant continued to rummage around and scratch at the ground and at me, I silently reached my hand into my pocket. I don't think he was even aware of the possibility that I might still be alive when I stuck the gun into his neck and pulled the trigger.

The chaos that ensued turned the campus and the community upside down. I used my cell phone to call Emily and the police. She in turn called an ambulance, which I had somehow forgotten to do. I was shocked to be alive, and even more shocked to find out that it was my father who had inadvertently saved me, on the very day I laid him to rest. I had put his journal in the breast pocket of my jacket, and the .38 slug had gone all the way through it and penetrated my chest, but not deep enough to pierce my heart.

In the days that followed, I saw my picture on the front page of the newspaper and on the television as well, when Emily would come up to the hospital to sit and visit with me. I had cracked the case all right, but it was not the one I thought I was working on.

My assailant had turned out to be Dr. Henry Rose. He was unaware of my father's treasure hunt, and was instead worried that my dad was getting close to unearthing and exposing something even more shocking. Not twenty paces from where he shot me were the final resting places of his wife and son, whom he had murdered two years prior. It seems that they had left him all right, as he had always said, but not without some assistance from the chairman of the history department. The scandal rocked the entire community, and I became something of a local celebrity.

Within a week, however, the news cycle turned over and I was on my way back to Austin. I had grown quite close to Emily Elliott, and she had kissed me like she meant it when I said goodbye.

Now, looking back on the events of three years ago, I feel much more at peace with the memory of my father, and much more worthy of the love he gave me. When I returned to Austin, I tried to resume my life there, but nothing seemed the same. The person who returned from Las Cruces was a different person than the one that left on that fateful day. I finished my master's degree and then raced through the doctoral program, and I am now teaching, as I'm sure my father would have wanted.

Emily also finished her doctorate and now teaches history at NMSU, and uses the same office my dad used. She also headed up a petition drive to rename the History Building the Herbert Green Building.

I teach across campus in the English department. Sometimes, we carpool to work, but often we take separate cars, if one of us has to work late. Emily and I were married last year. I still play songs at the occasional open mike night, and some faculty colleagues of mine get together and jam once a month or so.

I often think of my father and of the twists and turns in my life that brought me to this place. I can't say if this was all destiny or some grand design, some bigger wheel that turns the cosmos. I don't know if I made certain choices, or if some hand was guiding me to make those choices. I am reminded of what Albert Einstein once said, "The real question is whether God had a choice in creating the Universe."

The bullet through my dad's journal had all but destroyed the maps and diagrams and notes. The secret of the Padre La Rue treasure is probably safe for now. But my father knew something that it took me a long time to learn. The real treasures in life are family.

A student of mine came into my office the other day and we were discussing the meaning of some literary conundrum, and now, as I recall this story in my own leather bound journal, I will just say what I told him. As Isadora Duncan told one of her students, sometime before her scarf caught in a car wheel and broke her neck, "If I could tell you what it meant, there would be no point in dancing it."

CPSIA information can be obtained at www.ICGtesting.com
Printed in the USA
LVOW111522060412

276509LV00003B/130/P

[8]